THE AWFUL MESS

THE AWFUL MESS

A LOVE STORY

SANDRA HUTCHISON

SHEER HUBRIS PRESS
AVERILL PARK, NEW YORK

Sheer Hubris Press

96 Gettle Road

Averill Park, NY 12018

www.sheerhubris.com

Publisher's Note: This is a work of fiction. Names, characters, places, and incidents are a product of the author's imagination. Locales and public names are sometimes used for atmospheric purposes. Any resemblance to actual people, living or dead, or to businesses, companies, events, or institutions is completely coincidental.

Cover design by damonza.com

The Awful Mess: A Love Story / Sandra Hutchison – 1st Print Edition
ISBN 978-0-9911869-0-7

To my parents,
Alexander and Jackie Hutchison

"But, all this while, I was giving myself very unnecessary alarm. Providence had mediated better things for me than I could possibly imagine for myself."

— Nathaniel Hawthorne, from his introduction to
The Scarlet Letter

CHAPTER ONE

IT WAS THE warmest day since she'd arrived in Lawson, New Hampshire, a sunny day in March of 2003, and the Took River was swollen with melted snow. For the first time since Mary had begun these daily walks, there were other people clustered on the Main Street Bridge to watch the river. Uncomfortably conscious that she knew none of them, she considered hurrying past, but told herself that it would be ridiculous and stopped at her usual spot at the bridge railing.

"Impressive, isn't it?" a man said, and settled in next to her at the railing.

It was hard not to stare at him in appalled fascination. His face was extraordinarily craggy — almost like a gargoyle, or Abraham Lincoln at his most depressed. The rest was not bad. He had a healthy shock of salt and pepper hair, large grey eyes, a friendly smile. The French had a term for it, she thought. *Laid-beau,* ugly-beautiful.

He leaned towards her and lowered his voice to a compassionate murmur. "Forgive me for intruding — but would you, by any chance, need some help with food?"

She blinked. "I beg your pardon?"

"Sorry. I should have started with introductions. I'm Arthur Tennant, the rector of St. Andrew's. Just there." He gestured up at the old Episcopal church that sat overlooking the Main Street Bridge, then stuck out his hand.

Mary shook it automatically. She hadn't realized he was a cleric. His collar, if there was one, was covered by a scarf.

"And you're Mary Bellamy, of course. Everyone in town knows about the young divorcée from Boston who bought Miss Lacey's house. I didn't mean to pry. It's just — well, it seems to me you've gotten rather thin, and we all know how expensive a new roof can be. I thought I'd take the opportunity to check. Because we can help, you know."

It was true, she had a new roof. And she'd lost some weight. But surely it crossed some sort of boundary for him to admit he'd noticed it, even if he was a priest? "I'm fine, thank you. I don't need help."

"I've been meaning to call on you at home, actually. But since you haven't shown up in any of the churches, I suspected you wouldn't particularly welcome it."

"No, that's true, I'm a heathen."

He grinned. "Heathen? Well, there aren't that many churchgoers these days, you know, even in a little town like this. That's probably why my colleagues and I keep such close tabs on newcomers. We're all hoping it might be somebody new for our own congregation—"

"I'm Catholic, actually."

"Ah, a Catholic heathen. St. Mary's would be the church you're not attending, then. But you would certainly still be welcome at St. Andrew's. We have quite a few Catholics in our congregation, actually. Some heathens, too, I expect."

"Well, it was very nice to meet you, Father, but I'm afraid I need to get back to work…"

"Yes, yes, of course." He raised his voice to hold her there a moment longer. "I'm in the book if you need any help or just want someone to talk to! Arthur Tennant. Please don't hesitate. It can be very lonely being new in a small town."

"But I'm not lonely at all." It was, in fact, a tremendous relief to be alone. But he couldn't know that.

As she walked up the hill, she had the disagreeable feeling that she was being watched.

During the divorce, Mary had comforted herself with a fantasy of living in a quaint little house in charming little Lawson. She would have a beautiful and affectionate ginger tabby (her ex was allergic), take long walks, and listen to National Public Radio whenever she wanted. The yellow winter sun would stream onto her kitchen table and illuminate a vase of wild flowers which, if she had thought this through, could not have come from the nearby field covered in a foot of snow, but whatever. The fantasy had sustained her. Reality was quite different, of course — the house was draftier than she had hoped, even a little dank, and the winter sun never made it onto her little kitchen table. And flowers from the supermarket weren't really in her budget. But it was fine. She was fine.

It was true she had lost weight, but she was hardly starving. Mary put the odd encounter out of her mind and sat down to work. She liked to think she had been granted permission to work from home because she was a talented editor who could take garbled manuscripts turned in by deranged authors and gently and diplomatically shape them into books. The manuscript she was working on right now, though, was for a book called *Healing Yourself with Amazing Supermarket Cures*, and it had obviously been written by a hack copywriter claiming to be a medical expert instead of the usual sincere nutcase on a crusade to save the world with wheat berries and flaxseed. While this meant it was remarkably easy to edit, Mary suspected the author had simply made up his anecdotes of miraculous recoveries, especially when she got to Chapter Six ("Amazing Cures in the Pet Food Aisle!") and read about catnip tea curing a couple's infertility.

Should she challenge this? Or would that simply betray her sensitivity on the subject? Her boss had made it clear that this was an important title for which Shanley was projecting strong sales. Mary was uncomfortably conscious that in having been allowed to work from home, she had been granted a favor.

As she sat there contemplating the mysteries of catnip, it occurred to her that she hadn't yet acquired the ginger tabby from her fantasy. A nice warm cat in her lap would do nicely about now. And if somehow, beyond her control, her face was betraying something that inspired strangers to inquire after her wellbeing, perhaps having another living creature in the house would help.

At the shelter they didn't have any ginger tabbies like the one she'd imagined, but they did have a sweet-looking black cat that meowed in a personable and not overly needy way. According to the tag, he was named Bob. That seemed like more of a name for a shoe salesman than a cat, really, but there was no one she needed to impress with a clever pet name.

"Do you have any other pets at home?" the clerk asked. She was a tall, brisk woman who wore her hair in a practical silver bob and kept her reading glasses on a chain around her neck. Mary didn't need glasses yet, and still wore her hair long, but she could imagine looking like this in not so many years. A brisk, efficient, cheerful, independent woman — this was exactly the life Mary was aiming for.

"No, no other pets."

"Children?"

"No." Comforting, really, that someone in town didn't already know this.

"Well, you'll have no problems, then. He's even been declawed. You don't plan to let him out, do you?"

"Shouldn't I?"

"No, since he's de-clawed. And Hill Street is murder on cats, I'm afraid."

"Okay, I'll keep him in," she agreed. The woman asked her to wait while she went to fetch a carrier. All the cats of Mary's youth had either died under the wheels of South Boston traffic or disappeared into the night. It might be nice to have the same one around for more than a year or two.

"I live near you, you know," the woman said when she returned. "Agnes had such a beautiful garden in front of the house there, before she got too frail. Do you garden?"

"A little."

"You'll find a wonderful perennial garden under all those weeds if you work at it this spring. If you need help telling what's what, just look me up. Carrie Woodbury at Number Four, Old Street Road. I'd be happy to help you out, especially if you could let me have some divisions from her peonies. It was really something to look at, her garden. Shame how it went to ruin when she couldn't take care of it anymore, but she wouldn't accept help. Such a pity."

Mary couldn't tell if the pity was for Agnes Lacey or her garden. "Well, thank you." She hoisted Bob in his cardboard carrier.

"You take care, now. Hill Street can be murder on cars, too, in bad weather. They say there's a big one coming in tomorrow."

"Oh, that's right — thanks." Bob's meows grew more alarmed as Mary neared the door. She knew about the forecasted Nor'easter, but now she needed to stock up on supplies for Bob before it arrived. It had been months since she had needed to worry about taking care of anybody other than herself.

"Got a new cat?" the woman at the market asked.

"Yes," Mary said, with a tight smile. She was probably spending twice what she should for the single flimsy plastic litter tray she'd found. Lawson General Market dealt with its limited display space by stocking only one or two of almost anything anyone could ever need.

"I'm a dog person myself."

"Dogs are nice," Mary said diplomatically.

"But they're a lot of work, especially if you live on your own."

"You live on your own?"

"Oh God no."

*

The cat spent the evening slinking around the house, nosing into nooks and crannies, eventually disappearing. When Mary woke up in the morning, however, he was lying next to her on the bed, purring.

"It's nice to have someone in my bed, Bob."

Bob stretched, exposing his belly.

"And you're a slut!" Mary said happily, and petted him. This would do fine, she thought. This was all she needed.

CHAPTER TWO

THE NEXT AFTERNOON when it started snowing and she still hadn't gotten in her daily walk, Mary added an extra layer of waterproofing and headed out.

Not counting the state highway that skirted the center of town, Lawson proper had grown up along the convergence of two rivers that ran between the area's low hills. Mary's section of town was not densely populated because a quiet religious retreat of some kind owned most of the property behind the string of modest houses on Hill Street. There were trails crisscrossing their woods and a complete absence of NO TRESPASSING signs, and she had gotten into the habit of taking a wooded path down the hill to town instead of the sidewalk because it was pretty and private.

She was about halfway through the woods when the silent snow changed over to the muted rattle of freezing rain. Undeterred, she walked down to the library to choose some books for the weekend. Mary had nearly exhausted the Lawson Free Library's section on home décor and still hadn't decided how to paint her interiors. By now Roger would have hung drywall over the cracked plaster and painted everything white. She didn't miss his color palette, but she did miss the free labor and the way Roger just barged ahead and got things done. Every time she thought she had decided on a color, she began to doubt herself: what if that sunny yellow turned bilious once it was up on the wall?

She moved from the books to the magazines, looking for articles on wall color and flea market furniture finds. Agnes Lacey's heirs had thrown her old furniture in with the deal, happy to avoid the chore of clearing it out. Mary knew most of it would have to go, especially after smelling it for two months, but in the meantime she had somewhere to sit and sleep. She also hoped some of it might be salvageable with paint or stain or upholstery. The days were gone when she could go out and buy a new sofa or even a bedspread without a second thought.

She jumped when the librarian tapped her on the shoulder. "The town just called, dear, and said we'd better shut down. It's getting slick out there."

Mary checked her watch. Just past four. She got into her winter gear while the librarian waited anxiously by the door. "Careful, now!" she clucked, when Mary stepped out and almost slid off her feet. In the time she'd been inside, the sky had darkened, the wind had picked up, and a thin, treacherous layer of ice had coated every surface.

Occasionally struggling for balance, Mary navigated the sidewalk and crossed the bridge. She paused a moment to admire the grey, pounding river before heading down River Road to the entrance of the forest path. Under the trees the footing was sure to be easier. But when she got there, the trees were groaning in the wind and the path into the woods looked ominously dark. She heard a sharp crack and a bough landed heavily on the path ahead, showering the ground with broken twigs and tiny slivers of ice. She backed away. She'd be safer on the street — at least there someone might notice if a tree fell on her.

She tramped back along River Road, crunching her way along snowy lawns where she could, the drumbeat of the freezing rain on her outerwear punctuated by choruses of screaming crows.

Hill Street was where it got steep. She caught herself from slipping a couple of times before she got to the long stretch in front of St. Andrew's church and rectory. No doubt many people considered the sooty chiseled granite and Romanesque arches of the church elegant, but it reminded Mary of intransigent state agencies and bleak college administration buildings. A prickly barberry hedge along the sidewalk blocked better footing on the lawn, and there was no sidewalk at all on the other side of the street, just an impenetrable wall of evergreens, as if whoever lived there didn't care to admire the building either. She stepped into the road to see if that would be better, but had to scramble out again to make way for a car that went fishtailing up the hill like a drunk in an alley.

She had stopped to assess her chances of actually making it the rest of the way up when she saw another car slowly descend, blinking for a left turn into the rectory, just ahead. As she watched, it gently slid downhill out of its turn and landed with a *whump* in the hedge.

She instinctively stepped forward to help and her feet slipped out from under her. She landed jarringly on her tailbone and thumped the back of her head on the sidewalk.

She lay there, stunned, wincing up at the clouds while freezing rain peppered her face, listening to the excited cries of the crows. She knew she should move, but for the moment it seemed easier to just lie there. Her tailbone throbbed and her head hurt in a thick, blocky kind of way.

She heard a car door slam and then someone was looming over her. Arthur Tennant. Well, it was his church.

"You okay?" he asked.

"I'm fine."

There was a pause. "Can you get up?"

"Sure." She took a breath, then rolled over onto her hands and knees.

"Better come in the house," he said, extending his hand.

She looked up at him, then over at the rectory a good hundred feet away, and accepted his help getting up. On her feet again, she brushed herself off and said, "Thank you, but I'm on my way home."

"Nonsense, you'll never make it. Come in the house."

She sighed, eyeing the glazed sidewalk, not eager to depend on the kindness of a man who was likely to examine her even more carefully than he already had for signs of malnutrition or potential choir membership.

"Come on," Tennant said firmly, gripping her arm. "There's a break in the hedge there, and then we can go across the lawn."

"What about your car?" It was still sitting cockeyed at the entrance to the driveway, barely off the road, flattening the end of the hedge.

"Not much point trying to move it now. With any luck it will ruin the hedge and we can finally rip the damned thing out."

They crossed the lawn and he ushered her into a mud room, where he helped her get out of her gear, and then into a large, steamy kitchen. "Have a seat," he said, and gestured to an old kitchen table. She was relieved to find a cushion on the bench that served as seating and eased herself down.

He bustled around gathering and measuring ingredients into a pot. "The perfect afternoon for hot cocoa, I'd say. What were you doing out in this weather?"

"Walking home from the library."

"You're quite the determined walker. I see you all over town."

"What were you doing out in this weather?"

"One of my parishioners is in the hospital." He stirred his mixture and adjusted the heat. "They thought she was going, but she rallied."

"You must be relieved."

"Well, she sinks and rallies pretty regularly." To her surprise, he prepared three mugs, not two. He placed one before her and said, "Drink up. I'll be back in a minute." Then he took one of the others and left the room.

She'd finished only a few sips when he returned. "My wife enjoys hot cocoa, too," he explained.

Ah, that was right. Episcopal priests could marry. "Will she be joining us?" Mary asked. The wife of a priest might be a formidable woman.

"I doubt it. She seldom feels up to company."

Not so formidable, then. "She's ill?"

His air of authority faded for a moment. "Yes." The moment strung out between them and she felt he was considering telling her more. But then he said, "So how are you finding things? It must be lonely, being so new in town."

"No, not at all." He sure liked that *lonely* idea. Mary saw no point in starting to feel lonely only a few months into what she expected to be a lifetime of solitude. After a moment, she added, "I have a cat."

He smiled as if this amused him.

"So, how do you suppose I can get home?"

"Once they get some salt on the hill here, I can try to give you a ride in the car. Worst case, this is supposed to turn to back to rain tomorrow."

"Tomorrow!"

"Don't worry, we have plenty of room."

"But — I need to feed my cat..."

"Oh, I'm sure a cat can survive missing a meal or two."

Mary winced and tried to find a more comfortable position. Her tail bone was throbbing and the ache in her head was intensifying. "Do you have any Tylenol?"

"Oh, of course! How thoughtless of me." He left and returned to place several pill bottles in front of her. "Take your pick," he said, and handed her a glass of water. He sat down on the opposite bench. "My last church was in South Carolina. When we moved up here, I wasn't used to ice and fell on my backside in front of the congregation my very first week. There was the most awful silence. I just kept imagining the headline: *Priest falls down on job.*"

Mary smiled.

"No children?" he asked.

"No." She said it as curtly as she could.

"Perhaps a good thing, considering the divorce."

He either hadn't heard the warning in her tone or had decided to ignore it. "If I'd managed to have them, I might not be divorced."

"Oh, I'm sorry. That can be very painful. We have a couple in the parish…"

"You have children?" Mary interrupted. She'd heard more than enough stories of people in similar straits. It didn't help that so many of those stories ended with *they adopted a lovely baby girl from China* or *now they have twins*, or her least favorite — *as soon as they adopted a baby she got pregnant, just like that!*

"We have a 16-year-old daughter who's away at boarding school right now — Lucy." He looked down. "We also had a boy, Matthew, who died when he was nine."

Good God. "I'm so sorry."

"It was some time ago now. Not long after we arrived here. He had an undiagnosed heart defect."

"You must have been devastated."

"Well, yes, of course." He drained his mug and stood up. "I'd better get dinner started." He began to pull items from the cupboards and the refrigerator. "Is chicken all right?"

"Yes, fine. This is very kind of you."

"Not at all — it will be a pleasure to have company."

"Doesn't your wife eat dinner with you?"

"Not very often."

"Then she's an invalid?"

"I suppose. That sounds rather romantic, doesn't it?" He dredged chicken in flour. "The diagnosis has been a tad elusive. One doctor thought she had MS, but we were able to rule that out. Another diagnosed Epstein-Barr. Fibromyalgia has been floated about."

"Does she make it to church?"

"Oh no. Not in years." He whacked a clove of garlic flat with the side of a cleaver.

When dinner was ready, Arthur took a tray upstairs, after inviting Mary to help herself from the skillet of chicken breasts in a rather nice lemon caper sauce. She peered out the window. The wind was howling as fiercely as ever and frozen rain crackled against the panes.

He came down looking a bit peevish, served himself a plate, and sat down with a quick prayer: "For what we are about to receive, Lord, let us be truly grateful."

How annoying it must be to have to be grateful all the time to a God who has treated one so badly. This man's losses would have pushed her completely into atheism, or worse. Perhaps she would have started worshipping golden idols, just because God was supposed to really hate that.

"This is delicious," she said, and he smiled. He had a nice smile. It mitigated the cragginess. She wondered whether a married Episcopal priest was a figure of fantasy to the ladies of his congregation the way the younger Catholic priests had always been at her own childhood church.

"I'm relieved to see you eating. There's a young woman in my congregation who has had been battling anorexia for years. I thought perhaps —"

"I'm not anorexic. I just forget to eat."

"Forget? Why? Are you depressed?"

"No. It just hardly seems worth the effort to prepare meals for just one person."

"How long ago did you say you were divorced?"

"Two months. But we were separated for several months before that."

He frowned. "Most people need time to recover from that kind of loss."

"Maybe it wasn't that much of a loss." She coughed uncomfortably.

"How long were you married?"

"Eight years."

"You don't see that as a loss?"

"Well, the years, maybe." Her *youth*, she thought, but didn't say — he would feel obligated to tell her she was still young. "At this point I'm just glad to be out of it."

"You know, Lawson has a rather well-organized ecumenical counseling service which is completely free—"

"I'm sorry, but I wouldn't be caught dead doing anything ecumenical."

"Why ever not?"

"I already told you — I'm not religious."

"I don't believe there's any great expectation that you will actually be religious," he said, but then he looked uncertain. "Well, it depends on the particular counselor, I suppose. If you don't mind me asking, why aren't you religious? Are you mad at God? Angry with the church?"

"I just don't see any rational reason to believe there is a God."

He regarded her with an expression she couldn't quite fathom — speculation, perhaps? "Pity. Faith can be a comfort."

"I can comfort myself just fine." It sounded petulant even to her, but she wasn't the one who'd turned this into a religious discussion.

"How exactly do you do that? I'd like to know."

Mary hesitated. She had never mastered the art of ignoring questions she didn't want to answer. "Well. I take walks. I listen to music. I pet my cat…"

"Walking, music, cat," he murmured. "And this does it for you?"

"It's enough. I don't have to wonder when the next bad thing will happen anymore. Living alone is paradise compared to what I had before." She looked away, embarrassed to realize she was on the verge of tears.

"I'm sorry."

Now he was probably going to hit her up with God's redeeming grace. But all he said was, "I was being far too intrusive. Please forgive me."

Mary nodded, thrown off. She felt oddly stirred up, perhaps because this was the most intimate conversation she'd had with anyone in months.

"Can I get you anything else?"

"No thank you."

He took her empty plate and started getting the dishes together.

They had no dishwasher. Neither did she, in her new house. "I'll dry," she said.

He handed her a clean towel. "So what do you do for a living?" he asked.

"I'm a development editor. Have you heard of Shanley Publishing?"

"Oh, yes. Sharon's a big fan of Shanley vitamins. No doubt she has some of your books up there next to her bed." He flushed. "*Our* bed."

There was an amused snort from the door, and Mary turned to see a tall, pale woman in a bright red robe.

Arthur's flush deepened. "Sharon! Here's the woman I told you about, Mary Bellamy. Mary, this is my wife, Sharon."

"Hello," Sharon said. She spared Mary a brief smile and a handshake. Her hand was cold and she did look ill, with dark circles under her eyes. Her long hair — nearly black, with a few streaks of silver — was neatly combed but in need of a wash.

"What can I do for you?" he asked.

"I need my pills."

He looked irritated. "I was going to bring them up shortly. When I collected your dishes. Left them all up there, did you?"

"I told you I was tired today." She sank down into the chair at the head of the table and sighed. "Doesn't it seem as if winter will never end?"

"Yes," Mary said. "It's so icy—"

"It is staying light later, but that just gets our hopes up. And on a day like this it's dark all day anyway. Could you get my pills, Arthur?"

Mary watched as Arthur took bottle after bottle of what looked like vitamins, many indeed featuring green Shanley labels, and tapped capsules out of each. He brought them to Sharon with a glass of water, and she took them one by one while they watched.

"Well, it was a pleasure to meet you, Mary." Sharon slowly pushed herself up from the chair. "You're new in the parish, I suppose?"

"Actually —"

"She may need to stay over, dear," Arthur said.

"Oh, I wouldn't think so!" Mary said.

Sharon gave Arthur a sharp look. "You must use your own judgment, Arthur. I'm off to bed now." She turned to Mary with a stiff smile. "Good night, then."

"Good night," Mary said. She turned back to drying dishes.

He finished his washing without comment. Dishes and cutlery clinked. Water splashed. She was conscious of the silence as rather awkward, but had no idea what to say. When he'd handed her the last dish, he turned and smiled thinly at her. "Excuse me. I need to go get hers."

Mary dried industriously. She lived less than half a mile up the hill. She would simply have to hold firm about getting home for the night. This might be New Hampshire, but it was hardly a wilderness.

CHAPTER THREE

"YOU'RE NOT THINKING of going *now?*"

Mary looked up from zipping her parka. "I'm sorry, but I really must."

"Well. If they've gotten some salt down, maybe I could get you up in the car." He shrugged into a coat and hat and grabbed a bucket of salt by the door.

As soon as they stepped out, Mary realized it was impossible. The wind was howling. Heavy snow streamed nearly horizontally, and tall drifts had half-buried Arthur's car and hidden the road. Except for the wind, the town was silent — no traffic, not even a snowplow.

"This is bad. I really think you'd better plan to stay."

"But — "

He turned and disappeared through a doorway, so she followed him into a small room crammed with an old computer, books, photographs, and religious figurines. He noticed her looking at a plastic Madonna nightlight and smiled. "Gag gift," he said. He punched numbers into his phone. "One of my parishioners is a town cop. I don't know whether he'll be able to help you out tonight, though."

Mary waited. She surveyed his shelves. Just how many

of these assembled items were gag gifts? She leaned in to examine the holographic postcard of a Jesus whose arms moved up and down as she shifted her position. *Come unto me* read the caption.

"It's ringing. They must be busy. Hey — Eunice! Art Tennant up at St. Andrew's. Is Winslow there?" A pause. "Thing is, I've got a pedestrian stranded here. Mary Bellamy. You know, the woman who bought Miss Lacey's house." A longer pause. "Oh, I didn't know that. Well, good luck. Ask Winslow to give me a call if he gets a chance, okay? Thank you."

He hung up. "Power's out on the other side of town and the state roads are a mess, people stranded in their cars. Your chances for tonight look pretty slim. But our guest room is fairly comfortable, I assure you. Sharon does skulk around a bit, but she won't burn the house down like the first Mrs. Rochester or anything. Come on up and I'll show you."

She followed him up the narrow stairs. That had been a rather disloyal thing to say about his wife. Perhaps he'd intended it as a kind of secret code from one reader to another. Perhaps he was hoping to talk about books all night.

She hoped he didn't fancy himself a Mr. Rochester. Though his looks did kind of fit the part.

He led her up the narrow stairs to the guest room, which had a bleak monastic look — white chenille bedspread, worn braided rug, simple cross on the wall. She sat on the bed and wondered if she was expected to go to sleep now. There wasn't even a good spot for reading, not that she had a book. She pulled out the drawer in the bedside table, half expecting to find a Gideon Bible, but there was nothing.

But Arthur reappeared at the door with a flannel night-gown and a robe and a set of towels. "Would you like to take a shower?"

"Maybe later," she said, unwilling to lounge around in someone else's nightwear.

"Well, come on downstairs, then. You could watch TV. I have to work on my sermon, but I'll get you settled first. You won't think it too rude if I leave you alone?" He gestured her into a living room.

"No, not at all." She was actually quite relieved.

"I reward myself with dessert when I've finished a draft, but you can have some earlier if you'd like. We have ice cream, and an apple pie from one of my parishioners."

"I'm still full from your delicious dinner."

He smiled with such delight she got the idea he wasn't used to compliments.

Left alone, Mary turned on the television for weather news and surveyed the room. Essentially off-white, it was decorated here and there with colorful pillows and afghans of unfailing good taste. Mary wondered whether they were gifts from grateful parishioners or signs of life from Sharon.

There were numerous photographs on the baby grand piano: Sharon, looking young and slim and chic in an artistic black and white, with a baby who could have been either a boy or a girl; a young girl who was presumably their daughter with a younger, paler boy who was presumably the lost son — both on the gangly side, like Arthur, as if they still needed to grow into their bones. An older school picture of the same girl. Black and whites from older generations, and a formal wedding picture of Arthur and Sharon. There were already distinctive crags evident on young Arthur, though he also had a cute mop of dark hair and an appealing smile. Sharon looked elegant and poised, nothing like the tired woman in the bathrobe.

Mary sat down on the sofa with a coffee table book on gardening. The book was soporific, the drone of the television lulling, and before she knew it she was being lightly tapped on the arm. She gasped as she awoke to Arthur Tennant's face, horror-lit by the lamp on the side table.

"It's only me," he said mildly. "Would you like a piece of pie, or perhaps you'd prefer to go straight up to bed?"

"I think I'd better eat so I can take some more Tylenol." She followed him stiffly to the kitchen. "Did you finish your sermon?"

"First draft." He brought her the Tylenol, then served them both slices of pie. "Milk?"

"Yes, thank you."

They ate in silence for a few moments. The pie was stodgy. Mary sucked down milk to wash it down.

"This would probably be better heated up," he said.

She nodded, still chewing.

"Although I have heated up some of Bertha's pies and it hasn't really helped much. She's so persistent. You have to admire a woman who never gives up making pies from scratch no matter how badly they turn out."

"Sounds like the devil's work to me," Mary said, getting a startled laugh out of him. "How often does she inflict these pies on you?"

"Every week. Even in Lent. Not all prayers are

answered, you know." He grinned, then looked anxious. "Don't get me wrong — she's an excellent woman."

"No, of course."

"So many excellent women," he sighed.

She smiled. "Not me."

"I don't know. I sense that you are potentially excellent."

"I never bake."

"But you're Catholic. And you have a cat."

"Lapsed Catholic. Determined heathen. Sorry."

He snorted. "I love that word, *heathen*. It's so old-fashioned. Probably I ought to try to hold you here and feed you doctrine until you get over this lapsed business."

"I don't think that's too likely to work."

He smiled. "No, probably not. Though if I combined it with extreme social isolation, perhaps a little sleep deprivation… that seems to work for cults and monastic orders, anyway. Maybe I should just threaten you with additional pieces of this pie." He got up and looked out the window. "Do you want to watch some TV?"

In the living room she sat down on one end of the sofa and he sat on the other and clicked on the television, watching the weather news. The whole Northeast had been shut down by ice and driving snow and sleet.

"I've always found storms exciting," Arthur said.

"Awe-inspiring Acts of God?"

"I don't connect God with the weather. It's just exciting. When I was a child we lived in coastal North Carolina — hurricane country. When one was bearing down on us, we'd gather in the sturdiest house on high land and have a wonderful time. To us kids it was as good as any holiday. Maybe even better, because of that little thrill of mortal danger. Of course, we never lost our roof, and we never got flooded out. I believe that might have changed our attitude."

"You don't have much of a Southern accent."

"Boarding school. My mother came from old money in Boston."

"And you left hurricanes and old money behind to become a priest in New Hampshire?"

"There wasn't much of the old money left. Lucy got some when my mother died. She has a *trust*," he said mockingly. "It pays for her schooling. I swore I'd never send any child of mine to boarding school, but now I think it does her good to get out of the house."

Mary smiled uncomfortably. He was surely being a little too forthcoming.

"So what brought you to Lawson?" he asked.

What indeed? As winter ground on, Mary had occasionally wondered why she'd given sway to her fantasy of the table and the cat and the little house near the river. "I thought it was a pretty town. And I needed a change."

He looked as if he thought there must be more. "And how do you like it?"

She hesitated. "I still think it's very pretty. I'm surprised, though, at how much everybody seems to know everybody else's business."

He snorted. "I take it you've never lived in small town before?"

She shook her head. "No. So how do you like it?"

His face turned careful. "I think it's a lovely town. Very good people."

He doesn't really like it at all, she thought. "So you're here until you're reassigned?"

"No, that's not how it works in the Episcopal Church." He shifted in his seat. "I'd have to find another church willing to call me, or switch to another kind of job."

"So you're likely to stay until retirement?"

"Well, no. It's possible to get stale with a parish. But we've only been here six years, and I don't happen to be in a great position to move anywhere else right now. Sharon's not keen on moving again." There was a touch of bitterness in his tone.

Mary fell silent. Better to stick to safe subjects like the weather, really.

She was tired, the news was repetitive, and she realized without much ability to do anything about it that she was in great danger of dozing off again.

"Mary."

She turned her head into the light caress.

"Mary."

She opened her eyes, disoriented. Arthur was peering down at her with a quirky smile.

"You dozed off again, my dear. Let's get you upstairs."

She got up slowly, surprised at how stiff she was, still in a fog. Why was he smiling? Had she drooled? Snored?

The stairs were steep and strange. He turned down the bed clothes before whispering "goodnight" and closed the door softly behind him. Mary barely managed to unlace her shoes before she fell into bed and a deep sleep.

*

She awoke in darkness. Sharp gusts of wind were rattling the windows. She put together where she was and wondered if she'd left any lights on at home and whether Bob had managed to chew his way into the cat food box.

She was still wearing her watch. Just past three in the morning in a strange house and she needed to pee, damn it. Fighting stiffness, she got up and cautiously opened the door. She was thankful to find the long hall lit by a dim lamp.

She crept back to her bedroom and gasped. A ghostly figure stood there in the dark.

"Oh," the figure said. "I wondered who was using this bed."

Sharon, of course.

"Your husband invited me to stay because of the storm."

Sharon shrugged. "I see he loaned you one of my nightgowns."

"Yes. I hope you don't mind."

"You might as well be comfortable for the duration. That's my philosophy." Her tone was flat. She leaned in closer. "Have you seen his room?"

"His room?"

"My son's." Sharon opened the door directly across the hall and pulled Mary after her, turning on a blinding overhead light.

Mary blinked desperately. When she could see again, she found herself in the carefully preserved room of a young boy, heavy on red and blue, well-stocked with toys and models.

"I stripped and sanded and painted this room myself."

"It's lovely."

"He was a beautiful boy. You see?" Sharon handed Mary a framed school picture from the bureau. "He was playing in the snow after school when he collapsed. He had a heart problem we didn't know about."

"I'm so sorry."

Sharon gave her an oddly satisfied smile. "Well, good night." She padded off down the hallway and down the stairs.

Mary turned off the light and shut the door of Matthew's room. Her pulse was racing. She lay in bed and listened to Sharon below, who seemed to be walking around restlessly, then channel-surfing on the television. Later, Mary thought she heard the door across the hall open and the light flick on again. Eventually footsteps receded down the hall and quiet reclaimed the house.

She woke to the sound of a ringing phone. The morning light was grey and the radiators were thumping. It was impossible to see much through the fogged up window, but she had an impression of whiteness. She dressed and walked stiffly to the bathroom, where she washed her face and tried to smooth her hair with her fingertips. She could smell coffee, so she headed down to the kitchen.

She couldn't help a little yelp when she walked into the kitchen and there was a policeman standing in the middle of it.

She stared a moment longer than she should have, a little awed by his blond curls and blue eyes. He really was one fine looking man.

"Ah, good morning," Arthur said, bustling in from his office, fully dressed in suit and collar. "Mary Bellamy,

29

Winslow Jennings. This is the fellow I told you about last night."

She'd expected a grizzled old Yankee. Who named a kid Winslow? "Nice to meet you, Officer Jennings."

"Winslow," he said, and shook her hand with a strong grip. She had the feeling he was checking her out, though politely, and she was conscious of being in a particularly disheveled state. Not that it mattered, she reminded herself. She was done with all that.

"Do you think I can make it up the hill now?" she asked.

"We're all going momentarily," Arthur said. "We'll drop you off. Winslow already helped me get my car off the hedge, but I need some coffee first so I won't murder anybody." He handed her, then the policeman, steaming mugs and gestured at a bakery box on the table. "Winslow brought donuts."

She sat down carefully as Winslow swung onto the other end of the bench. Arthur quietly placed a bottle of Tylenol at her left. "How did you sleep?"

"Fine." After a swallow of coffee, she said as casually as she could, "I ran into Sharon during the night."

Arthur nodded. "She wanders. Too much sleep during the day."

"She showed me Matthew's room."

His face darkened, but he said nothing.

Winslow shifted uncomfortably.

"My sick parishioner, Olive Cantwell, is Winslow's great aunt," Arthur said. "So he's not only here to rescue you, but to ferry me over to the hospital."

"You bought Miss Lacey's house," Winslow said. "It was in pretty bad shape."

"Yes, I have plenty of work to do."

"Fixing it yourself?"

His blue eyes were watching her carefully. Had she neglected something in terms of building permits? "I hired a roofer. The rest I'll be doing myself, bit by bit."

"Sharon did a lot of redecorating when we first got here," Arthur said. "Annoyed the hell out of the building and grounds committee. They're supposed to approve any changes to the rectory. Maybe that's why she loves to scare poor innocent women with Matthew's room in the middle of the night. As I recall they weren't at all thrilled about the red trim."

The phone rang again and Arthur went to his study to answer it.

"I don't think it was the trim," Winslow said.

Mary felt a little thrill at being included in any flow of town gossip. "No?"

"She just wasn't popular. Didn't join the altar guild. Never volunteered for clean-up."

Mary wouldn't be caught dead joining an altar guild either, but her mother had belonged to one. "Ah, the hanging offenses."

Winslow grinned.

Arthur bustled back in with the phone in his hand. "Lucy is having a small crisis at school. Winslow, perhaps you could drop Mary and then swing back for me?"

Winslow nodded and they stood up. Arthur clasped Mary's hand, looked her in the eye, and gave her a warm smile. "It was a great pleasure having your company, Mary."

"Thank you for taking me in."

Yes, she was quite sure there were women in his congregation who swooned for him. He knew how to shake her hand as if she were the only other person in the room. No doubt it was a useful job skill. She watched as he patted Winslow on the back as if they were old, dear friends. Were they really, or was that also part of the job?

She navigated a narrow canyon of shoveled snow to Winslow's monstrous sport utility vehicle and climbed into it using the steps and handholds. "Big," she observed.

Winslow grunted. "This is Lawson's official unmarked police vehicle. Also its official all-weather, all-terrain vehicle."

"You must have been very busy last night."

"Yes. I've only been home for a shower. After I drop Father at the hospital it's back to work."

"Sorry about that."

"I'm not complaining. But that's why we couldn't help you out last night."

"I guess I'll think twice before I set out in bad weather next time."

"Perhaps it was meant to be. God works in mysterious ways."

She expected that kind of sentiment from silver-haired old ladies, not handsome blond policemen. "You think he had me fall on my ass to save my soul?"

"I was thinking more that Father Arthur might have needed the company." The SUV climbed easily over the mound of plowed snow at the end of her driveway. Now it would be even harder to shovel, but she could hardly complain. Winslow put the car in park and gave her an assessing look. "You're not religious?"

"No, not at all."

"Still, you'd be welcome at St. Andrew's."

"Thank you, but that's not likely to happen." She peered at the drifts covering her front walk. She was going to have a bit of a job just getting in the house.

"Do you have a snow blower?" he asked.

"No, but it's a small driveway. Thank you for the ride. I'm sorry about your great aunt."

"Why don't you let me help? I carry an extra shovel in the car."

Mary met his eyes. There was something there — a touch of wistfulness, perhaps? For some reason she thought: *with this one word, my whole life could change.*

"Oh, no," she said. "No, but thanks anyway. I'll be fine."

Chapter Four

THE SNOW AND ice melted quickly in the longer days of late March, and in her walks Mary noticed buds swelling on the trees. Crocuses bloomed on southern slopes and skunk cabbages unfurled on the forest floor. She cut forsythia from overgrown bushes in the yard and forced it into bloom in the house. Spring was coming, but first they had to get through mud season.

She was summoned to a meeting at work to discuss her willingness to train as a web editor. "According to their fancy new consultant, this is where our business needs to go," said her boss, Carmen. "Anyway, it's a good marketable skill to pick up."

"And I can do it from home?"

"Yes, once you learn it. The training isn't that far from you — Nashua."

Yes, that wasn't too far. "Since when did they hire a consultant?"

Carmen scowled. "Apparently our revenues are 'trending down'. People in suits have been nosing around. There's a rumor the book group is up for sale."

"But they wouldn't send me to training if they were

planning to sell us, would they? I mean, what would be the point?"

Carmen shrugged. "I stopped trying to figure out the point of anything we do around here awhile ago."

Back home, Mary walked around her little house. She tried to reassure herself that nothing happened quickly at Shanley. But John Shanley Senior, passionate vitamin enthusiast and fastest two-finger typist in the building, couldn't live forever. And John Shanley Junior, with his freshly-minted MBA, was already an object of terror.

Even if the division was sold, wouldn't the new employers need skilled employees, too? How was she supposed to find another publishing job within commuting distance of Lawson, New Hampshire?

Calm down, she told herself. Worst case, she could just sell the house and move again. Thanks to Roger, she already knew how to move on with her life.

She wasn't expecting anyone on the East Coast to wish her a happy birthday that year, though she did get a lottery ticket inside a nearly-pornographic birthday card in the day's Fed-Ex from Carmen. *Hope you strike it lucky on your birthday*, she'd written. Mary didn't win anything, but it was nice to be remembered. That evening when the phone rang, she expected it to be her mother or her sister. But it was Roger.

"Happy Birthday," he said.

"Oh. Thank you." How had he gotten her phone number?

"Doing anything to celebrate?"

"Not really."

"Why not? You should go out."

"Did she have the baby yet?" she asked.

"No. Any minute now."

"You must be excited."

"Yeah." He didn't sound excited.

"Well, I hope it all goes well."

"Mary…" He breathed heavily, apparently in the grip of some emotion.

"You know, Roger, I'm really enjoying the peace and quiet. Things worked out for the best, just like you said they would. Bye now!"

She hung up. Her heart was pounding — she'd never simply cut him off like that before. She waited, but the phone didn't ring again.

She leaned down to pet Bob, who was enticing her with a wanton display of his belly.

All in all, a cat was much easier to live with than a man.

Her training wouldn't begin for another week, so Mary enjoyed the improving weather on her walks while she could. She got frequent waves from Winslow on patrol, but she hadn't seen Arthur Tennant in days.

When she did see him again, she almost walked right past. He was sitting limply, eyes closed, on a bench in the little park at Underwood's Folly, surrounded by the brown remains of the previous summer's perennials. The Folly was the ruined foundation of a mill built on the modest falls where the smaller Cattigutt River dropped out of the hills to the west to join the Took. The Catgut, as locals sometimes called it, often dried up during droughts, but

John Underwood apparently hadn't known that when he built his mill. Bankrupt, he'd hanged himself in it one hot, dusty autumn in the late 1800s. Lawson celebrated his tragic end with a tidy historical marker, extensive plantings from the Lawson Garden Society, and the sturdy bench where Arthur now sat, so still and pale that Mary feared for a moment that he might be dead, too.

Given his own tendency to intrude, he could hardly object if she checked on him. She coughed, but he didn't react. She tapped his shoulder. "Father!"

He opened his eyes and peered at her. "Ah. Mary. Hello."

"You okay?"

"Bit under the weather. Today was so warm — I thought, let me get some sun." He coughed. "Arthur will do, you know."

"Oh, sorry — Father Arthur."

"No, just Arthur. Or even Art," he said, with a little laugh and another, deeper cough.

"Have you seen a doctor?"

He looked blank and coughed again. Unless she was much mistaken, that was a moan he stifled as he hunched over.

"How about I help you get home?"

"I'm fine. Rectory's right there." He gestured irritably.

She looked and realized the rectory *was* there, barely visible through a stand of bare trees. "That's not really that close, unless you're planning to swim across the river." The late afternoon sun was no longer providing much warmth, and the wind had picked up. "I don't think I should leave you here."

He leaned his head back against the bench and closed his eyes.

"Arthur?"

"Peace be with you," he muttered, without opening his eyes.

"And also with you," she replied, annoyed at being dismissed so liturgically. She returned to her walk, then thought better of it and detoured to the town's small police station.

"May I help you?" asked a young woman wearing a startling amount of make-up.

"Is Officer Jennings here?"

"Winslow!" she bellowed into the back. "There's a lady asking for ya."

Winslow smiled when he saw who it was. Mary blushed. Yes, she was done with men, but this guy was so damned attractive it was like trying to act natural with a movie star.

Conscious of the woman's avid stare, Mary moved off to the far end of the front desk. "It's about Arthur Tennant."

"Father Arthur?" Winslow seemed to be correcting her, and Mary fought a ridiculous urge to argue the point with him. "What is it?"

"He's sitting in the park looking rather ill. I'm not sure he can get himself home."

"Well, let's go see." He raised his voice. "Eunice, we may have a citizen in difficulty at the park. I'm taking the SUV."

"Who is it?" Eunice asked, wide-eyed.

But Winslow strode away silently.

"He'll be annoyed," Mary said.

"I wouldn't worry. Why don't you come along?"

She hesitated. "Okay." Having ratted Arthur out, she felt bad just slinking away.

The ride to the park took less than thirty seconds. Winslow didn't put the siren on, to Mary's relief. When they got there the sun had disappeared behind a cloud, and Arthur's face was tucked down into his jacket.

"Good afternoon, Father," Winslow said.

Arthur lifted his face, blanched in cold or fatigue, and focused on Mary. "You're back."

She nodded. "Getting cold out here."

He grimaced. "Yes, it is. I will take a ride home, Winslow, if you're offering."

"That I am," Winslow said, and helped Arthur get up from the bench. They shuffled slowly over to the SUV.

"Bit off more... than I could chew," Arthur said breathlessly.

"Are you sure he doesn't need the hospital?" Mary whispered to Winslow.

Winslow raised his eyebrows.

"That cough sounds bad. I think he may be wheezing."

"What are you whispering about?" Arthur complained.

"Have you seen a doctor?" Winslow asked him.

"Marsha stopped by."

"Marsha's a podiatrist."

Arthur coughed and moaned softly. "It's just that it hurts a bit."

Winslow looked at Mary, shrugged, and opened the back door for her. She hesitated, then got in. Somewhat to her surprise, Winslow drove off away from the bridge. Arthur, apparently preoccupied with breathing, didn't appear to notice until they'd pulled into the small local hospital. Then he looked up and paled. "God help me."

"Let's just get you checked out," Winslow said. "Once they say you're fine, I'll drive you home."

The intake nurse listened to Arthur's chest and shepherded him back into an examining room.

"Shouldn't we call Sharon?" Mary asked Winslow.

"Let's see what the story is first."

"She'd want to know he's here."

"You can try calling if you want. If you leave a message she might get it. She won't pick up the phone."

"How do you know?"

"Everybody knows." He gestured at the small, nearly empty waiting room. "Why don't we sit down? This shouldn't take long."

She took a seat. "You've never been married, have you?"

An older woman across the room perked up at the question and looked over expectantly.

Winslow stared at the woman until she turned back to her magazine. "No, I haven't."

The woman quite distinctly snorted.

Winslow sighed and started working on a report.

Mary picked up a magazine. Perhaps there was also something that everybody just knew about Winslow.

Eventually a doctor came out and looked curiously at Mary, who was munching crackers from the vending machine and thinking that Arthur Tennant was a bad influence on her cat's feeding schedule.

"Who are you?"

"A friend," Winslow answered for her. "How is he?"

The doctor frowned. "Is there a family member available?"

"Not at the moment."

"We've got a bunch of new HIPAA rules. I need Sharon."

"I'll take you over there if you want to talk to her."

"You know I can't leave right now."

"If she's willing, I'll bring her back. I wouldn't count on it, though. I take it you're keeping him?"

The doctor nodded.

"Can we see him?"

"Yeah, but don't tire him out."

"I'll wait here," Mary said.

"Don't be silly," Winslow said, and gestured her to go ahead of him.

Arthur looked much diminished in a pale blue hospital gown. He was dozing against the lifted back of the examining table. There was oxygen attached under his nose and an IV tube snaking into his hand.

"Father Arthur?" Winslow said.

Arthur barely opened his eyes.

"I'm going to go tell Sharon you're here and make sure she has some dinner. I'll tell Marsha too. Don't worry about a thing."

Arthur nodded almost imperceptibly and closed his eyes.

"Feel better, Arthur," Mary said gently, and squeezed his hand. She was pleased to get a little smile, though he didn't open his eyes. Winslow, she noticed, looked a trifle taken aback.

"Poor man," she said, once they were in the car.

"He's had more than his share of crosses to bear."

"Who's Marsha?"

"She's our warden. Of the church."

"Keeps the inmates in line."

He smiled. "She tries."

When he stopped at the rectory, Mary climbed out of the SUV and tasted freedom. "If you don't mind, I think I'll just walk up from here."

"I was hoping you'd come in with me."

Mary lowered her voice. "I think that woman is scary."

"I know. Come on, I need back-up." He knocked on the side door and walked in. Sharon was fully dressed and sitting at the kitchen table in front of a bowl of soup and a loaf of bread.

"Hello, Sharon," Winslow said.

"Hello, Winslow." She looked curiously at Mary. "Do you have a new deputy?"

"No. She's —"

"Mary, isn't it? Would either of you happen to know where my husband is?"

"That's why we're here," Winslow said.

She put down her spoon and gave them her full attention.

Winslow recited the facts with the precision of a man used to giving testimony.

Sharon looked relieved. "I knew he wouldn't just forget dinner."

"Would you like me to drive you back there so you can see him?"

Sharon paled. "I don't like that place."

"But —"

"He'll be fine. You just said so. You'll look after him, won't you, Winslow?"

"Dr. Potter would like to be able to talk to you about his condition."

"But you just told me his condition."

"It could change—"

Her face turned hard. "He can call."

Winslow grimaced. "Is there anything you need?"

"No, I'm fine. Thank you for asking." She took another spoonful of her soup.

Winslow just stood there.

"Is there something else?" she asked.

"Maybe I could take him his toothbrush or something?"

"He keeps a travel kit in the bathroom closet."

Since she made no move to get it herself, Winslow ran up the stairs. He'd left her alone with Sharon. Mary smiled awkwardly.

"So how are you finding St. Andrew's?" Sharon asked.

"I've never been there."

Sharon paused. "You're in one of the ecumenical groups?"

"I don't go to church at all. I just keep bumping into your husband."

"Must be God's will," Sharon said dryly.

"I'm not religious at all, actually."

Sharon looked at her with new interest. "No? Good for

you! I think it's just the most amazing load of crap, don't you?"

Winslow came back down, kit in hand. "Is this it?"

"Yes, that's it." Sharon winked at Mary. "Thank you, Winslow. Please tell Arthur I hope he feels better soon."

"She seems happy to have the house to herself," Mary said, heaving herself back up into the SUV. What exactly had that wink signified? Was it from one unbeliever to another? One woman to another? Was it something connected to Winslow? She eyed him critically as he backed the car out of the rectory.

"She kind of lost it when their son died," Winslow said. "Hasn't been right since."

"Seems pretty lucid to me, if not all one could hope for in a wife."

He gave her a sidelong look and pulled into her driveway.

"Well, it sounded like they might send him home tomorrow," Mary said. She put her hand on the door handle.

Winslow cleared his throat. "Would you like to go out sometime?"

She stopped and stared at him. "Out?"

"Yes, out. On a date." His eyes fell on her in that assessing way they had.

"Oh, I can't do that. I only just got divorced."

"Then how about a cup of coffee sometime?"

"Just a friendly cup of coffee?"

He nodded.

"Okay, sure. Coffee sometime."

"I'll call you," he said, as she got out.

She hadn't given him her phone number. But then, everyone in town probably already knew it.

CHAPTER FIVE

MARY HADN'T ANTICIPATED needing to fend men off.

A man like Winslow wasn't part of her dream of the little house and the ginger cat and the sun falling on the table. She could adjust to minor changes, like a black cat and a table that didn't get any sun. Add a tall, blond policeman and the house got too small and cramped and fussy. Arthur Tennant she could imagine fitting in occasionally — visiting priest has cup of tea, behaves impeccably, leaves promptly. Priests were practically half women to begin with. But Winslow was a cop, which made him twice the masculine threat of the average man. He wore a uniform and carried a gun and probably knew exactly how to murder her and safely dispose of her body.

On the other hand, she'd have to be dead not to feel gratified that she'd been asked out by anybody at this point in her life.

He called later that evening and asked her to join him for coffee at the hospital the next day. While they were there they could also check on Father Arthur.

"Okay," said Mary, disconcerted. Perhaps he was

actually just trying to keep her involved in the tortured life of Arthur Tennant.

But she didn't mind checking on Arthur. Somebody should.

The next day was warm and sunny, so Mary decided to hike to the hospital even though it sat on the ugly state road that bypassed the center of town and provided a home for two apparently warring tire stores ("We'll match ANY competitor's price!!!"), a used car lot, and the town's only strip mall, populated by a Freihofer's bakery outlet, a propane dealer, a Goodwill thrift store, and the town's lone pizzeria.

Winslow was already there when she arrived breathlessly, the walk having taken longer than she'd expected. He smiled and laid aside a sheaf of reports.

"I'll just get my coffee," Mary said. She didn't want him to think for a minute that this was a real date.

He had started to rise, but sat back down. "I believe Margie just made a fresh pot." He nodded towards the pretty blonde working the counter. "She's one of my cousins."

Margie's gaze was frankly appraising when Mary came up to get her coffee, though she didn't say much — just looked over at Winslow with raised eyebrows.

Mary took a cautious sip when she sat down again. "Not bad."

"Margie's a good kid."

Mary guessed that Margie was at least in her late twenties. How old was Winslow? He had one of those ageless Scandinavian physiques. "How long have you been a policeman here?"

"Awhile now," he said, not very helpfully. "I joined the force a couple of years after I left the Marines."

"You were a Marine?" A Marine was even less likely to fit into her cottage than a cop. Mary was not exactly a snob — she'd grown up in a working class family herself — but she immediately slotted Winslow into a category of guys she would never consider dating even if she wanted to date, which she didn't.

"I enlisted after college."

Okay, perhaps she'd been a little hasty. "What did you study?"

He looked embarrassed. "Philosophy."

"Philosophy!" She'd never known anyone to actually major in that. "Why?"

Winslow shrugged and hunched over his coffee. "I liked it. What about you? What did you study?"

"Oh, English." She had long felt mildly embarrassed by her English degree, but compared to philosophy it was practically vocational training.

"And you're an editor."

"Yes."

"Do you get free books?"

"Nothing too exciting, unless you're into amazing vinegar cures or wheat grass shakes."

He wrinkled his nose. "No. I'm a cop, I eat donuts."

She was about to ask him where he'd studied when he said, "So you were married?"

It didn't really matter how old he was, because after this conversation it wouldn't matter. She smiled tightly. "Yes, for eight years. But he wanted kids, and I couldn't have any."

"You couldn't adopt?"

"We never got to that point. Anyway, he's already remarried and expecting a baby."

"That must hurt."

"It did at first." Politeness perhaps required that she ask him about his own romantic history, but what was the point? She drained the tepid remains of her coffee. "Shall we go see the patient?"

Arthur appeared to be dozing when they first walked in, but roused when Mary whispered, "I think he's asleep."

"I am not!" He scooted up on the pillows. "You think people can sleep in hospitals?"

"You look better," Mary said.

"I've coughed most of my lungs out already. Anything left has got to be much healthier."

"Praise God," Winslow said and Mary cringed inwardly. Who talked like that?

"I'll praise God when they let me out of here," Arthur said. "I'm hoping they'll discharge me this morning."

"Is that likely?" Mary asked.

"Damn well better be." But he ruined the effect of his declaration by coughing.

Winslow's police radio squawked and he excused himself.

She sat down in the side chair. "Pneumonia?" she asked. He nodded.

"Did they get the culture back?"

"Culture? You seem to know more about this than I do."

"My mother was a nurse. We got to hear all the gory details."

"She died?"

"No, she moved to Arizona."

He lay there, smiling oddly at her.

"What?" she asked, patting her head. "Is there something in my hair?" Once she'd gotten home and found a rather large twig entangled there.

He flushed slightly. "No. I was just thinking that you are a lovely woman."

She felt a little involuntary thrill. Perhaps he thought ministering to her might involve shoring up her feminine self-esteem. Or maybe he was just a hopeless flirt. "We stopped in and saw Sharon yesterday. Have you been able to talk to her?"

He rolled and unrolled the hem of his blanket. "I left a message."

"Does she have agoraphobia?"

"Does she? I suppose it's possible. Preferable to thinking she just doesn't give a damn."

"She did ask about you. She does appear a bit...." Mary was about to say *detached*.

"Mental?"

She was shocked into silence.

"Well, I hope that's it. I hope she's mentally ill, and not just spiteful. She didn't want to move here, you see. She argued, among other things, that the health care would be primitive. And then Matthew died right here in this hospital." He coughed, then winced. "Maybe she was right. Or maybe he would have died anyway. We'll never know. But she'll never forgive me."

"Losing a child is probably enough to unhinge any mother."

"Oh, no doubt, but it gets old, especially when there's another, living child in the picture." He shook his head. "I'm sorry. This is far more than you want to know."

Mary was wondering what to say to that when Winslow returned. Arthur asked him something having to do with the church, then started coughing and didn't stop. A nurse leaned in the door. "Bringing anything up, Father?"

Arthur was too busy coughing to reply, but the answer was obvious.

"Very good!" the nurse said. "I'll be right back."

"You'd better leave," he managed to gasp out, tears in his eyes.

"I'll check in on you later, Father," Winslow said hurriedly, and put his hand on Mary's shoulder.

"Feel better," Mary said. She squeezed Arthur's hand briefly. He gave her a plaintive look before he was overtaken by coughing again.

Winslow had to get back to work. She accepted a quick ride to the police station, but refused his offer to drop her at home.

"Would you like to try this again?" he asked, as they pulled up in front of the station.

It had been a quiet drive, which she'd attributed to the effects of hearing someone gag his lungs out, or her infertility disclosure, or his mind already running ahead to work. But apparently he was still trying to enlist her in The Friends of Father Arthur. "You mean visit Arthur again?"

"No, I meant coffee. Or lunch or something."

What could he possibly see in her now? "Well, the thing

is, I have out-of-town training coming up next week. I'm going to be kind of busy getting ready for that."

"I see." He got out of the car.

"I enjoyed the coffee, though!" she said, after she'd joined him on the sidewalk in front of the police station. This felt all wrong. Groping for a way to put it right, she stuck out her hand for a handshake. "Thank you, Winslow. It was a pleasure getting to know you better."

He raised an eyebrow and shook her hand formally. "Likewise, Mary." She had the impression he was mocking her, but figured she deserved it. Stupid handshake! She was terrible at all this and always had been. It was just as well she had put it all behind her.

CHAPTER SIX

SPRING FINALLY ARRIVED in earnest: trees flowered; tulips blossomed; frogs peeped in the marshes. Mary watched the front garden erupt in shades of green and red and wondered how anyone could tell what was what.

Carrie Woodbury was walking up the hill that Saturday afternoon while Mary was unloading groceries. Mary waved eagerly to her. "You wanted some peonies. I think they must be coming up."

"Oh, you don't want to be getting in there yet, dear! You'll compact the beds!"

Mary felt rebuked. Gardening, it seemed, was even more mysterious than web design.

She was doing well with the Internet training — learning the relevant programs and the basic principles and pitfalls of web design. Her favorite new concept was *graceful degradation,* the principle of designing a web site so that essential content could get through relatively intact even on outdated or eccentric web browsers. It struck Mary as applicable to life in general. She certainly didn't want anyone in Lawson to get the wrong idea about her. But what should she be trying to get across? *Quiet spinster-type — no threat to you — only wants to be left alone?*

Though it could be the message had gotten out. Certainly Winslow had not called again, though he still waved when he passed by in the SUV. Mary waved back, sometimes with a pang of regret that was wholly irrational.

Saturday afternoon was pleasant and she decided to tackle the backyard, which was matted with the remains of at least two years of autumn leaves. She raked and peeled the half-rotted layers into soggy piles and surveyed the muddy traces of what had once been a lawn. She had just gone inside for a drink of water when her doorbell rang, and there was Arthur Tennant, meticulously neat in a suit and clerical collar.

"Hi," Mary said, conscious of her muddy sweats and unwashed hair. Arthur looked much healthier this time, though still a bit gaunt.

"Hello." He smiled and extended his hand.

"Better not," she said, and held up a hand still crusted with muck. "I've been raking out the back yard."

"Is that why I haven't seen you walking lately?"

"No. I was off getting some training."

"I wanted to thank you for helping me when I was ill."

"It was the least I could do."

"Why don't you show me your garden?" he said.

"Oh, stuff is just coming up; I don't even know what most of it is."

"I could help you with that." He took off down the few steps to the terraced front garden. "You've done some work here already, I see," he said. "It must have pained poor Agnes to see the weeds taking over."

"She was in your parish?"

"No, Unitarian."

"You know everybody in town, don't you?"

"I know the ones who get on the radar of our community groups. We were very concerned about Agnes, but she wouldn't accept any help."

"She was an independent woman."

"She was also a lonely woman."

"How do you know that?"

"She was lying dead in this house for days before they found her. That strikes me as pretty damned lonely."

Agnes Lacey lay dead in this house for days? Mary reviewed her memory of the rather distinctive smells of the house when she'd first seen it. "Do you know where?" she asked faintly. Even her bed had come from the estate. Surely they wouldn't have left her a bed someone had died in? Goddamn Yankee frugality — what if they had?

Arthur looked distressed. "You didn't know?"

"No, I didn't. Do you know where she was when she… passed?"

"I have no idea. Winslow could tell you; he was there."

"Oh." She could hardly call him.

"I'm sure he'd be happy to hear from you."

Would her budget stretch to a new bed, and how soon could it arrive?

"What happened there, anyway?"

"Mmm?" Really, it was only the mattress that mattered, right? Keene must have mattress stores. Still, the thought that a corpse might have been lying in her bed for days —

"He told me you turned him down for coffee."

With difficulty, Mary focused again on Arthur. "I was

just trying to get stuff finished up before my training began." She was glad she remembered the excuse she had used.

"I think he interpreted that as a lack of interest."

"Well, there was little point."

"Why not?"

Was he actually here on a mission for Winslow? "I told you I can't have children."

"Good grief, Mary. Infertility is hardly a reason to withdraw from all hope of a loving relationship."

"It's not just that. He's also too religious."

"Oh, that's just the way he talks, you know. He grew up in a family of Evangelicals. You should hear his dad talk."

"Then he's not actually religious?"

"Well, no, of course he is."

"Well, that's my point, isn't it?"

Arthur just looked at her for a moment, then pointed at an eruption of curly red fronds. "That's a peony."

"It is?" Mary was interested despite herself. "There are an awful lot of them."

"Oh, yes. Agnes put cages up every spring to keep them from flopping over."

Oops. So that's what all those rusty wire things had been. "I think I just tossed them all out. Anyway, there's a woman up the street who wants to dig some up."

"Carrie? Tell her to wait until fall. That's the best time to divide peonies, as she well knows. As for cages, you just need to get a roll of wire fencing at the hardware store — I can show you how to make them."

"I'm sure I can figure it out."

"I'm sure you can, too, but let me help anyway."

She sighed, feeling bullied.

He gave her a look that was unsettlingly intense. "Look, Mary, here's the thing. I need a friend and so, I suspect, do you."

She stared at him. He gazed back steadily, grey eyes earnest.

She softened her automatic response a bit. He was a nice man. There was no need to be cruel. "Leaving aside the issue of whether I actually need one, how can we be friends?"

He looked taken aback. "What do you mean?"

"You're a priest — and a married man. I'm a single, divorced woman. I don't even believe in God. Unless you believe that I am one of the community's hard luck cases, somehow requiring your specific intervention — which would really annoy me — you have no good reason to ever be seen with me. I already feel like the whole town is discussing what brand of kitty litter I buy. I don't want to generate more gossip."

He looked amused. "I sincerely doubt anyone in this town cares about your kitty litter. And I don't think a platonic friendship between a man and a woman is going to raise too many eyebrows these days. If it did, I would point out that Jesus himself hung out with tax collectors, prostitutes, and other riff raff."

"Jesus also got crucified."

Arthur grimaced as if she'd just said something distasteful.

"Not to mention he was trying to save the riff raff, and I would be deeply offended if that's what you have in mind."

59

"I'm not trying to save you, though I can't deny it would make me happy to see you experience God's grace— "

She huffed impatiently and turned away.

Arthur's voice rose as he pursued her. "It's just — do you think there's anybody else in this town willing to tell me I'm full of shit when I start throwing around allusions to Jesus? There's nobody here that I can talk to on an equal basis, except other clergy, and that gets old."

"There's your wife."

"You've met her," he said dismissively.

"So that's what you want, someone to argue with?"

"No, I want a friend." He looked discouraged, now, and stared out across the yard. "But I can't make you be a friend, obviously."

She sighed. "People don't decide to be friends. It happens naturally."

"And you have already been a friend to me. Although it may seem like little to you, it meant a great deal to me. All I'm asking is that you allow me to be a friend to you. Please."

She didn't know how to say no to such a direct plea. "All this so you can help me build peony cages?"

He smiled. "Actually, I thought you might enjoy a climb before the bugs get bad. Have you been up Monadnock yet?"

"No," she said, intrigued. Although she couldn't see it from her home, Monadnock was the major landmark in this part of the state, a mountain with a distinctive silhouette made all the more striking by the way it rose out of relatively flat land.

"You just need decent boots for getting across the muddy bits."

"Are you sure you should be climbing a mountain?"

He scowled. "I've climbed it dozens of times. I do it every year at this time. But it would be nice to have company."

She looked doubtfully at him, but agreed to go with him the following Saturday. Then he told her what was in her garden, providing far more information than she could absorb. She eventually reminded him that she had raking to finish.

As he walked off down the hill and Mary returned to her raking, she thought she saw a curtain fall in her neighbor's window.

It just figured.

CHAPTER SEVEN

SATURDAY FOUND MARY grumpily pulling on her hiking boots and berating herself for agreeing to a hike with Arthur Tennant just because the man wouldn't take no for an answer. She still had doubts whether he should be attempting this hike. She had been doing her research, and although Monadnock was quite accessible — climbed more than any other peak in the world, some sources claimed — it was still a mountain. She also couldn't help the suspicion that Arthur wanted to recoup his manhood — establish that keeping house for a cranky wife, lying in a hospital bed, and choking down bad pie was not all he could do. And this was a bit worrisome.

Could he actually have a little crush on her? Mary found it rather sweet the way even aging, educated men longed to be perceived as strong and virile by at least one woman — but she had no desire to be that woman herself, especially in this case. So when he arrived she was wondering about his motives and not feeling particularly gracious. He was not wearing his collar, she noticed, but instead was layered up in wind gear.

He seemed jaunty. "Don't bother filling up your water

bottle. There's a spring right on the trail with water that's not to be missed."

"I can always empty it out when we get there." She felt so oppositional it was almost a physical sensation, and she considered canceling right then and there. "I have to get some homework done this afternoon, so we'd better get going."

"Smells like you've been painting?" he asked, beginning to head down the hall in the direction of the fumes.

"That's a mess!" she yelled after him, not wanting him in her bedroom, where she had been painting the walls and even the bed, which now had a new mattress, in bright cheerful colors unlike anything Agnes Lacey lived and died in.

He turned back, for once getting the hint.

She picked up her pack, still reluctant. "You're sure this isn't a bit too strenuous so soon after pneumonia?"

"But I'm fine," he said, looking surprised.

Ahead of her, Arthur suddenly stopped and leaned, pale and trembling, on a damp boulder. He looked as if he might pass out. He had done fine on the early stretch of the trail, which had a moderate incline and more mud to deal with than anything. Once they had broken the tree line, though, he had started coughing. He'd kept insisting he was fine. Now he was clearly wheezing.

"Maybe I'd better go get some help," she said, though where she would get it, she had no idea. But surely someone would be able to help.

He shook his head. Eventually he managed to gasp out, "Just need a minute."

Perhaps someone in the parking area would have a cell phone? Would it matter? Her budget didn't allow one, but she'd heard service was spotty at best in this area.

Arthur just kept wheezing, embracing the boulder as if it could save him. She leaned back against it, close to him, staring out at the view, which was indeed lovely. Would he have attempted this hike if she hadn't agreed to go with him? Clearly she shouldn't have agreed. Still, it was probably better that he had someone with him. What would her mother the nurse advise?

She'd advise that Mary not go out hiking with a married man, that's what she'd advise.

"Arthur, I really think I should head down and get you some help."

He shook his head and whispered, "I'll be fine."

What if he died? She'd be that woman Father Arthur was with when he died. That stupid woman who'd let a man die on a mountain because she didn't know how to say no to a really bad idea.

A small clump of hikers approached — the first group she'd seen going down rather than up. She could send a request for help with them, couldn't she?

"You folks okay?"

A spry, white-haired man from the group had already stopped on the other side of Arthur, who nodded automatically and whispered, "Yes, fine," before coughing again.

"He's having trouble breathing," Mary said.

"Yes, I'd say so," the man said. "I'm a doctor," he added.

Oh thank goodness. "He was in the hospital with pneumonia a few weeks ago."

"Ah. Well, you certainly don't lack ambition, Mr. —?"

"Tennant," Arthur sighed.

"You have an inhaler with you, Mr. Tennant?"

Arthur shook his head.

"Well, it's your lucky day, because I have punky lungs, too, and I have an extra one with me. Let's have you take a puff, shall we?"

The transformation was dramatic. Arthur visibly relaxed as his breathing eased.

"That's better," the doctor said, and handed the inhaler to Mary. "You keep it in case he needs it again. He needs to follow up with a pulmonologist. He's actually done fairly well to get this far, but no more mountains until he's been checked out, okay?"

She decided not to correct his obvious misapprehension that she was Arthur's wife. It was almost a pleasure to feel so anonymous again.

The doctor turned to Arthur. "Make sure you sit for a while and then take it easy going down, okay?"

Arthur said "Thank you," with a poor attempt at a smile.

"Thank you for your help," Mary said.

"Oh, it's nothing," the man said, with a comforting pat on her arm, and continued down with his companions, a couple of robust-looking older women.

Arthur looked miserable.

"You were right that the views are beautiful," she said. "Do you want to eat a bit now, or head down first?"

"We haven't gotten anywhere near the summit yet."

She narrowed her eyes. "And we're not going to."

He waved his hand dismissively. "I'm feeling much better. On a day like this you'll be able to see all the way to Boston."

"You don't have to impress me, you know."

He frowned. "I'm not trying to impress you."

"If you insist on going up there, you're going alone. I'm going to sit here awhile and enjoy the view, and then I'll meet you down at the car. Here's that inhaler."

He took it, face turning red, but didn't make any move to leave.

She pulled herself up until she was actually sitting on the boulder he'd been leaning on, then pulled out her bag of trail mix and picked out chocolate candies to suck on. This little snit would probably put an end to the whole 'let's be friends' thing.

He followed her example and they sat, listening to his breathing as it steadied.

"Maybe I am trying to impress you," he said, finally.

She raised her eyebrows, surprised.

"Or myself. I don't know. God knows I've seen plenty of men go through some sort of crisis at middle age. I've always sworn that the one thing I would never do was just give up and sit in the recliner."

Mary frowned. "You're awfully young to be worrying about that."

He looked out at the horizon. "My father spent his last ten years sitting in a recliner — he had a war injury. He died at 52 when a piece of shrapnel traveled up to his heart."

"I'm sorry."

He shrugged and stared pensively out at the view. "It seemed so young. But of course, he had a very full life compared to my son's."

"It must be very difficult to go on after the death of a child."

Arthur sighed. "I don't feel I ever had any choice about it. Sharon fell apart, and Lucy still needed to be brought up and food still had to be put on the table. And, of course, it's hardly being a good role model as a priest, is it, to despair the loss of a child who has presumably gone to be with God?"

"Presumably?"

He gave her a crooked little smile. "Well, there's no proving the matter, is there? One must take it on faith. And I find that faith can wax and wane a bit."

They fell silent as another party of hikers passed by with friendly nods.

"I didn't think the average priest would have all that much waning to cope with."

"Lay people never do." He sounded bleak.

She stared. "How can you stand to do your job if you're feeling doubtful?"

He shrugged. "I find that ritual can carry me along when I'm feeling dry. I continue doing the things I must do, and sooner or later the feeling that I actually believe in what I'm doing, and that God gives a fig whether I'm doing it, returns."

"Huh," she said, surprised. Somehow she'd never imagined a priest having that sort of problem, but then Arthur was the first priest she'd ever talked to outside a church setting. She could think of a priest or two from her childhood who might have been just going through the motions, but she was certain they would never have admitted it. She slid off the boulder back onto the trail and brushed crumbs off her clothing. "Shall we?"

He followed her and hoisted his day pack. "When did

you lose your faith? When you found you couldn't have children?"

She snorted. "Oh, no, long before that. About the time I got confirmed. There was something about the way everything could be reduced to these ridiculous multiple choice questions."

Mary had forgotten how much she disliked descents, from the need to pick one's steps carefully to the strain it put on seldom-used muscles. But descending didn't take much breath, and Arthur didn't seem to be having any trouble. He hadn't said much either, though, except to point out occasional rock formations and trail heads.

The trail was increasingly busy. Some hikers they passed were equipped in expedition gear, while others wore sneakers, jeans, and sweatshirts. A number of groups had passed them when a girl just coming up the trail shrieked as only a teenage girl could and cried, "Father Arthur!" The two girls with her stopped and exchanged sullen glances, perhaps at the intrusion of God into their Saturday.

"Hello girls!" he said heartily. "Allison, you must bring your friends along with you to youth group sometime."

The girls looked really alarmed now.

Mary was standing a little aside when Arthur seemed to recollect that she was there. "Oh, girls, this is Mary Bellamy. She recently moved to town from Massachusetts. Turns out we share a fondness for hiking. Mary, Allison lives right up the street from you, in the big yellow house. Mary lives in Miss Lacey's house."

"Nice to meet you," Mary said, smiling bravely.

"Hi," the girls said. Allison's eyes were wide, and the other two girls smirked at each other.

"Well, see you tomorrow, Allison," Arthur said, and moved on. A burst of girlish giggles erupted behind them a few moments later.

"You're busted," Mary said, as the trail widened into an old logging road and they could walk side by side again.

He looked puzzled. "Busted?"

"Those girls. It will be all over town that you were seen lurking on the mountain with that divorced woman."

"I don't have anything to hide. If Sharon has no problem with it, I hardly see why anyone else should. This is not *The Scarlet Letter*."

"So you told her?"

"Yes, of course," he said, looking surprised. "Not that I expected her to care one way or the other. Nor did she, so long as I brought the paper up for her before I left."

"She must trust you."

He snorted. "She trusts me to honor my vows by maintaining her in relative comfort for the rest of her natural life."

"The Episcopal Church doesn't allow priests to divorce?"

"Oh, there are ways one can go about it. But it's not really the thing to do, is it, ditching your wife because she's ill? Besides, there's Lucy to consider."

"Henry the Eighth chucked his wives regularly. Isn't he the founder of your church?"

He smiled. "I suppose if I were Henry, Sharon would have been packed off to some distant castle by now."

"Or beheaded."

His mouth dropped open.

"Sorry," she said quickly. "Sometimes I just blurt out these things...."

"So I've noticed."

An awkward silence fell. They had reached the end of the trail — probably in more ways than one.

CHAPTER EIGHT

WHEN HER TRAINING ended, Mary took a week's vacation. She wanted to get the rest of the yard in shape. She had a stretch of beautiful spring days to do it in, too. But without the distraction of her regular work or her training, she began for the first time to feel that she really might be a bit lonely.

In her old neighborhood, she'd chatted with neighbors and attended the occasional block party or barbecue. Here she had yet to meet her nearest neighbors. She'd seen the Curtain Lady outside once or twice, getting into a car that had pulled into the driveway. The other house was home to a man and a woman and a young girl who could be seen coming and going, presumably to jobs and school. There had been a wave or two, but no conversation over the picket fence and overgrown roses that separated their small properties. There were no houses immediately across the street, just the fenced-in grounds of a crumbling estate further up the hill.

She hadn't seen or heard from Arthur, which was a bit irritating after that impassioned plea for friendship. But perhaps he'd decided that on second thought he really shouldn't hang out with a woman who casually mentioned beheading his wife. She went ahead and constructed cages for the peonies without his help. Perhaps this was what prevented Carrie Woodbury from stopping by to claim any divisions, although Mary would have willingly parted with a good many plants in exchange for some conversation.

One day she was weeding in the front garden when a familiar-sounding car stopped and idled in front of the house.

"What'cha doin'?"

The spade dropped from her fingers. Yes, it was him — Roger, smirking at her from inside his BMW.

"Cute cottage, Mary. Very quaint! What is it, a two bedroom?"

How could she have already forgotten how strong his Boston accent could be?

She straightened up slowly, brushing her hands off on her pants. "Where's your wife?"

"Home with the baby. How about a drink? Come on, anywhere you want."

"I don't think that's such a good idea."

"Or coffee. Whatever you want, wherever you want. I just want to talk."

She should tell him to go to hell. But she was also curious. This might be the very worst sign of how desperate she was for conversation. "Let me get cleaned up."

"Can I come in?"

"No. Wait out here."

Roger pulled into the driveway and listened to his favorite Boston sports station at excessive volume while she went in and scrubbed dirt off and changed her clothes into something more presentable, but not too attractive either.

"Where to?" he asked, when she came out.

"There's an inn just up the road."

"This is pretty country."

"Yes."

"So what do you do for entertainment around here?"

"Enjoy the pretty country, I guess."

He snorted. "Cultural wasteland, huh?"

"When was the last time you did anything cultural?" Roger's parents dabbled in the symphony and the arts, or at least the fancy dress balls associated with them, but Roger's passions were simpler: football, hockey, baseball, home improvement, beer, and BMWs. He had endured a few plays and museums with Mary early in their marriage before she'd understood the depth of his bewilderment that anyone could prefer anything like that to a bracing afternoon with the New England Patriots.

She watched him as he drove and decided he was still attractive — slightly impish looking with his dark unruly hair and long eyelashes. Roger's mother had once told her she thought he was too cute for his own good, and Mary was inclined to agree. She'd certainly been deeply flattered by serious attention from such a handsome, well-connected man.

"You're looking a little thin," he said, as they left the car.

"Lost a little weight," she agreed.

"But you look good." He sounded surprised.

In the inn, which was dark, quiet, and nearly empty, they sat down at either side of a rough-hewn table. Roger conducted his usual interrogation as to which beers were on tap, and the waitress confirmed his cultural wasteland theory by listing only domestic brands. After some fussing, he chose an acceptable bottled import. Apparently his drinking hadn't yet reached the point of requiring a cheaper supply. They were given a bowl of peanuts to go with their drinks and Mary ate them eagerly, having once again forgotten lunch.

"So Darlene had the baby," he said.

"Congratulations."

"I don't think it's mine."

Mary blinked, surprised at how casually he was sharing this with her.

"It doesn't look anything like me. And she named it David. I told her I wanted Roger Bellamy Jr., but she insisted on David."

Mary wasn't a big fan of the name Roger either. But she had focused on the sexy French undertones of it, occasionally even pronouncing it *Rojh-AIR* — which he hated. "Maybe he just looks like one of the grandparents. You know, recessive genes."

"I don't think so. I ordered a paternity test. When she found out she acted all pissed off, like how dare I not trust her, but I think it's just an act." His face darkened. "She's been playing me all along. That's what I think."

"Could he be yours?"

He shifted in his seat. "Yeah, of course. But I'm pretty sure I'm not the only candidate."

Mary was suddenly very glad she'd already tested negative for the various social diseases.

"Anyway, she has this Puerto Rican friend, Gabby — Gabriel — supposedly her sister's friend, but he's always around. Her low-life friends talk about him and then shut up when I come in the room. And if you ask me, this baby looks a lot like him."

"Sounds like you two could use some counseling."

"Fuck that." He drained his beer and signaled for another one.

She sighed. Once the language started it was always downhill.

He wiped his mouth and cocked his head at her. "Come on, admit it. You're thinking, you're getting your just rewards, asshole."

"No." And it was true, somewhat to her surprise. It was such a pathetic story — for Roger and Darlene, but especially for poor little baby David. If there were a God, she might ask why he saw fit to bless so many messed-up women with so many infants while withholding even one from her. But she didn't believe in God. She also assumed that if she'd slept around in her teens and early twenties she might have gotten pregnant, too. "Are you sure you're not making too much out of this? Like, maybe you're feeling a little guilty or something?"

"Guilty? Yeah, so okay, I know I put my desire to have a family ahead of my marriage vows, but it's not like you can't get an annulment in that kind of situation. And it still doesn't excuse her for being a lying slut." He leaned back, legs spread, and chugged his beer.

Had she really once loved this man? "So what are you going to do if he isn't yours?"

"Toss the bitch out. Let her boyfriend support her and his little brat without making more of a fool out of me."

"And if he is yours?"

77

"I'll cross that bridge when I get to it. I don't think I'll have to, though." He gulped down the last of his beer.

"This is really sad, Roger."

"I know. It's fucking pathetic." He signaled for another beer.

"If you drink that, I'm driving."

"Whatever." He waved his hand at her dismissively.

"And you're on your own once I'm home, I don't care how drunk you are."

"Jesus, Mary, it's just three beers! What makes you think I'd want to stay, anyway?"

"Maybe the way you're chugging beers miles away from home while you complain to me about your slutty wife."

He gave her a disgusted look. "You have a boyfriend yet?"

"No."

"Big surprise there."

"Why bother? I can do what I want when I want. No sitting around bored while someone channel surfs, no freezing cold tailgates at football games I don't care about. No more listening to your relatives asking me when we're going to have a baby."

"How nice. Just you and your empty bed."

"I sleep like a baby. I have a cat now, too."

"Jesus. Why'd you get married in the first place if you like being an old maid so much?"

She'd wondered this herself. "I guess it seemed like a good idea at the time. It's what people do. You know, like that lady in *Airplane* — 'At least I have a husband!'"

He laughed. They had always shared a weakness for low comedies. He chugged down the rest of his beer and signaled for the bill. "Okay then, Miss Mary. Let's get you back to your kitty cat."

"I'm driving."

"Yeah, yeah, yeah, I know. You just miss the Beemer." He tossed her the keys.

Eight years of marriage, and he didn't know her at all. She'd always thought it was a stupid, pretentious car.

"How about a cup of coffee?" he asked, when she'd pulled into her driveway. "That beer is making me sleepy."

"If you're entertaining any idea that I might have sex with you for old time's sake, you can just forget about it right now."

"Sex? Jesus Christ, Mary, it's just a cup of coffee."

"And I don't want to hear anything about how I should be hanging drywall. I'll get to it when I get to it."

"Got yourself a fixer-upper, huh?" He rubbed his hands together.

Against her better judgment, she let him into the kitchen through her side door. Roger peeked into the adjoining rooms and winced. Bob slinked in and took a long look at the new guy.

Roger sneezed twice.

"He's shedding. The bedroom would kill you," she added, just in case he had any ideas.

"You really do need to hang some drywall. Jesus, and that's just the start. I hope you didn't pay a lot for this shack."

She focused on the coffee. The sooner he drank it, the sooner he'd leave.

"I could help you fix it up, though."

"I don't think so."

Bob, after peering in from the doorway, decided to brave the stranger so he could come in and curl himself around Mary's legs, something he seldom neglected to do when she was anywhere near food. Roger sneezed again. His eyes had gone all watery. If Mary had ever doubted his allergy, she didn't any longer.

"Not so long as you have that fucking cat, anyway." He sneezed again.

Mary shooed Bob down the steps into the cellar and closed the door.

"Thank you." He blew his nose on a paper towel.

"Drink your coffee."

He sat at the kitchen table and drank while she leaned against the counter, sipping her own. "You make great coffee," he said wistfully.

She doubted it was anything special. "Darlene doesn't?"

"Darlene likes those awful sweet instant coffees. The better to mix in a little vodka."

"Even while she was pregnant?"

"Not in front of me — she knew I'd freak. I'd find empty bottles, though."

"Is she all alone with the baby right now?"

"Nah, her mother's there. Probably supplying the vodka."

Just how sordid could his life get? "Sounds like this kid could really use a good father."

"I'm not Mother Theresa. I didn't sign up to raise some stranger's kid." He drained his coffee. "You hungry? You want to grab some dinner?"

"No, thanks." She folded her arms and leaned back

against the counter. The beer and peanuts from the inn were coming back on her. The taste reminded her of long afternoons spent in sports bars with Roger and his buddies.

"She can't cook worth crap, either."

"You weren't always a big fan of my cooking."

"I guess I just didn't know how good I had it."

"I guess not."

"You're prettier than her, too."

She sighed. "It's time for you to leave, Roger."

"Oh come on, Mary." He waggled his eyebrows at her suggestively.

She went to the door and held it open, wondering uncomfortably what she would do if he refused to go. Walk out of her own house?

Thankfully, he gave in. "You're being very cold, Mary," he said, as he stalked past her. "Very cold. And you know what else? Your house smells like somebody died in it."

CHAPTER NINE

AFTER ROGER LEFT, Mary no longer felt even the slightest bit lonely, but she was in a mild panic about how her house smelled. She threw out rugs and drapes, left windows open, and put dishes of potpourri, vinegar, or baking soda in all the rooms. She carried the old coffee table out to the driveway and reconsidered her first impulse to sand and paint when the bright sunlight revealed beautiful wood grain under the darkened shellac. Since it was blessedly free of curves, she decided to strip it instead, and was soon scraping curls of old finish onto newspapers spread on the driveway.

"Whatcha doing?"

Mary looked up. The old lady from next door had come up the driveway and was leaning on an aluminum cane with three rubber-tipped feet, her eyes sharp and inquisitive. Her hair was an unlikely shade of orange, with a clear demarcation at the white roots.

"Stripping a table."

"That looks like a lot of work!"

"It's really not difficult. I'm Mary Bellamy, by the way."

"Yes, yes, of course. I'm your neighbor, Cecille

Corbierre. Cici, they call me. I'm waiting for my daughter to pick me up. She's late, as usual. You've been doing such a lot of work around the house!"

"Well, it needs it."

"Oh, don't I know it! Agnes let it go to pot the last few years. I'd just gotten my hip replaced when she passed, or I would have noticed something wrong much sooner. I don't get around much, but I like to keep an eye on things."

Mary smiled grimly. Yes, she'd noticed that.

Cici coughed gently. "And are you settling in well at St. Andrew's?"

"St. Andrew's?"

Cici's bright orange lips pursed as if she were flustered. "But I thought — I've seen their Father Arthur here, you see. Quite frequently."

Mary gave her a sharp look. "He did seem quite intent on welcoming me to town, at first, but he hasn't dropped by in a while."

"Oh no, dear. He was here just yesterday."

Mary blinked. "He was?"

"Walked up just after you went driving off with that young man, I believe. I told him you'd gone off with a fella in a fancy car. He seemed quite disappointed."

Mary was more dismayed than she'd expected at having missed Arthur. But Cici was looking intently at her in a way that got her guard up. "I guess he hasn't given up on getting me to church."

Cici sighed heavily. "I used to attend St. Mary's faithfully, but I can't get there now. The judge took away my license after a minor fender bender that wasn't even my fault! For years I drove around my friends who couldn't drive, and there's not one soul left to drive me around now that I need it."

"That must be frustrating." Mary resisted the impulse to offer a ride herself. She had done favors like that for an older couple in her old neighborhood, but this woman struck her as someone to be cautious about. "But you still get out, I see."

Cici sniffed. "My daughter's always saying she's busy. It's a terrible thing to be an old widow, you know. I hope you'll be luckier than me and have many loving children to take care of you in your old age. Perhaps you'll start a family with that young man."

"That was my ex-husband. And I can't have children."

"You can't? Oh dear, I am sorry. Of course, children can be a bit of a disappointment, like my daughter. Still, she's so much better than nothing."

Mary returned to scraping finish off with new intensity.

"And there she is at last — Annette, darling! Over here!" Cici yelled, waving with considerable vigor. "Well, I'll be going. So glad to meet you, Mary. Now that winter's over I'm sure we'll see much more of each other." The old woman headed down the sidewalk at a fast clip, banging her cane down firmly.

Mary watched the unsmiling daughter get out of the car and open the front passenger door. So Arthur had stopped by, and knew she'd driven off with a man. She wondered what he'd made of that. Still, what did it matter? If he really wanted to see her, as a friend, why not call? Of course, as Arthur's friend, she could also call him. But she couldn't see herself doing that. He was the one who wanted to be friends here. It wasn't her idea. She didn't even think it was a good idea.

When Mary came in from a walk that Friday morning, she had a cryptic message waiting from her boss. When she called back, Carmen sounded strained and suggested a meeting as soon as possible.

Mary put on work clothes and drove to Framingham, wondering if for some reason she was being fired after just completing training. When she arrived, the parking lot was nearly empty. Inside, a number of cubicles had been stripped of all personal possessions.

Her heart started pounding. "I'm fired?" she asked Carmen.

"No, you're not. Not yet." Carmen ran a hand through her thick salt-and-pepper curls and sighed. "Look, I'm sorry to ruin a vacation day, but I wanted you to hear it from me. They've laid off eighty percent of the publishing group. You're the only development editor left."

Mary sat down, weak with relief. "I still have a job?"

"Yes. But Mary, I think it's only a matter of time."

Mary absorbed this with dismay. "Why send me to training if things were so bad?"

"I don't know. Maybe they hope to put you to work on the vitamin side. But if I were you I'd get a resume circulating ASAP."

"Are they giving severance?"

"Two weeks for every year of service. Plus unemployment, of course."

So she might be out the door with twelve weeks of pay at any moment. Three months. And her savings were at a particularly low point after buying a home, a new roof, a winter's worth of heating oil, and a divorce. Shanley Publishing Company had been in business for 75 years. She had never counted on this.

She left the building in a daze and drove around aimlessly until she found herself, with some surprise, in front of her old house.

It was garbage day and trash bags and discarded boxes for baby items were heaped in front. As she idled there, wondering whether she should drop in on old neighbors or just head back to Lawson, the front door opened and a slender man in a black leather jacket appeared. He pulled a cell phone out of his pocket and checked it. Could this be the infamous Gabby? He was darkly handsome, with tight jeans and long straight hair pulled back in a long ponytail. As he opened the door to his car — an old Chrysler that had seen better days — he noticed her watching and stared at her. She decided to pull away. Although she deliberately avoided eye contact she sensed he was still staring intently as she passed by.

Eight blocks away, on her route to the highway ramp, she noticed a pair of old bookshelves and a potentially useful floor lamp put out with the trash and thought of her success with the coffee table. When she had actually lived in this neighborhood she had been too embarrassed to do any trash-picking, but she was from New Hampshire now.

It was awkward getting the bookshelves into her backseat. It was even more awkward when an old Chrysler

THE AWFUL MESS

slowed and pulled over just in front of her car. The man
who'd so intently watched her leave got out and sauntered
over. Mary's heart began to pound in her chest.

"You need some help there, *mamacita?*"

"No, thanks, I'm fine." She smiled weakly.

He smoothed his hair back, shuffled his feet, looked
both ways. "There wasn't no furniture where you were
looking before."

"What? Oh, no." She gave a false laugh. She wrestled
ineffectually with the second bookshelf, which wouldn't go
in far enough for her to shut the door.

"Better let me do it," he said, and took the shelf from
her without waiting for permission. He turned it around
and easily fit it in the car. Then he closed the back door and
turned to her, suddenly intent. "Did that *cabrón* ask you to
watch his house?"

"No. I was just — I used to live there."

His expression changed. "Wait a minute. I know you.
We found your wedding pictures up in the attic. You don't
want your wedding pictures?"

"No."

He leaned into her face, so close that she could smell his
cologne. "Then what you doing there?"

She stared at him. The truth was she had no idea
what she'd been doing there. "I guess I was curious." She
grabbed her keys out of her pocket and let them jangle in
her hand, the universal signal for *I have to go now.*

He didn't back off. "I hope you're not going to tell that
pendajo anything. Darlene's not the smartest girl I ever met,
but she never want to hurt nobody. That *pendajo* threw you
away like the garbage, didn't he? He told her you couldn't

88

give him no children. But you know what I think? I think the *cabrón* is the one who isn't able." He gave her a leisurely, leering once-over. "He's not like me." He smiled ruefully, straightened to his full height. "Sometimes I think I can make a woman pregnant just by looking at her."

"Do you *mind?*" Mary hissed, recovering her will through sheer indignation.

"Hell, you could be pregnant right now, just from standing next to me!"

Mary flinched. "Get away from me!"

He laughed and backed off, raising his hands as if in surrender. "It wouldn't take much, that's all I'm saying!" He blew her a kiss and sauntered back to his car.

She stood there and breathed in short, angry spurts as he drove away with a jaunty backwards wave.

The neighborhood was quiet. Still nobody came out. She got back in the car and sat for a moment, trying to get her nerves under control. Then she took off for the highway, driving too fast.

Chapter Ten

A S SHE DROVE up Hill Street she passed Arthur Tennant walking down. He turned to watch as she drove up the street, but she didn't acknowledge him. She was in no mood for waving at anybody.

At home, she changed into her jeans and collapsed onto Agnes Lacey's sloping sofa, its threadbare upholstery not very effectively disguised by an Indian bedspread. She sniffed, trying to decide once and for all whether it was just giving off old-lady mustiness or the lingering aroma of decomposition. Bob jumped up. Mary petted him absently and wished she had stopped for a bottle of wine on the way home.

The doorbell rang.

Groaning, Mary got up. She checked through the living room window.

It was Arthur.

She opened the door and said, "Hi" rather curtly.

"Hi." He smiled. "How are you doing?"

There was a pause as she considered how to answer. "Well, I've had kind of a bad day, actually." She was disgusted to feel tears rising. She retreated to the sofa and hugged a pillow to her chest.

He closed the door behind him and hovered uncertainly a moment. Then he lowered himself into an ancient upholstered rocker also from the Lacey estate. The springs had collapsed, so he ended up perching on the edge. "You want to talk about it?" he asked.

"Not really. How are you doing?"

"Me? I'm fine."

"I haven't seen you around." It sounded more aggrieved than she'd intended.

"Well, you know, Easter. Such a marathon."

Oh, Easter. She hadn't realized it had already passed. In childhood, it had been so terribly important — all those religious movies on television, all those somber masses. In adulthood, if she noticed it at all it was because she could buy pastel-colored candy half-price when it was all over.

"After Easter, Lucy and I always take a little trip — we went to Charleston this year."

"And Sharon?"

"Oh, Sharon doesn't travel. Her sister came to stay with her while we were gone."

He was looking rather tanned, wasn't he?

He cocked his head at her. "So you had a bad day?"

"I just found out they've laid off most of the staff at my company, and apparently my job is about to go, too."

"That's terrible. You must be very worried."

She nodded, again blinking away tears.

"But you have excellent skills, don't you? You could find work."

"Around here?"

"You might be surprised at what's tucked away up here. Besides, didn't you say you can do it all on the computer? And you've been getting all this training."

She didn't say anything. She didn't want to be cheered up, damn it.

He cleared his throat. "I tried to stop by yesterday, actually, but I believe you were just leaving. I'm glad to see you're getting out." But his eyes shifted away and she thought, *no you're not.*

"That was my ex."

"Oh." His next question sounded cautious. "Is that a good thing?"

She sighed. Should she bother trying to explain? "He wanted to tell me he doesn't think the baby his new wife just had is his."

Arthur's eyebrows rose.

"He says she has this boyfriend, this guy named Gabriel. The thing is, I just drove by my old house on the way home — you know, just to take a look — and I had a kind of unpleasant encounter with him. At least, I assume it was him."

"What do you mean?"

So she haltingly related what had happened, which she knew didn't really amount to much. Some guy had helped her put furniture in her car. But when she remembered the way he'd suggested Roger had thrown her away like the garbage, she suddenly stopped and started sobbing.

"Mary?" Arthur left his perch to kneel in front of the sofa.

It was so pathetic. So insulting! To be pitied by a guy like that!

"Mary! Did he hurt you?"

She shook her head and rocked, arms crossed protectively across her chest.

He laid his hands gently on her knees in front of him. The contact was startling.

She took a long shuddering breath. "He said he could make any woman pregnant just by looking at her." She half laughed, half sniffed. "He said that I might be getting pregnant right there!" She shook her head. "It was stupid."

"He scared you."

No, not exactly. Though she had been scared.

Arthur sat back on his heels. "I think there's at least an implicit threat there when a strange guy suggests he can make you pregnant." His mouth twitched. "Did you say this guy's name was Gabriel?"

"Yes. At least, I think so."

He looked bemused.

"What?" she demanded.

"It's just… it's a little funny, you know. Mary… Gabriel? The annunciation?"

"Are you serious?" Did he really have to make some arcane connection to a Bible story?

He drew back. "No, I'm not serious. Obviously not. I'm sorry, I was being tactless. Of course you're going to be a little sensitive about anything related to pregnancy—"

"Sensitive?" Her mouth dropped open in outrage. "I suppose you also think your wife's a little too sensitive about losing her son!"

His face closed in. On another day she might have felt contrite, might even have apologized, but today she'd had enough. "Look, perhaps you should go. Like I told you, I've had a really bad day."

He nodded briefly, looking bleak, and left.

Afterwards, Mary sat in her darkening living room, petting Bob and brooding. It occurred to her that she had just managed to alienate the only friend she had made in town. Since the divorce, she had developed quite a talent for isolating herself.

Eventually she noticed that she was sitting in the dark. She got up and went into the kitchen, tugging the chain to turn on the old fixture, which threw a dingy yellow light on the uneven plaster walls. She should eat, she thought, opening the old refrigerator and staring at the nearly empty shelves.

Why the hell hadn't she stopped for wine?

Moving to Lawson had been a terrible mistake. It didn't even have a state liquor store! She'd never fit into such a small town. She'd always be that divorced, childless woman living in Agnes Lacey's house. She'd never find a decent job here. If she stayed, she'd never have friends again, she'd never have sex again, she'd never be able to eat anything but dried beans and rice and whatever the government gave away free to poor people. (Spam? Lard?) Someday Arthur Tennant might find himself discussing her in detached tones in committee meetings devoted to the town's struggling poor. And when it was all over, she'd probably die alone in her house, lying there decomposing for who knew how long, until whoever was living in Cici's house finally noticed the smell.

Okay, well, perhaps she was getting a bit carried away. Still, it was about time she seriously considered the possibility that she'd taken a wrong turn in coming here. She could sell this place and still have enough for a new start somewhere within easier distance of her profession. Some place where she could do a better job of starting her life over than she'd been doing here.

Maybe this had just been a trial run.

Two hours later Mary still hadn't eaten anything but an apple and some cashews, but she had a plan. It was not a very detailed plan — write new resume, network, find job, move — but it would do. She didn't feel like implementing it yet, however, so she moved back to the sofa with Bob and idly flipped channels on the TV, wondering whether cable was something she should drop immediately to save money.

The doorbell rang.

She turned on the porch light and checked through the window, surprised but not entirely displeased to see Arthur back again. He was shifting from foot to foot.

She opened the door and he held up a bottle of wine. "I brought a peace offering."

She took the bottle and nodded him in.

He took off his coat and draped it over the back of a kitchen chair while she searched for the corkscrew. It finally occurred to her that she might not even have one.

"Don't worry, I got it," he said, rummaging in his pocket. He produced a Swiss army knife. "You know what they say about Episcopalians and wine."

She didn't actually know any jokes about Episcopalians. "What do they say?"

"Well, that we drink a lot, I guess."

"I didn't know that."

"Personally I make it a rule to never have more than a glass. I think, in my situation, that it is too great a risk."

He poured them both full glasses — she was relieved that she at least had wine glasses. Now that she thought about it she had probably left the corkscrew for Roger because she'd always considered it an ugly plastic thing.

She took her wine and headed back into the living room. She shut off the television. He followed uncertainly.

"Were you watching something?"

"No." She flopped down on one end of the sofa. He eyed the broken rocker and instead chose the other end of the sofa. He looked relieved when it didn't sink under him.

"Agnes Lacey's furniture," she explained.

"Ah."

"I was hoping to get some new stuff this year, but that won't happen now."

"You never know. You might end up much better off."

"I'll probably just leave it when I move."

He nearly choked on his wine. "You're moving?"

"Any decent publishing jobs are likely to be in Boston or New York."

"There are jobs out here. They don't pay as well, but you don't need as much to live."

"I just don't think this is working out the way I hoped."

"No? What did you hope?"

She shook her head. "I don't know. Not this."

"You haven't given it enough time. It's always lonely, moving to a new town. It will be like that at first no matter where you go."

"Actually, I'm not sure it's lonely enough. I just want to live out my days peacefully, enjoy a simple, quiet life. But everybody in town seems to know who I am. It's claustrophobic. But at the same time, it's...."

"Lonely," he said, with certainty.

She sighed deeply. "I guess."

They sat in silence for a moment. "Look," he said. "I need to apologize. About what I said earlier. I'm sorry."

She looked into her wine glass, which was nearly empty. "I know you didn't mean to hurt me. That's more than I can say for myself."

"It was provoked."

She smiled. "I think maybe you are too used to putting up with crap from people."

"Perhaps. But some people give better crap than others."

Startled, she gave half a laugh. "What are you saying? That I give good crap?"

"You give excellent crap."

She laughed again.

"And if you left, I would really miss your crap." He picked up the bottle of wine, which he had brought in with his glass, and poured more into both their glasses.

"I thought you had a rule about one glass."

He growled, "Fuck the rules."

CHAPTER ELEVEN

THEY DRANK WINE and she asked him about Lucy (who had just asked him if she could pierce her nose), Carrie Woodbury (animal lover, except when it came to groundhogs in her garden), and Cici. "Is she one of the community's sad cases?"

"Only if you think awful people are sad. She'd like you to believe she's a poor suffering old widow, but she's sitting on a fortune and she's too cheap to pay for the services that would make her life better. Plus she's a terrible busybody. We once got a letter from her expressing her concern that the senior center in town is dominated by trailer trash, her words. We didn't fire the director, as she suggested, so she won't set foot in there anymore, though it must kill her to miss all those free health checks."

"She told me you were here yesterday."

"I'm not surprised. She once reported Agnes Lacey to the town for replacing her bathroom sink without a permit."

"She probably knows you're here now, too." He'd been there over an hour.

"Are you trying to get rid of me?" He gave her a bland look and stretched his arm across the back of the sofa.

Was she drunk? Because craggy Arthur somehow looked downright appealing tonight. "No. I'm not trying to get rid of you."

He frowned and pulled his arm back. "But you probably should." He stood up and finished the rest of his wine in a gulp. "I'd better go."

She followed him into the kitchen. She was disappointed that he was leaving and yet conscious that this was what should be. She picked up his coat from the chair to hand it to him. It smelled musky in a pleasant way, the smell of a man who used the same soap and deodorant every day. It was a smell she had missed without even realizing it.

He put it on, standing in front of her — in her space, really, though she didn't feel threatened. He was a little taller than she had realized.

"Thank you for the peace offering," she said.

"Thank you for accepting it."

The moment drew out.

"Well, goodnight." Should she offer a handshake? It seemed feeble.

"Mary, I'd hate to see you leave," he said in a rush. "I really would."

She decided to offer a hug instead.

He seemed surprised at first, then relaxed into the hug.

She was the one who prolonged it when she felt him start to pull away. Later, she might wonder what on earth she was thinking; right now all she knew was that she didn't want him to leave. He took a long shuddering breath and murmured, "What are we doing here?"

She lifted her face and kissed him.

"Oh God," he said, but if it was a prayer for self-control it didn't work. He kissed her back, hard and sure, and she opened her mouth to him and met his wine-soaked tongue with her own. He clutched at her, hands roving from her hair down to her ass and back again, grinding his pelvis into her with unmistakable intent.

When they came up for air he stared wildly at her. "We shouldn't." But she could tell his heart wasn't in it. For one thing, he still had both hands on her ass.

"Come on." She pulled him back to the bedroom, and he followed without resistance. She let go of him to pull off her shirt and bra, watching to see if he'd make his escape, but he just stood there and stared hungrily at her.

"How long has it been, anyway?" she asked. She pushed her jeans and underwear and socks down to the floor in one movement and stepped out of them.

He didn't answer, just moved forward suddenly and gathered her up. He latched onto a nipple and sucked it hungrily. She closed her eyes and thrummed with pleasure as he switched from one to the other. When she reached out and cupped him through his pants, he moaned.

"Take off your coat, stay awhile," she whispered.

Wordlessly, he obeyed, shrugging off his coat and then struggling out of the rest of his clothes. His body was lean and had more hair than she'd expected.

She shooed Bob out of the bedroom and closed the door. She was willing to bet Agnes Lacey had never fucked a priest in here, and the thought made her want to giggle, but she stifled it. She'd never known a man who responded well to unexplained giggling in the bedroom.

Arthur was staring at her with an odd expression — lust mixed with terror, maybe. She went to kiss him. As their tongues dueled, his fingers searched her out. He had a nice, gentle touch.

"You sure you want to do this?" he asked.

Instead of answering she dropped to her knees and took his dick into her mouth. Always Roger's favorite part, she thought, annoyed that she was letting thoughts of Roger intrude now.

He moaned in appreciation. "I guess you do." He threaded his hands through her hair. Eventually he pulled gently back on her head. "Get on the bed."

She complied.

He went to work between her legs with an enthusiasm that put Roger to shame. She fell back. Goodness. Perhaps it was true what a friend had once told her, that ugly men made better lovers. Before she could quite help it she was coming, and it felt wonderful, but she was a little disappointed, too — too soon, too easy. He smiled proudly at her.

If he was like Roger, he'd want her to finish him off with a blow job — sometimes she'd wondered if Roger was just so sick of all the failed attempts at procreation that he wanted to make sure it wasn't even on the table. But Mary wanted a man inside her. "Get in there," she said, and tugged on his head, pulling him up. He entered her with a groan of pleasure. He thrust steadily, producing a pleasant echo of what she had felt before, until she was surprised to find herself coming again. Then he sped up and came, too, with deep, satisfied groans.

He slowly withdrew and lay, softly panting, next to her.

"Holy Mother of God," she said.

"I'd rather not bring her into it. But I know exactly what you mean."

She pointed him to the box of tissues on her bedside table so he could clean up, while she just lay there, immensely satisfied and unwilling to move.

He leaned down and gave her a kiss. "You are so beautiful."

"But?" she prompted.

"But what?"

"But we can never do this again, right?"

He looked dismayed. "You don't want to?"

She sat up. "I was just assuming — I mean, I know we had too much wine, and I kind of jumped your bones..."

He smiled. "You did, didn't you?"

"And you're married... and you're a priest."

He took a deep breath. "I'm still a man, aren't I?"

"Well, yeah. Obviously." She waggled her eyebrows at him.

"I know that this is supposed to be wrong. But it doesn't feel that way. It feels like manna from heaven." He got up and started to put on his clothes.

"I doubt Cici would understand that."

"Cici needs to get laid."

Mary laughed.

He touched her face with his hand. "You have no idea how grateful I am for this."

"That goes both ways."

He leaned down to kiss her, then straightened up. "I'd better go. I'll lock the door on the way out." As he opened the bedroom door, Bob slipped through it. He meowed and jumped onto the bed. "Jealous," Arthur said.

She snorted. He left with a smile; she heard his footsteps walking down the hall, then the snick of the front door opening and closing. Who knew when she'd see him again, or how he would act when she did. Distant? Eager? Ashamed? It didn't matter. Neither of them had made any promises.

She lay there and petted Bob. She supposed she should feel that a change had come over her: She had slept with a married man. She had cast her lot on the other side of a line she had respected all her life. But if anything, she merely felt a wanton satisfaction that she had just had the best sex of her life.

Normally fastidious in these matters, Mary dozed off without even getting up to go to the bathroom.

At three in the morning Mary woke up parched. She sucked down a glass of water in the moonlit kitchen, hoping to avoid the worst effects of too much wine. Then she went back to bed and lay awake, brooding.

Arthur hadn't been all that hard to seduce, had he? And he was the one who'd shown up with the wine. How could she be sure he didn't do this kind of thing all the time?

And how could they have been so irresponsible? Neither had hesitated even a moment to think about protection. Not that she had any. Okay, there was no way she was going to get pregnant, but she hadn't even inquired about dread diseases.

More fundamentally, of course, what was she thinking, sleeping with a married man — a priest, for God's sake? It was not only depraved; it was pathetic. It didn't say much for her self-respect. It also didn't say much about his respect for the marriage vows that had supposedly prevented a divorce for so long.

She really had to leave town now.

Eventually she fell asleep and when she woke again, light was streaming in the window and the sky was a perfect blue. How could she leave? It was so beautiful here. And Arthur, in his ugly way, was beautiful, too.

She could not summon the slightest inclination to work on her resume, so she decided to walk down the hill to the diner and admire the river. But it was still early, too early even for a man who might think of walking there himself to be up, so she took a shower, then did some chores — cleaning out the cat litter, taking out the trash. When she went around the house to the garbage can she heard a door slam and eager slippered steps head her way.

"Why hello, neighbor!" Cici, in a purple house dress. No aluminum cane this time.

Mary smiled tightly. "Hello."

"Is everything okay, dear?"

"Why do you ask?"

"Well, I saw Father Arthur here twice yesterday."

Mary shoved down the bag of garbage with more force than was really necessary. "I just found out I'm about to lose my job. I guess he was concerned about my state of mind."

"How awful," Cici said without the slightest trace of sincerity. "You know, I didn't realize you even had a job."

"Well, yes, I do. I work from home."

"It must be nice being able to keep the hours you choose." Cici still sounded skeptical.

"Yes, you can imagine why I'd hate to lose a job like that." Mary turned to go back in the house.

"I'm surprised Father Arthur takes such an interest. Seeing as you don't even attend his church."

Pushy old bitch. "I guess he's just a really nice man."

"You do realize a woman can't be too careful. I say that as a friend, of course."

Mary decided to play dumb. "What do you mean?"

"The way it looks, entertaining male guests in the evenings."

"Why, Cici! You know Father Arthur is married."

Cici sniffed.

"Well, I'll keep it in mind if he shows up again." She scooted into the house before Cici could offer any more advice. Vicious old bat. She'd be sitting there spying on her for the rest of her days. Why couldn't she just die and leave the world better for her absence?

Oh dear, what a slippery slope she was on. First she'd committed adultery, and now she was wishing little old ladies would drop dead.

Chapter Twelve

MARY TOOK THE path through the woods to get to town. The forest was full of birdsong, and a spring brook gurgled and sparkled in the dappled sunlight. She would have been tempted to loiter there, but clouds of gnats and flies kept her moving.

There was no sign of Arthur when she stopped at the bridge, so she walked on to the diner for a grilled blueberry muffin and a cup of coffee. The usual crowd of contractors and laborers was reduced by the weekend, so Mary decided to indulge herself in a booth seat even though she was only one person. She spread the *Boston Globe* out on the table. Sunday was a better day for employment listings, but she might as well take a look.

"Hello."

She looked up to see Winslow looking down at her, splendid in full police regalia, large Styrofoam coffee cup in hand.

"Hello," she said, and felt herself blush. She could just imagine what he would think if he knew what she'd been up to the night before.

"Are you expecting someone?"

"Um, no."

"May I join you?"

She hesitated, feeling the absence of any reason why not. "Sure."

He slid in. "Why are you reading the classifieds?"

"I'm about to be laid off."

"Oh. I'm sorry. For local jobs, you'd do better with the *Sentinel* or the *Union Leader*."

"I don't really expect to find a local job."

He looked perplexed, but let it go. "So what have you been up to? Have you seen Father Arthur at all since the hospital?" He took a sip of coffee and looked so neutral that Mary was suddenly quite sure he knew the answer.

"Yes, I have. He dropped by last night, in fact. It was awfully nice of him; I'd just found out about my job and I was pretty upset." She was blushing again, goddamn it.

"He seems to have a fondness for you."

"Is that a bad thing?"

"No." He cleared his throat and looked out the window.

What the hell? She leaned forward. "Does Father Arthur have a reputation I should know about?"

Winslow blinked. He looked surprised by the question. "No."

"So, what's the problem? Do the townsfolk think I'm leading him astray?"

"I have no idea what people think. We all know he has a difficult life." He used his nail to mark a crease in his coffee cup. "Still, in his position, it's risky to do anything that even hints at impropriety."

"You think he could lose his job over — what — mere rumors?"

"I'm not saying anything would happen in the absence of evidence. But there's a contingent that thinks Father Arthur is too liberal. Add a couple of families with grudges, and things could get unpleasant."

"So what are you suggesting? I should tell him we can't be friends?"

"I'm not suggesting anything."

"I thought you wanted us to be friends. It seemed like you were trying to keep me involved when he was in the hospital."

"Actually I was hoping that once you got to know me better, you might be willing to try dinner or something." He gave her an apologetic smile. "I'd still like that."

Mary stared at him. "I don't know what to say."

"Yes or no would do." That gently mocking tone was back again.

"Have you forgotten what I told you?"

"What? That you can't have kids? Of course not."

"So you know it can't really go anywhere."

He frowned. "Why is that?"

"I told you."

"If that were the only thing that mattered to me, don't you think I would have settled down by now?"

"By now? How old are you?"

"Nearly forty."

Forty? She'd assumed she was older than him, not the other way round. A handsome, well-employed guy in a small town who was still single at forty? "And you've never been married?" she asked, although he'd already told her the answer.

A twinge of annoyance crossed his face. "Would you prefer that I had been?"

"Refill, Winslow?" The waitress had appeared at their table.

"No thanks, Jeanette."

"Refill, hon?" she asked Mary, her coffee pot hovering.

"No thanks, I'm fine," Mary said.

"Oh, I can see that," the waitress said, with a conspiratorial smile and a wink.

Winslow waited until Jeanette had moved away. "Look, never mind. I'm sorry I bothered you. I just thought I'd give it another go." He reached for his hat.

Mary felt an odd lurch of panic. "Wait!"

He waited.

She swallowed. "I'd be willing — I mean, *happy* — to try a date or two. It's just, the timing is bad. I don't think this can go anywhere. Assuming you'd even want it to." She winced. She'd gone at least one sentence too far. But at least she'd officially disclaimed.

He looked at her for a long moment. "I suppose it might be interesting to date a woman with such low expectations. I'll call you Sunday when I get my schedule." He saluted her with his coffee cup and left.

Mary just sat there. Why had she been overcome by that sudden humiliating need to say yes?

Besides, if her friend's theory about ugly lovers versus attractive ones was correct, Winslow should be just awful. (Was that was why he was unmarried at nearly forty?)

Oh God. Here she was imagining this guy in bed, and

she'd only just enjoyed a night of adulterous passion with Arthur.

Overnight she'd become a hopeless slut.

"Not thinking of jumping in, I hope?"

Mary turned around and smiled. She had only been waiting a few minutes at the bridge, not even long enough to start feeling ridiculous. Arthur looked ten years younger than the first time she'd seen him, and not at all homely. "No. You?"

"Not even remotely." He joined her at the rail and they stared at the river, which was sparkling in the morning sun. "Wish I could kiss you good morning."

"Me, too. This is pretty odd. I've never had to, you know... sneak around."

"I wish we didn't have to."

"So how does it feel, being a big sinner?"

"Freakishly good."

She lifted her eyebrows.

"Maybe it will hit me in the gut any minute now and I'll feel just terrible. But this morning I feel great. I might feel worse if I thought Sharon actually gave a damn."

"Are you going to tell her?"

"Tell her? No, I hadn't planned on it."

Mary felt a twinge of disappointment. But what had she expected?

"Christ never suggested we can completely avoid sin," Arthur said. "Only that when we sin, we must repent and ask forgiveness."

Mary watched the water flow gently around the litter of rocks and boulders that had appeared again now that the spring floods were over. "I always figured that a really venal person would do the math and figure he might as well sin today and seek forgiveness tomorrow."

"Well, yes. But would such a person be capable of experiencing true repentance?"

"Have you?"

He shook his head, staring out towards the horizon. "I made a stab at it this morning during my prayers, but I couldn't carry it off. It didn't help when Sharon asked me to bring up her pills because she was too tired to deal with the stairs."

Mary had no particular illusions about their relationship, but it still stung a bit to think she'd been Arthur's way of getting back at his wife. She edged slightly away from him.

He stared at the water, hands gripping the bridge rail. "When can I see you again?"

"I don't know. Cici was practically flying out the door this morning to warn me I shouldn't have a man in my house or my reputation will be ruined forever."

He groaned. "Oh, and she'll spread it all over town, I assure you."

"I told her it was just friendly concern about my job. But she felt it was extremely odd for you to be taking such an interest in someone who's not in your church."

"It would be much worse if I were taking this kind of interest in you and you were in my church. Though we'd have more of a chance of pulling it off, no doubt."

Was he fishing? "You wouldn't actually want me to...."

"No, no, of course not. Though it would please me immensely, of course, to see you seeking God somewhere."

Failure to repent his own sins apparently didn't dampen

his ability to preach to others. Mary turned and leaned back against the bridge rail. Traffic was picking up.

A shiny Mercedes slowed in front of them. "Good morning, Father!" a man cried out, and waved. Mary noticed a keen appraisal of her from the woman in the passenger seat.

Arthur called "Good morning!" and waved back; the car continued up the hill.

"Damn," he said. "That was Dan and Alma Whitaker — and you never saw such a woman for gossip. What the hell do I think I'm doing?"

"Having a conversation on a bridge," Mary said. She was mildly offended by his use of *I* when she was standing right there. "You're not doing anything. Or at least, there's no need for you to do anything further." She turned back to the water, noticing for the first time the damsel flies swooping busily over the surface.

"What do you mean?"

She took a deep breath. She hadn't expected to reach this point so soon, but here it was. "It was a lovely evening, Arthur, very lovely, and I take full responsibility for what happened, but I certainly don't expect anything more."

"Full responsibility? Who brought a bottle of wine to a woman in an unusually vulnerable state, then proceeded to drink too much of it? I only hope you don't feel completely taken advantage of."

"How can you even think that?"

He pursed his lips.

"Let's say we were both... a little carried away," Mary said. "There's no need to attach blame. We can just walk away right now, and no harm done."

"Really?" His eyes searched hers. "No harm at all?"

She stared down at the river and felt tension fill the space between them.

"Perhaps it's best, then." It sounded hollow; he was still studying her face. "Not a very romantic resolution."

"Sooner or later it would have to end. I take it you don't plan to leave your wife."

"I couldn't do that. Not while she's like this."

"So there's little point, is there?"

He slumped. "I'm going to miss you," he said softly. "You've been a comfort."

"You, too." She choked up, realizing how much she meant it. She held out her hand.

He took it in his for a moment, without looking up, then turned and walked away.

She watched and wondered when she'd see him again. It occurred to her that she had failed to warn him about her date with Winslow. She hoped he wouldn't take it the wrong way when he heard about it.

Still, what would be the wrong way, in this situation?

Back home, she walked into the bedroom, scene of their misadventure. She hadn't made the bed yet and Bob stretched wantonly in the middle of it. Mary sniffed for evidence from the night before, but she had left the windows open and now she really couldn't detect any trace of sex or of Arthur. He hadn't left anything behind, like a sock or a tie. Just the empty wine bottle, she remembered, walking into the living room and collecting it. The smell of stale wine reminded her of grim morning-after scenes from college debaucheries. She rinsed the bottle and put it in the recycling bin. Hardly worth getting sentimental now, although she found it depressing that there was nothing left in her life to mark this relationship.

Perhaps someday, after she'd made friends at her new job in her new city, she could go out drinking with them and say, "Did I ever tell you about the night I screwed a priest?"

CHAPTER THIRTEEN

MARY SPENT THE weekend cleaning out old manuscripts, taking stock, beginning the process of yet another major life move. She resisted the nagging urge to walk down to the bridge and see if Arthur was also having second thoughts.

Winslow called late Sunday afternoon and suggested dinner on Friday. Was Italian okay? "That sounds fine," Mary said. Maybe he'd help her stop thinking about Arthur.

The phone rang again. It was Roger. He sounded as if he'd been crying. "I was right," he said. "It's not mine."

Mary stood there holding the phone. This was certainly an unusual etiquette situation.

"Hello, hello, are you there?"

"I don't know what to say. I'm really sorry."

"I don't expect you to be sorry." He sniffed.

"You're quite sure?"

"Yeah, I got the results Friday. I already talked to the lawyer."

"You must be feeling pretty bad."

"Tell me about it. I'm still paying for the first divorce."

She paused. "I mean about the baby and Darlene."

"That miserable cunt? I can't believe I was so stupid."

Cunt? Apparently he'd already started drinking, but this was a new low. How had she ever allowed herself to fall for a guy like Roger? Did she have pathologically low standards? Is that why she'd slept with a married priest?

"Can I see you?" he sniffed, when she didn't reply.

She sighed. "Where are you?"

"In front of the house."

"Jesus, Roger!" She looked out and saw that he was indeed parked in front. "What if I say no?"

"Oh come on, Mary! Please! I'm begging you!"

"Have you been drinking?"

"I wish," he said fervently.

What to do? "I guess we can walk into town for some coffee if you want. Wait out there, I'll get my jacket."

When she went out he was still in the car, blowing his nose. He rolled down the window. "Hop in."

"I'm not getting in your car. You want to walk or not?"

"Jesus Christ! I'm not drunk, you know." He shut off the motor, then got out, slammed the door, and glared at her.

She started down the hill. She waved at Cici's house, sure that she was being observed. And yes — there — the curtain dropped.

"Jesus, slow down!"

"This is downhill, Roger. This is the easy part."

"What are these freaking bugs?" He was trying to bat them away.

"Black flies. Walk fast and they won't bother you as much."

"Shit," he said, huffing. "What was I thinking?"

"What *were* you thinking?"

"I thought I needed someone to talk to, for Christ's sake."

"What about your brothers?"

"They don't understand."

"And I do?"

"You know what it's like. When you want that kid. You know how crazy it makes you."

She was silent.

"It made me crazy and I did a crazy thing because of it. I admit it. I looked for the first girl I could find with nice big hips and a smile on her face, and I tried to get her pregnant. Unfortunately I never noticed she was a conniving little whore."

"Guess it's a good thing the baby's not yours, then."

He scowled, and it occurred to Mary she had just said exactly what she had always resented people telling her — *thank God you didn't have children.*

Mary noticed a small group of people milling around outside the church as they walked past. The evensong service advertised on the church's tasteful little sign must have just ended. And indeed, there was Arthur in his vestments, standing at the door shaking hands.

Arthur looked over as she passed down the sidewalk, and their eyes met. She nodded. He nodded back, raising his eyebrows at her companion, then turned back to the silver-haired lady in front of him.

"You know that guy?"

"He's the Episcopal priest." She said it as diffidently as she could, but she could feel herself blushing. "We run into each other in town sometimes."

"You're not attending church?" He sounded horrified.

"No, of course not." She took a quick peek back over her shoulder and caught Arthur watching her again. It gave her a little thrill. How pathetic was that?

They squeezed into the last free booth in the tiny diner. The same waitress who had refilled Winslow's coffee waved them to their seats. There was no wink tonight, just a tight smile and a professional recitation of the night's specials. Mary decided she might as well get a meal over with and ordered a BLT to go with her coffee. Roger told her he hadn't eaten all day and ordered fried eggs and bacon, French fries with gravy, and a chocolate malted.

"They make great French fries here," she said.

"You gonna steal 'em from my plate like you used to?"

Oh God, was he trying to flirt with her? "I'm not that hungry."

"You still look a little skinny."

She eyed him. He looked unusually unkempt and hollowed out. "So do you."

"These days I'm living on nuts and pretzels."

"Bar food."

"Don't start."

She sighed and folded her arms. Why had she agreed to this?

The food arrived and Roger's red-rimmed eyes lit up. He quickly stuffed in a dozen French fries, then washed them down with a long drag on his malted. He sat back and gave her a speculative look. "Actually, Mary, I've been thinking — why don't we get back together?"

"You've got to be kidding."

"We had a good thing going, before."

"Well, it's not going anymore."

"I heard about Shanley. What are you going to do when they shut it down?"

"Get another job."

"Publishing sucks right now."

He'd always felt qualified to pronounce on these things. Unfortunately he was often right, if only because companies in depressed industries made poor prospects for new commercial real estate projects.

"I just learned web design," she said, though it suddenly occurred to her that she hadn't practiced her new skills even once.

"Tech sucks even worse than publishing."

"Then I'll collect unemployment."

"Look, I admitted to you that I made a mistake." He leaned over his food towards her, either to impress her with his sincerity or to keep the people around them from hearing his admission.

"You just got egg on your sleeve."

"Aw, fuck." He attempted to get the stain out with a napkin soaked in water from his water glass. Mary watched and resisted the temptation to help.

The bells on the front door jingled and she looked up to see Arthur Tennant, still in clerical collar and suit but free of his vestments, step in behind a teenage girl. Lucy, undoubtedly. Tall, like both parents; thin, like her father. Prettier than she had expected.

Scanning for seats, Arthur spied Mary and froze.

She gave him a small, careful smile. His smile in return was more of a wince.

"There's just the counter for the moment, Father," the waitress said, pointing down at two empty seats across from Mary and Roger's booth.

"We can wait, Jeanette," Mary heard him say, but Lucy said, "But I'm starving, Dad!" and pulled him down the aisle.

"Hello," he said awkwardly, as they approached the booth.

"This must be Lucy," Mary said.

"Yes!" He spoke with a touch too much enthusiasm. "Lucy, this is Mary Bellamy. She moved to town recently. She was kind enough to rescue me in the park when I got sick one day."

"That was nothing," Mary said quickly, noticing that Lucy looked shocked, presumably at the news her father had been ill.

Arthur held out his hand to Roger. "I'm Art Tennant. And you are — ?"

"Roger Bellamy." Roger wiped his hand and shook Arthur's.

"My ex," Mary explained.

"Ah. In town for long?"

"No," Mary said sharply.

Roger opened his mouth, looked at Mary, and shrugged.

"Well, it was nice meeting you," Arthur said. He gave her a quick, inscrutable look before taking a seat at the counter.

"When were you sick, Dad?" Lucy demanded. Mary could hear him quietly explaining and Lucy's low, urgent voice in reply.

"What did he mean, you rescued him?" Roger asked.

"It was nothing," Mary said. "I came across him in the park when he was sick and I got the police. That's all."

"So that's how you know him?"

"He and his wife also put me up in the rectory one night during an ice storm. I couldn't get up the hill."

"Oh, so he's married."

"Yes, his wife's name is Sharon."

Lucy's voice rose. "But I want you to call me!"

Arthur's reply was too soft for Mary to hear.

"Anyway," Roger said, "I don't see why you're so quick to reject the idea of getting back together. Wasn't it good before all that infertility stuff got in the way?"

Hell no. "I don't see how that's changed."

"Well, it has, kind of." Roger's face flushed.

"What do you mean?"

"I finally went and got tested." He'd leaned in again and dropped his voice. He was embarrassed, obviously. They'd run into this embarrassment before, when the fertility specialists had wanted him to supply a specimen and he'd insisted there was no point if Mary wasn't fertile anyway.

"And?"

"Well, so maybe we're in the same boat."

Mary's mouth fell open. "What do you mean? You can't —?"

He checked to see if they were being overheard, and whispered, "Not without an operation."

While Mary stared, Roger took a long pull on the chocolate malted until the straw was sucking air. He sat back. "Anyway, I'm not so sure I'm cut out to be a father."

"You bastard," she hissed.

"What?" He looked taken aback.

"I went through all those humiliating tests and treatments and you wouldn't even consider the possibility that it was you."

"Well, it wasn't just me, was it? And look at my brothers! It's not like it runs in the family. I mean, how was I to know?"

"It doesn't run in my family either!"

"Yeah, but you know the statistics. Women in their thirties… "

"You wouldn't even consider that your own precious self might be less than perfect, would you, you son of a bitch!" Her voice had risen in anger and the diner silenced as all heads turned their way.

Roger, oblivious, matched her volume. "Don't you think I'm already feeling bad enough about this?"

Mary ducked her head and took deep calming breaths.

"You okay, Mary?" Arthur asked. He'd left his seat to lay a hand on her back.

She nodded, both soothed and embarrassed by this unexpected gesture.

He left his hand there and asked, "You need anything?" Judging from the pissed off look on Roger's face, he was really asking if she wanted him to get rid of Roger for her.

"No, I'm fine. Thank you."

She looked briefly up at him and wished the rest of the world would disappear so she could take refuge in his arms. But then she noticed Lucy watching and reflexively smiled at her. Lucy flushed and turned back to her dinner.

"I'll be right here," Arthur reminded her — or perhaps he was reminding Roger — before returning to his stool.

"Jesus Christ!" Roger said in disgust, and Arthur's back twitched.

"Look, I'll get dinner," she said. "Why don't you just head out? I don't feel like talking to you right now."

His mouth opened in outrage. "What?"

"Or you stay and I'll go." She spoke as calmly as she could.

"You're not paying for my dinner," he said loudly, standing up, digging out his wallet and putting down enough money for half the people in the diner to eat a good meal. "I can't believe I have to walk back up that freaking hill!"

Arthur circled round on his stool. "We could call you a taxi," he suggested.

"Go fuck yourself!" Roger said, drawing outraged stares from just about everybody in the diner. "I just can't win for losing, can I?" he hissed at Mary, then stalked out.

After he left, conversation slowly resumed to normal levels, then climbed well above them. Mary sat in a daze, reflecting that now she'd be known in town as the woman with the ex-husband who told Father Arthur to go fuck himself.

She noticed Arthur tilt his head as if to suggest to Lucy that they join Mary in the booth, but Lucy hunched her shoulders over her meal expressively and stayed put. "You okay?" he asked, from the stool.

"Yeah, I'm fine."

The waitress refilled her coffee and took the money Roger had laid on the table. Mary sipped slowly, letting Roger get well ahead of her.

"There's way more than you need here," the waitress said, coming back and holding out a small wad of bills.

Mary regarded it with repugnance. "I don't want it."

The waitress insisted. "Honey, this is a lot of money."

Mary sighed. "How about you give yourself a nice tip and then give the rest to him?" Mary pointed at Arthur. "You guys must have a food pantry or something, right?"

He smiled. "We sure do."

"Then I'm sure you can put it to good use." She took a last swallow of coffee. "I'm going to head home."

Arthur looked concerned. "You sure it's safe? Let's call the police, get you a ride."

"I'm not worried. Sorry we messed up your dinner. Lucy, it was nice to meet you."

Lucy bobbed her head awkwardly.

"Thank you for your help, Arthur."

"You're sure you'll be fine?"

She nodded. He'd been sweet, really, but she was sure she would do even better if she could just avoid her ex-husband and the married priest — and father — she should never have messed around with in the first place.

CHAPTER FOURTEEN

SECURE THAT ARTHUR was not watching from his office, Mary paused to enjoy her favorite spot on the bridge, but the swarming flies soon drove her up the hill. As she walked up, batting insects away, she hoped that Roger had already driven off.

That bastard. Putting all the blame on her for all those months when he was infertile all along.

Did this mean she might not be? But after a couple of rounds of Pergonal the doctors had concluded that her ovulatory response was weak. She could not forget the instinctive shame she'd felt at that first suggestion of IVF with donor eggs, as if she'd somehow let her own rot in the back of the refrigerator. And then, once she'd begun to work her way around to the idea, she'd run straight into Roger's refusal to jerk off into a cup.

As if the asshole never masturbated. As if he didn't at least get an orgasm out of it.

She batted angrily at the flies. What would she do if he was still there?

She was surprised when Winslow pulled up next to her in the SUV.

"Hop in," he said.

"Thanks, but I think I need to walk off some dinner."

"The flies are going to eat *you* for dinner. Come on."

She opened the door and heaved herself up. "They are making me nuts. To think I was looking forward to warmer weather!"

"It's only this bad for a week or two." He accelerated up the hill.

"So you just happened to be passing by?"

"No, Jeanette at the diner called and said maybe we should make sure you got home safe. This is official police business."

"Oh." She was both annoyed and gratified. "Well, thank you."

"Even if your ex didn't bother you, I was sure the flies would."

"My tax dollars at work."

"Is that him?" Winslow asked, as they approached her house. Roger was sitting in his car, radio blaring.

"Yeah," Mary said, with an unhappy sigh.

Winslow slapped a light on his roof and let off a yelp from his siren as he crossed into the other lane to pull up alongside Roger's BMW. Roger's car was so much lower than Winslow's that Mary couldn't even see the roof.

Roger's radio cut out. His voice was squeaky. "Yes, officer?"

"Could you state your business here, sir?"

There was a pause. "I'm waiting for someone."

"Would that be Ms. Bellamy, sir?"

There was another pause. Mary imagined Roger's look of consternation.

Winslow's cop voice had an extreme neutrality about it, an absence of expression of any kind, and yet the message was clearly *don't mess with me.* "It's my understanding that Ms. Bellamy doesn't wish to speak to you any further this evening. May I see your registration?"

"She called the police?"

"Your registration, sir."

After a moment, Winslow had it in his hand. He scanned it into some device and information streamed up. Mary recognized her old address.

Winslow leaned out of the window to return the registration. "Very good, sir. Please move along now."

"Move along?" Roger sounded outraged.

"Yes, sir, move along." There was a clear warning in Winslow's tone now.

A pause, then, resentfully: "Yes, okay, officer, I'm leaving."

There was a short silence while Roger drove down the road.

"Well. That was fun in a sick kind of way," Mary observed.

"He ever get physical with you?" Winslow was back to his normal voice. He pulled into her driveway.

Mary flushed. "Not really."

He turned and regarded her, clearly waiting for more of an explanation.

"Just... nothing serious. A slap now and then." She felt her face begin to burn.

He watched her, still waiting.

"Mostly just broken dishes. Tantrums. Especially if he'd been drinking."

"Was he drinking just now?" Winslow reached for his radio.

"No," Mary said, and Winslow let his hand drop. She hoped she was right. For all she knew Roger kept a supply in the car. "It's just, he's had a run of bad luck recently, and he's not very good at dealing with disappointment." She sighed. "And now he thinks I called the cops on him."

"Do you care what he thinks?"

"I guess I just don't see the need to make him feel worse than he already does."

Winslow said nothing, just regarded her.

"You want to come in for a cup of coffee?" she asked uncertainly.

"Better not. I'm on duty."

"Oh. Well, thank you for the ride." She opened the door.

"You call 911 if he shows up again. Ex-husbands can be dangerous."

"Isn't it the ex-husbands who *don't* want you to leave who get dangerous?"

"What was he doing here, then?"

Oh, right. "He said wanted to get back together."

Winslow's eyebrows went up and the next question sounded like it might not be entirely a matter of police business. "Does he have any reason to think you'd want to do that?"

"No!"

"Then why was he waiting for you?"

She sighed. "Because he hates to take no for an answer."

"Not taking no for an answer isn't really a good sign in a man." The cop tone was back.

She sighed. "Okay. If he comes back I'll call 911."

"Good. See you Friday."

She had been dismissed. She got out and waved good-bye. He waved back at her, but remained parked in the driveway, talking on the radio and filling out a report. She went in and turned on the lights, hovering near the window, wondering how long he'd be out there. It was weird to have a police car idling in her driveway, radio occasionally squawking. It made her front yard feel like a crime scene. She didn't relax until he finally backed out ten minutes later and headed back down the hill.

Damn, she could use a glass of wine. Oh well. She didn't have a corkscrew anyway, she reminded herself. It wasn't worth going out. She put on the kettle for a cup of chamomile tea.

Her phone rang.

"I can't believe you called the fucking police!" Roger said.

She didn't say anything.

"Hello, hello?"

She hung up.

It rang again, insistently.

She picked up the phone and said, "Look, Roger, just leave me alone!"

"Mary?"

She sighed, realizing with a flutter that it was Arthur on the line, not Roger. "Sorry. I thought you were him."

"He's still bothering you?"

"No, it's fine. Winslow got rid of him."

"I wanted to make sure you got home safe."

"I did, thank you."

Arthur had looked out for her. And now Arthur had

called her on the phone. This was a new thing. Yes, they'd had sex, but they'd never spoken on the phone. It was ridiculous, surely, to feel that somehow *now* a line was being crossed?

"I just wanted to make sure you were okay."

"I'm fine."

"Well, that's good, then," he said, his inflection rising into a goodbye.

"Was Lucy upset?" She was suddenly unwilling to let the conversation end.

"About what?"

"You know, all the yelling."

"She didn't say anything about it. She's angry nobody told her I was in the hospital."

"Perhaps she's old enough now to handle that sort of thing."

"I don't want her to have to. She deserves to have her childhood."

Mary remembered what it was like being sixteen and felt the ideal of childhood in the teenage years was over-rated. For her, at least, it had amounted to boredom and frustration and feeling dangerously out of the loop.

"I'm taking her back to school early tomorrow morning," Arthur said. "I was wondering... would you like to meet me somewhere for lunch? Just to talk?"

She paused, considering.

"Or perhaps that's not such a good idea. You must have work to do — "

"No, I don't, actually." They weren't going to do this, but what harm could talking do?

*

She went out the next morning and surveyed the garden. The peonies had largely outgrown the cages she'd erected, and many had swollen round buds on them, with tiny hints of pink and red at their seams. There was almost something obscene about the way they were so clearly getting ready to unfurl their enticements to the bees, or whatever peonies wanted to entice. Ants?

She had worked hard on this bed, weeding and putting down mulch. She bent down now, pulling out some grass and wild strawberries that had made a new run for it. She dubiously surveyed a few plants she'd suspected were weeds, but had given a stay of execution in case she was wrong. She still didn't know. They looked healthy and possibly smug at having fooled her. It would have been handy to be able to ask Arthur about them again.

Of course, any work she did to this garden now was really just going to help her sell it to the next owner. Any investment she made in her relationship with Arthur was even less likely to pay off. Or with Winslow, for that matter. More than ever, now, she needed to start over somewhere else.

A proper sense of closure, then. That should be the goal for her lunch with Arthur today.

Closure. Not sex.

"Sorry I'm late," she said breathlessly a few hours later, slipping into her seat. Best not to do the kiss on the cheek, she'd already decided.

Arthur, half out of his chair, lowered himself into it again. "Did you get lost?"

"I went right past."

"It's easy to miss."

She looked around. It was an elegant place — not what she had expected from a modest exterior in a modest town. There were few other diners. She turned back to Arthur. He was not wearing his collar.

She hadn't expected to feel this awkward. She studied the menu without quite seeing it, except to note that the prices were breathtakingly high. "Have you ordered already?"

"No, I wanted to wait for you."

The waiter came up, took their drink orders, and described the specials. "Are you ready to order?" he asked, with excessive patience, as if he were the one Mary had kept waiting.

"I need a minute." Mary wondered if she could get by with an appetizer.

"It's my treat," Arthur said, perhaps guessing her concern.

"That's not necessary."

"I invited you, remember?"

"Okay then. Thank you."

"Do you like seafood? I recommend the salmon."

"That sounds fine," she said, disheartened. This felt like dating, with all the awkwardness and fumbling over issues like money, but without the excitement of getting to know someone who might just turn out to be special. Or at least available. This was perhaps her just reward for sleeping with a man before he even knew whether she liked seafood.

"I'm quite hungry, actually." Arthur signaled the waiter. After he intoned "Very good, sir," and glided away, they regarded each other.

"You okay?" he asked.

"I guess it's sinking in with me that now I'm a slut."

He laughed. "I know what you mean. Not that you are, of course."

"I don't know about that. This might be an objective fact sort of situation."

"To be considered a slut, I think you need to establish a general pattern of behavior."

"You mean sleep with you again?"

He smiled. "Well, yes — repeatedly, I should think." It was a joke, but there was a gleam in his eye.

The waiter arrived again to honor them with a basket of bread and a dramatic demonstration of the fine art of grinding pepper into a plate of olive oil. Arthur tore off a piece of the bread and devoured it.

"Arthur... have you and Sharon ever had any counseling?"

"Lucy and I each have therapists. Sharon feels it's a waste of her time." He ripped another piece of bread in half and stabbed it into the olive oil.

"So what does your therapist think about this?" Mary asked, using her hands to indicate the two of them.

Arthur looked sour. "My therapist is also my spiritual advisor. He's a priest."

"And...?"

"And I haven't told him. I'm sure he'd tell me that engaging in adultery is not a good thing." He smiled crookedly. "And I already know that."

"Then why are you here?"

"Well, I'd call this lunch rather than adultery. I just felt that we ended things a little too abruptly."

"So you want a better sense of resolution."

"Don't you?"

"Sure." She leaned back in her chair. "I guess I would like to feel I can stand at the bridge or walk past the rectory without wondering if you'll feel you must come out and talk to me."

"Exactly. That kind of thing."

"I suppose we could have handled that in a phone call."

"I wanted to send you flowers," he said abruptly.

She looked up, surprised.

They fell silent as their plates were delivered with a flourish.

"But I couldn't see how to do it," he said, when they were alone again. "Everybody in the local flower shops knows me. And your neighbor there would notice if I showed up at the door with a bunch."

"It was a nice thought, though."

"I'll buy you some after lunch. You can take them home, and no one will know."

"And then we'll be all resolved."

He smiled.

"I can see it," she said. "You repent, you seek forgiveness, life goes on and all that. And my life moves on, too. Friday night I have a date with Winslow."

He coughed. "What?"

"I seem to recall you lobbying on Winslow's behalf at one point."

Arthur covered his face with his hand. "I can't believe how jealous I feel."

"I'm sorry. Look, I don't expect it to go anywhere, if that makes you feel any better."

"It shouldn't, if I were truly a friend to either one of you. He's a good man. You could make each other very happy."

Who ever really made anybody happy? And yet people seemed to be able to make each other miserable with very little effort.

"Mary," he said softly. "Hypothetically — if I divorced Sharon — would you marry me?"

She paused, fork in midair. "Marry you? I barely know you."

"Then you're not in love with me." His tone was flat.

"I hardly know you well enough to say. And you can't possibly be in love with me, either. You barely know me."

"I know you well enough."

"It's a midlife thing. I look good because you're lonely and you're trapped in a bad marriage. That's all."

"I'm quite sure that's not all," he said stiffly.

She sighed. "I was positive that I was in love with Roger and he with me when I married him. But that turned out to be nothing. I like you very much, Arthur, but I don't trust my own judgment anymore." *Not to mention you're cheating on your wife.* "We can't even explore the possibility of a serious relationship without sneaking around, and that's not going to work, is it? Not unless you do get a divorce. I think you should, personally. But not for me, for yourself."

"I can't." At her look, he sighed. "Marriage is a sacrament. And she's sick. In sickness and in health, I promised. It doesn't say anything about being able to get out of it if one of the main features of her illness is that she doesn't want to get better."

"But you're miserable. Why are you sitting here right now? It's almost like you hope you'll get caught."

He frowned. "As I said before, it's only lunch."

There was a painful silence.

The waiter swooped in. "Coffee, dessert?"

"No, we're done," Arthur said heavily.

She nodded in agreement, gathering her purse. "If you don't mind, let's just skip the flowers."

He looked stricken. "This really wasn't what I had in mind for today."

No, she thought, you were probably hoping to get laid again. Not that she should get all moralistic about it, since she'd had the same not-quite-formed idea. She could still do it, probably — just lay a hand on his arm. It would be as easy as that.

He sighed, counting out bills. "I also meant to ask you about Roger, whether he's likely to be a continuing concern."

"I don't think so. I hope not."

"Why were you so angry at him in the diner?"

Mary took a breath. They shouldn't still be sharing secrets, but it was hard to stop. "He was right about his new wife's baby. It turns out he's infertile. So now he wants to get back together."

"He's infertile?" He looked alarmed. "Then isn't it possible you aren't?"

"Oh, the doctors were pretty clear on that. I don't think you need to worry."

He stared at her for a moment as if fertility might be something he could determine just by looking, then shrugged and turned back to his wallet. "Well, and anyway, what are the chances?"

CHAPTER FIFTEEN

IN THE DAYS that followed, Mary felt restless. Having mentioned the bridge to Arthur, she doubted he would come out just because she was standing there. Still, she felt she ought to wait a decent period before taking up her old habit of stopping to watch the river, which had turned quite placid as the days warmed. So she walked, but avoided lingering there.

The black flies had finished their worst swarming for the year. They'd had their one or two weeks of frenzied mating. She'd gotten one night. Of course, she still had Winslow taking her somewhere Friday night, but she felt determined to keep him at a safe distance.

It didn't help her sense of restlessness that she had completely run out of work. Carmen was sympathetic, but said she had nothing to send her, and neither of them wanted to call Nat, the only surviving acquisitions editor, to see if he had more. A Shanley brother-in-law, he was so profoundly lazy he was just as likely to send over his travel and expense receipts for tallying. With the editorial list left solely in his incapable hands and no sign of anybody coming in to fix things, Mary could see that the publishing arm of the company was doomed. Her boss agreed it only a matter of time.

"You must be job hunting," Mary said.

"No, not yet. I'll get almost a year of severance, and I've always wanted to see what it's like to stay home, pick the kids up at school. Joe can carry me for a while if he has to."

Mary felt a sharp stab of envy. Kids to pick up from school. A husband who could carry her. Carmen actually seemed to be looking forward to being laid off.

She scoured the Internet for jobs. There weren't many that sounded promising, but she sent out resumes and began calling old colleagues.

It was a depressing afternoon. Two old friends appeared to have disappeared from the face of the earth. The awkward conversation with another reminded Mary why she hadn't felt the need to keep in close touch with him in the first place. By the time she picked up the fourth one's message about being on maternity leave, she was longing for a stiff drink.

Mary dressed in black slacks and a black shirt for her date with Winslow. She was feeling petulant. He couldn't know she had been procrastinating about finding a job, but she somehow felt it was partly his fault. After all, she'd had to clean the house in case he came in, and think of something to wear, and even dig out some make-up, all reasons not to be doing what she should have been doing.

"I just need to grab my shoes," she told him.

"You look like you're dressed for a night in the West Village," he commented, when she returned from her bedroom in low pumps — a gigantic fashion step up from her usual sneakers and hiking boots. "I'm only taking you to Manchester."

She felt a surge of irritation. "Is this not appropriate for Manchester?"

"No, no, it's great. You look great." He smiled his appreciation and she immediately felt much better. She'd never considered herself attractive — her mother had always said she had an 'interesting face' (whereas her sister Patty was a 'natural beauty') — but Mary supposed that in her mid-thirties she might be attaining some sort of appeal by default, if only because she hadn't gotten fat yet.

She watched him survey the living room, which adjoined the kitchen. She expected a grimace or a raised eyebrow, but his face was dispassionate. "You kept the furniture?"

"It seemed like a good idea at the time. That was before I noticed the smell."

He sniffed. "I don't smell anything. But then I was just locking the chickens away for the night."

"Chickens?"

"I live with my dad on the family farm. You didn't know that?"

"No." So Winslow was actually a cop-slash-farmer who lived with his dad? Perhaps that was why he was unmarried at nearly-forty. "How come you know how people dress in the West Village?"

"I lived in New York for a couple of years after I got out of the Marines. I sublet my sister's apartment. She didn't want to let it go until she got tenure."

"Were you there for 9/11?"

"No, by then I'd been back here a while."

That had been a year and a half ago. "So why did you come back here?" Surely it couldn't have been the chickens?

"Mom got sick and Dad needed help." A shadow crossed his face.

"Oh, I'm sorry. Is she okay?"

"She died."

"I'm sorry."

"It was a relief by the end, really. Are you ready to go?"

"Oh, of course! Sorry!" Mary ran to scoop up her little going-out-on-a-date purse and shook it, trying to remember whether she'd put her keys in it yet. There was a lack of comforting key-jingle and she started patting her pockets down.

"There's no rush."

She quickly surveyed the kitchen and shook out her regular purse. "Roger always hated how long it took me to get ready."

"I'm not Roger. Take your time." His tone was so soothing that she could just imagine him crooning reassurances to a recalcitrant cow: *There, there, Bessie.*

"You have any other livestock on the farm?" she asked, finally discovering her keys right where they were supposed to be, in the little purse.

"Not recently, praise God. Well, some ducks. Why do you ask?"

"No reason." If she could just ignore that oddly habitual 'Praise God,' Winslow's calm, soothing voice was rather seductive. Then again, even the kindest-hearted farmer had his own reasons for soothing the cow.

Winslow was driving his own car, a Toyota older than her

Nissan, but much better kept. "Wave to Cici," she said, as they pulled out.

He looked puzzled, but waved. Mary watched the curtain drop.

"Do you always wave to her?"

"I just want her to know that I know she's spying on my every move."

He laughed. "Maybe she's finally met her match. She had poor Agnes totally intimidated."

"I can't believe she didn't notice her death earlier."

"Oh, she did. She shared her suspicions with enough people that it eventually got to us. She wasn't going to call us directly, though. In her eyes we're the town and the town refuses to do her bidding."

"Arthur told me you were there."

He nodded, wrinkling his nose.

"So where was she?"

He frowned. "What do you mean?"

"Where did you find her?"

"Oh. On the floor outside the bathroom."

"Poor old woman." So the new mattress hadn't been strictly needed.

"There are worse ways to go."

"Are you thinking of your mother?"

He shook his head. "No. When I was a kid my cousin John got pinned by a tractor." He clenched his hands on the steering wheel.

"I'm sorry," she said yet again. "I read somewhere that farming is a dangerous occupation."

"It can be. But I'm not really a farmer. I'm a cop."

"Which is so much safer."

He smiled.

"Do you see a lot of death on the job?"

He gave her a bemused look. "Not a lot. Accidents, of course. Old folks like Agnes. Couple of heart attacks. Carbon monoxide once, took out a family of seven."

"How horrible."

"Yes."

"Any murders?"

"We had one a couple of years ago. Man stabbed his wife to death when she tried to leave him." He gave her a significant look. "Heard anything more from your ex?"

"No. Did you see any death when you were in the military?"

He pursed his lips. "This conversation is getting pretty morbid."

She flushed, chastened. "You're right. I'm sorry."

They drove in awkward silence along the curving mountain highway. Finally, Winslow said, "I was in Somalia. They'd had a famine, a civil war. People were starving to death."

"Oh. Wasn't that also —?" She had a vague idea that bad things had happened to U.S. troops in Somalia.

"That *Black Hawk Down* stuff happened later. But it was bad enough when I was there. Humanitarian mission, supposedly, but some days I wished we could just blow the whole place off the map."

She noticed he'd flushed an angry red just talking about it.

"But you got through it okay?" Was she actually dealing with a traumatized combat veteran rather than a laconic small town cop?

"Spending time in the city helped. I think I might have started thinking the corn was out to get me if I'd come home straight from Mogadishu."

"Ah."

"But as I said, I don't really farm. Dad's the farmer."

"But you must help." He'd just told her about putting the chickens away.

"Well, there are things that need to get done. Dad's getting on, you know, but every year he comes up with some new scheme. This year it was Asian vegetables." He shook his head. "I'm trying to talk him out of buying a pair of llamas."

"So do you expect you'll sell the farm someday?"

The car lost speed. Winslow looked shocked. "Sell the farm?"

Mary said nothing, conscious that she'd struck a nerve.

"It's been in our family for generations," he said, as if that explained everything.

"Oh, I see," she said, although she didn't.

Winslow lapsed into a ruffled silence, and she sat in her seat and watched the increasing signs of habitation as they headed into Manchester's suburbs. Had she somehow managed to say something unforgiveable? It would be pretty awkward if he was this silent all night.

Then again, what did it really matter if he was?

None of this really mattered, she reminded herself. It was just dinner.

CHAPTER SIXTEEN

M ANCHESTER WAS CLEANER and brighter than she expected. As they left the car, Winslow cleared his throat. "Tonight is on me."

"There's no need," she said automatically, although she was relieved.

"Please. I asked you." An echo of Arthur. She wondered whether Winslow also hoped to get laid tonight. Well, of course he did. He was a man, after all.

They were soon seated at a small table with a view of the Merrimack River running between old brick factory buildings. After they ordered their drinks he looked out pensively for a moment, perhaps girding himself for the rest of the evening, or perhaps just appreciating the view. Mary watched and appreciated her own view: Winslow had a classically handsome face, beautiful golden curls, blue eyes flecked with green. But in the slanting golden light she could also see signs of age: faint crow's feet around the eyes, worry lines across his forehead, strands of white amid the gold. He reminded her vaguely of a Wyeth painting she had once seen in a museum in Maine.

He caught her watching him and gave her a quizzical smile.

"So you went from farm to philosophy major to globe-traveling Marine to the big city and then back to the farm," she said.

"I guess that pretty much sums it up. And your whole existence?"

"Oh, mine is so much duller. Boston Irish to UMass to various editorial jobs and a failed marriage. And looming unemployment." She almost wished she could throw in the part about sleeping with his priest — at least it would be more interesting.

"Do you have any hobbies?"

"Hobbies?" Reading and walking didn't count as hobbies, did they? "I don't think so." God, she really was dull. "I don't even collect anything."

"I don't either. Unless you count restaurants. Do you know what you want to order? People rave about the tortellini here."

But he asked the waitress for a calamari fra diavolo extra spicy. Mary stuck with penne in vodka sauce, something she had often enjoyed in her old life.

"Tell me about your family," he said.

"Dad died about five years ago and Mom moved out to Arizona. She wanted to be closer to my brother and sister. They have kids, so she gets to have all her grandkids around."

"You've never thought of following them out there?"

"No."

"Why not?"

"I don't know. I guess I never really thought about it."

She simply wasn't that close to her siblings, at least not since they had married. She also would never admit to him or anybody how depressing she found it to be an aunt and not a mom, for she knew that was terribly small of her. "Let's just say my mother has always been very good at zeroing in on all my faults."

He smiled. "Seems to me you're pretty good at zeroing in on things yourself."

"I guess so," she said, stung. She didn't like the idea of being in any way like her mother. It didn't help that among her father's last words to her had been "Just because you're thinking something doesn't mean you need to say it, missy."

Or as Roger had once put it, "Don't be such a fucking bitch."

"Mary?"

She looked up.

"I didn't mean that in a bad way."

"No, I know, of course not." She gave him the best fake smile she could pull off. A new relationship was not on the agenda right now anyway. She looked around the restaurant at everything she could that wasn't Winslow and chewed her bread industriously, though it now tasted like cardboard. Would it be too transparent if she suggested she wasn't feeling well?

"Hey." He reached over and put his hand on top of hers.

She flinched. "What?"

"It's too early in the evening to clam up."

"As you've noticed, I tend to say things without thinking first."

"Maybe I appreciate having everything out on the table."

"Don't assume it's all out. I'm an even worse bitch inside my head."

He looked amused. "Really?"

She felt suddenly lighter. "Yes. I'm just horrible. Consider yourself warned."

"Okay, I will." He took a sip of his seltzer and watched her, still smiling. If nothing else, he appeared to find her entertaining.

"So tell me about your family," she said.

"My sister lives in San Francisco. She teaches political science. My younger brother works for Raytheon. He has his own family down in Massachusetts."

"Your sister has no family?"

He hesitated. "She has a partner, but no children. She's gay."

"Oh." She recalled Arthur telling her something about Winslow's religious upbringing. Conservative, she thought. "Does your father mind?"

Winslow snorted. "I'm sure he would if he knew."

"Do you mind?"

"No. It's just who she is. I confess I'm not a huge fan of her partner."

"Then you've met her?"

"I go out there and stay with them at least once a year. I love San Francisco."

This man was full of surprises.

The salad course arrived. Mary focused on the various greens and set aside the more exotic antipasto. The dressing was redolent with garlic and onions. Not so good for kissing. Not that she had any expectation that he even would want to kiss her after all this. Still, didn't one generally extend at least a quick little peck at the end of a date? There was a little frisson of fear and excitement at the thought of kissing a guy as physically imposing as Winslow. For all she knew he was a date rapist. Then again, unmarried at almost forty, he might just be a terrible kisser. Or tragically impotent. Or gay, like his sister. And the poor man had no idea what she was sitting there thinking about, she realized, and smiled at him to make up for it. He smiled back, but looked puzzled.

"Why does your ex want to get back together with you?" he asked. "I thought you said he was married again."

"He just found out his new wife's baby isn't his. In fact, he found out he can't have kids either."

Winslow raised his eyebrows.

She sighed. She really didn't want to spend the evening talking about infertility.

"Is he an alcoholic?"

Was he? Mary had often debated this herself. "He can be a problem drinker. It's not like he ever missed any work because of it, though. It's just..." she stopped herself.

"What?"

"You can't really want to hear this much about my ex-husband."

"Sure I do."

"Nobody enjoys listening to other people go on about that kind of thing."

"I'll tell you when I'm tired of it."

Mary shook her head, not persuaded. "The thing about Roger is that the drinking makes him mean. I mean, my father was a big drinker, too. But he wasn't a mean drunk, he was funny and charming. He only really got mean when he couldn't drink." She flashed back again to those last days in the hospital.

Winslow smiled sympathetically. "I suppose I'll never know what kind of drunk my dad would be. He considers alcohol the devil's snare."

"What about you?" Mary asked. Winslow had ordered a seltzer with dinner, so she had restricted herself to an iced tea.

"I enjoy a drink now and then. But not when I'm driving. You?"

"I probably need to be careful. It doesn't take much to make me stupid." She thought of the bottle of wine she'd shared with Arthur. But had that really been enough to get them drunk, or was it just an excuse to do what they'd wanted to do in the first place?

The food arrived. Mary, her appetite restored, ate to the point of discomfort without being able to make a noticeable dent in the huge serving. Winslow had no such trouble, finishing his platter. He offered her a bite before it was all gone, but she made a face and said no thanks.

"You don't like squid?"

"It tastes like rubber bands."

"Then it was overcooked. You should try it again."

"I don't think so."

"You're pretty conservative, aren't you?"

Mary had never thought of herself that way. "Actually, I'm an Independent."

"I mean you're cautious. Being an Independent is cautious, too. Not committing one way or the other."

Had he just implied she was a weenie? "What are you, then? A wild-eyed liberal? A Libertarian?"

"Moderate Democrat. But that's fairly radical for me, because my dad heads the local Republican party."

"Is that how you got your job?" The town of Lawson had been in Republican hands since the Civil War, as far as she could tell.

He grinned. "I'm sure it didn't hurt."

"And do you like being a cop?"

"Yeah, I do. I like being useful."

It was a charming sentiment. Mary realized with some alarm that Winslow was growing on her — which wasn't part of the plan.

"Do you want dessert?" he asked.

She shook her head. "I'm too full."

"Well, I'm going to order piece of cake. I think it's called for. As of today, I am no longer nearly forty."

She stared. "Today's your birthday?"

"Yes." He flushed. "Thank you for allowing me to have a date with a beautiful woman on my birthday." He lifted his seltzer glass and saluted her.

"Happy birthday," she said weakly.

"Thank you."

Mary wished she had something to give him other than sex, although at this point she was not as utterly opposed to the idea as she'd expected to be. "Why don't you let me get dinner, then?" she said, her voice squeaking.

"Thanks, no. We already settled that."

"But it's your birthday."

He shrugged. "I'm forty. Grown-ups don't even do birthdays in my family."

"We never did in mine either. Roger's family, though — God, you had to watch every single one of them blow out the candles and unwrap their presents, whether they were turning three or forty-three."

"Sounds like you don't miss it."

"Actually, I really liked his family. But they've made it pretty clear they don't want to keep in touch." She swallowed and looked out the window.

"This has been a pretty hard year for you, hasn't it?"

Her eyes filled and she nodded, not trusting herself to speak.

"We'll share a slice of cake," he said.

The ride home was quiet, Winslow intent on the dark curves of the road. At the house, he put the car in park and looked at her.

She thought of inviting him in for coffee, but feared that if he did come in it might be out of pity. So she just said, "Well, thank you for a lovely dinner."

"I enjoyed it. You want to go out again?"

He actually wanted to try this again? "Okay. Sure."

"How about a trip to the coast?"

"The coast? That's pretty far, isn't it?"

"We'll make a day of it. Go to Rye, take a walk on the beach, eat some lobster."

She hadn't been to the beach in years. "A walk on the beach" sounded suspiciously like a personal ad, but he struck her as pretty straight-up. "Okay. Sure."

He smiled. "Good night, then."

"Good night," she echoed. She leaned forward for the

obligatory kiss. He looked pleasantly surprised and gave her a fairly tentative one.

She drew back and checked for his reaction. In the dark, with the frogs peeping and Winslow steadily regarding her, she imagined leaning forward for another kiss. Perhaps, after Arthur, it had become easier for her to make sexual overtures. Perhaps, after Arthur, she was hungry for the next thrill of contact.

Perhaps, after Arthur, she really had become a slut.

But Winslow said, "I'll give you a call" in a final sort of way. She got out of the car and went into the house. She hadn't intended to agree to another date. She hadn't intended to like him at all.

Cici was all but wagging her tail the next morning as she intercepted Mary at the garbage cans. "Did you have a nice evening out, dear?"

"Yes, I did."

"That was Winslow Jennings' car, wasn't it?"

Mary didn't answer, determined not to get drawn in.

"I saw him get rid of that man for you the other night. You know, of course, that he was engaged to be married not so very long ago." Her voice dropped into a loud whisper. "Something happened, very hush-hush, and she's with another man now."

Mary was horribly curious, but didn't want to betray her interest to Cici. "Have a nice day, Cici," she said with a false smile, and escaped back into the house.

On Monday she got the call she'd been dreading.

"It's official," Carmen said.

"I'm laid off?" Even though she had fully expected it to happen, Mary couldn't help a feeling of sudden panic.

"As of the end of the week. Even Nat got the axe this time."

"And you?"

"They're keeping me on for an extra week so I can throw stuff out. When can you come in?"

"I really need to?"

"Yeah. Besides, you can sign up for unemployment while you're here."

Mary sighed. She felt too dazed to drive. "Tomorrow morning, I guess."

"Good, see you tomorrow."

Mary walked out her backdoor and stared at the back yard, where new grass was poking through the salt hay she'd laid down after reseeding.

Someone else would get to enjoy her new lawn.

Oh buck up, she told herself. After all she'd been through in the last year, it was just ridiculous to start feeling weepy over a patch of grass.

CHAPTER SEVENTEEN

ON HER WAY back from the office Tuesday, thick
packet of unemployment information crammed into
a box of office pickings on the passenger car seat beside her,
Mary felt something she hadn't expected: excitement. For
better or worse, her life must now change, and change was
not necessarily bad. Just because she had her savings sunk
into a little house in Lawson did not mean she had to stay
there; just because she had spent the last six years editing
books of dubious value did not mean something better
might not come her way. True, the busted tech-bubble
economy was rotten, but she had never been unemployed
for more than a few weeks before. She'd find something.

But when Winslow picked her up that Friday she was
subdued, anxious about leaving the phone when she had
so many resumes out. Half were for jobs that didn't really
sound terribly interesting, and half were just shots in the
dark at companies she knew. She was also a little wary of
the day's adventures. He'd told her to dress for a walk on
the beach, not swimming this early in the season, so she
was wearing light summer clothing and comfortable sneakers and carrying a jacket in case the shore was fogged in.

"What made you decide to move to Lawson?" Winslow asked as they set off, and Mary wondered if he'd prepared a series of interview questions.

"I always thought it was a pretty little town. And I guess I wanted a clean break." She hesitated, then added, "I suppose the infertility might have something to do with it. Most of my old friends have children. I could try to reconnect, but I just don't feel up to it right now."

"Most of my friends have kids now, too."

"I mean, I'm happy for them that they have their families, but... I don't know, I guess sometimes I'd just rather shoot myself than have to sit through one more baby shower."

He grinned. "My sister said the same thing to me just the other day."

"Maybe when I've moved back there it will change."

He gave her a quick look. "Moved back?"

"It's unlikely I'll find a publishing job close to Lawson."

Winslow lapsed into silence, and Mary sat and watched the scenery, wondering if he'd suddenly decided not to waste any more conversation on someone who had just told him she was leaving town. If so, this could turn out to be a really long day. But then he said, "You're that committed to a career in publishing?"

"No, I'm that committed to making a living."

"What if you fell in love? Wouldn't that change your plans?"

Startled, she looked at him, but he wasn't blushing or otherwise betraying more emotional engagement than she had expected. Apparently he just really wanted to know. "Honestly? I just don't trust the whole falling-in-love thing at this point in my life. I mean, it sure led me wrong the last time."

He frowned and drove on in silence. She said, "You said you'd had relationships before. Didn't you find that your feelings changed over time?"

His voice went a little flat. "Yes, but in hindsight I don't think those relationships were meant to be."

There was a sort of passive reverse logic there that irritated her; it was not unlike Roger's opinion, offered along with the news that his girlfriend was pregnant, that if he and Mary had been meant to be together, they would have been able to have a baby together. "God didn't approve of them?"

"You seem to think I'm some kind of religious nut. I just mean that in hindsight we were not well-matched. Things happened; we grew apart."

"I don't know. It seems to me that when it comes to relationships things often happen. And people often grow apart." She knew it sounded bitter, but it was the truth as she saw it.

The beach was lovely — the water and sky blue under a warm sun, mist hanging off the ocean at a distance. They walked up and down its length, comparing childhood trips to the shore. Mary kept her eyes on the sand, stuffing her pockets with sea glass. Maybe she should start collecting it and see if it made her a more interesting person. Winslow watched the water with an alert air, as if he didn't believe the life guards were really protecting those children, most of whom were simply going in far enough to get wet, shrieking at the cold, and running back out again. "Can be quite the undertow here," he said.

"Don't you want children of your own, Winslow?"

He shrugged. "If I'm blessed with children, great. If not, I get to sleep later."

"Really? That accurately sums up how you feel about it?"

He nudged over a clump of seaweed with his big toe and she caught herself admiring his feet, although this was not a part of the male anatomy she'd ever found enthralling before. "These days I count myself lucky if I can find a kindred spirit to go on a date. First things first."

"Cici told me you were engaged."

His head came up. "Yes, I was."

"What happened?"

"She had a miscarriage."

Mary frowned, unimpressed.

Winslow kicked the seaweed towards the surf. "We were only getting married because she was pregnant. It wasn't a great match. When she had the miscarriage, we both walked away. She has two kids now, and lives with their father."

"I see." Mary wondered if it had really been that simple.

"After that I changed my wicked ways."

"What do you mean?"

"No more sex before marriage," he said, and blushed.

She stared. "Seriously?"

"It's the only way to be sure. She'd told me she was using protection. And maybe she was; these things can fail. Anyway, when I returned to the Christian faith several years ago I also returned to the idea that sex outside of marriage is a sin."

"A sin." It sounded so quaint. Not even Arthur seemed

to see it in such antique terms. She was annoyed to realize that she was disappointed.

God, she really was a slut.

Winslow regarded her evenly. "I realize it seems old-fashioned. But I also think it's just too risky an act to be shared with someone who hasn't made a serious commitment."

"But you didn't always believe this." Really, there was something almost clinically fascinating about a man who'd rather get married before he got laid.

"No, not at all. I was raised in a very religious household, but I rejected all of it. I came back eventually, but in my own way."

"Is that why you don't belong to your father's church?"

He looked out to sea. "They mean well, but I believe they sacrifice the most important tenets of Christianity in their fervor over things like homosexuality."

"So you don't think that's a sin?" If you charted every aspect of this guy's beliefs, the line would be full of wild zigzags.

"No, not at all. I told you about my sister."

"Yet the idea that homosexuality is evil is found in scripture."

"So is the idea that eating pork is unclean and women shouldn't speak in church. It's hardly a major focus in the Bible. Jesus never even mentions it. Not that all Episcopalians agree, of course. What a flap we've been having over Bishop Robinson."

"So you accept homosexuality, but extramarital sex is a sin."

"Yes."

"But these homosexuals are having extramarital sex."

"But it's a catch-22 if they're not allowed to marry. So I don't judge them, unless they're promiscuous, in which case I suppose I judge them as I would anybody who sleeps around."

Mary winced, aware that her own recent behavior wouldn't bear close examination. Still, she appreciated that his views on this matter were now out there between them and settled. Obviously, he didn't expect to get laid tonight.

On the other hand, Arthur had had a personal rule about only having one glass of wine. She'd had a personal rule about having sex with married men. She had a bit less faith in resolutions these days. If she were truly evil, she thought, she might try to seduce Winslow just to see if she could.

"You're not anti-gay, are you?" He looked concerned.

"Me? No, not at all." She resisted the temptation to add that she was, in fact, pro-fornication.

The restaurant he took her to was a huge place crammed with long picnic tables covered with vinyl tablecloths and permeated by the smell of frying fish. Prices for various items were written in magic marker on paper plates tacked to the walls.

"The smelts are popular," he said. "And the fried oysters. We can get a side order of either, but I think we should start with a couple of lobsters. Or would you prefer a roll?"

"Roll, please." She was unwilling to take on a whole lobster under his scrutiny. Her parents couldn't afford lobster when she was growing up and Roger hated seafood, so she'd had little experience dismantling giant arthropods.

She also didn't want anybody telling her she should be eating the green stuff or the red stuff.

"Another conservative choice."

"I guess. But if you want to wrestle manfully with a lobster, you go right ahead."

"Don't mind if I do." He ordered a three-pounder.

"I still don't see why you haven't met a kindred spirit, as you put it, in all these years," she said. "Your one bad experience aside."

"Oh, I've met kindred spirits. I lived with someone in the city. I pretty much planned to marry her."

Pretty much sounded fairly tepid. "What happened?"

"I went home to help out when Mom got sick. Time passed. She met a guy from New Jersey."

"Were you upset?"

Winslow frowned as he cracked a claw open. "Yes, at first. But I couldn't really blame her. If I'd asked her to marry me, she might have waited longer. But she also had no desire to live in New Hampshire. So it was for the best."

"And there's been nobody up here?"

He tore apart the lobster's knuckles easily. "Well, Melissa, the woman I was engaged to. That scared me off dating for a while. Sometimes I wonder if the canceled wedding and my trips to San Francisco and my support for Bishop Robinson haven't gotten a few rumors going."

Mary regarded Winslow, now sporting a plastic lobster bib, and could see where that might happen. He was so pretty. Kept his car clean. Attended church. Had lived in the West Village. "You must feel like you just can't win."

"Not at all. You're here, aren't you?"

She smiled. "For awhile."

The trip back was quiet. Mary thought it was nice to be able to sit quietly with someone, then wondered if it wasn't too early to have run out of things to say. On a normal second date, there'd be the tension of wondering whether he wanted sex, or she wanted sex, or should they even be thinking of sex? At the least, there'd be the tension of whether he liked her, and whether she liked him. It hardly mattered in this case, though she did find him attractive and interesting and very likeable, if a bit hard to read. But, really, he might as well be an alien for all they had in common.

Of course, she'd thought that about Arthur, too.

She was glad to know that wasn't going to happen here, since Arthur had perhaps opened a floodgate of some kind and left her feeling that, hey, it could be fun having casual sex with men she barely knew. She watched Winslow's muscular forearms as he steered the car — the fine, blond hairs glowing in the slanting evening sun, his capable hands on the wheel. Before she knew it she was imagining those arms wrapped around her, those hands on her body.

He looked over at her and smiled, almost as if he knew what she was thinking. She flushed and stared out the window.

Once home, she asked, "Do you want to come in for a cup of coffee?"

He hesitated.

She added, "Cici will assume we're having sex, but that might be a good rumor for you at this point in your life."

He laughed. "You have a point there."

He followed her in and sat at the table, scratching Bob's neck like a man who understood cats, while she made coffee and hunted for something to serve with it.

"Do you bake?" he asked, watching her search her cupboards, then open the refrigerator and stare into it, willing inspiration to strike.

"No."

"Cook?"

"Sure, I cook. But I don't feel like bothering much just for me." She poured some crackers onto a plate, after surreptitiously tasting to make sure they weren't stale, and put out some cream cheese she'd bought to eat with a bagel, but forgotten about. She couldn't see any mold on it, so it must be okay. "What about you?"

"Dad does most of the cooking. I do the baking."

"Really? Desserts?"

"No, bread."

"Bread from scratch?" Her saltines must seem really pathetic to him.

"We've always baked our own bread."

How wholesome. But who baked bread these days? Really, it was just another reason for people to think he was gay.

She served the coffee and he drained his cup long before she'd gotten more than a few sips of her own down. He spread cream cheese with great concentration, probably trying not to break the cracker.

"This was a really nice day," she said. She already felt nostalgic about it because of the job-hunting she'd need to pick up in earnest the next day.

"Come have dinner at the farm Sunday. I want you to meet my dad."

"Your dad? Why?"

He cocked his head. He looked amused. "Because I like you."

She just stared at him. "But —"

"But?" Those eyes didn't give much away. It wasn't at all obvious that he liked her in particular. Found her interesting, yes, like some sort of unusual bug or something.

"You can't like me *that* much," she said, though she was not really sure she meant it. He might. It might be just one more odd little turn in his unique exploration of life. It was strange that she was more willing to believe this of Winslow, with his inscrutable eyes, than Arthur, whose emotions seemed much closer to the surface. "You hardly know me. And I don't think I'm the right sort of person for you."

"Why would you say that?"

She thought for a moment, assembling her list. "One, I'm not religious. Two, as you have noted, I'm more conservative than you are. Three, I'm planning to leave town soon." *Four, I slept with your priest.*

"I don't have a problem with any of those things."

That's because you didn't hear four. "How can you not mind that I'm not religious?"

"That's between you and God. It would be nice if you were a believer, but I don't require it so long as you're a good person. We might have had issues about raising children, but that hardly seems relevant."

She shook her head as if to clear it. Was he already

talking about what he seemed to be talking about? "What makes you so sure I'm a good person?"

He looked surprised. "Aren't you?"

She felt a little choked up at the realization that she couldn't honestly and without hesitation say *yes*. "I've made some bad choices."

"So has everybody. You're kind to strangers. I've seen that myself."

"If you mean Arthur, he wasn't a stranger."

"You're kind to your ex-husband."

"I wouldn't say that."

He smiled. "You're modest."

Oh please. She got up to rinse the cups at the sink.

He followed her. "I don't mind a conservative nature. It suggests you don't get bored quickly. And you chose to move here, so you must like it at least a bit."

She looked down at the cups in the sink as he hovered next to her, wondering with some resentment what conclusion he would draw if she washed them immediately, or if she decided to put it off. "I get the feeling you're fitting me to some profile."

"Maybe what I like most of all is your honesty."

She sighed. He had no idea.

He leaned down to her ear and whispered, "And I think you're gorgeous."

She looked up in surprise and he took the opportunity to kiss her. Soon his coffee-flavored tongue was probing her mouth while his hands explored her hair. Then he pulled back, panting slightly, and watched her.

She just stared at him, her mouth hanging open, panting

a bit herself. That had been a very good kiss. Not at all what one might expect from a man who had given up sex before marriage.

"I'd better go now," he muttered.

She felt dizzy from the sudden change in direction. "What?"

"I'll call with directions." He gave her a quick peck on the cheek and ran out the door.

Weak-kneed, Mary sank into the kitchen chair. So much for all her resolutions not to get involved.

CHAPTER EIGHTEEN

HOWEVER MUCH MARY liked Winslow, she told herself to come up with an excuse why she couldn't go to Sunday dinner. What was the point? She had no desire to live with a cranky old fundamentalist and a bunch of chickens in an ancient farmhouse, looking forward to the weekly bread bake. However, she was a little curious to see the whole catastrophe for herself. And she wanted to stay friends with Winslow, not only because she really liked him, but because at the moment it seemed he was the only friend she had. So when he called with directions, she only hesitated a moment before confirming that she would, indeed, drive out on Sunday.

She reassured herself that she was sure to be found wanting by his puritanical father, which would help Winslow restrain his enthusiasm, and if she was lucky she'd still have someone to go to dinner with occasionally before she found a job and left town.

Unfortunately, she hadn't had a response to a single resume, with one exception. Someone with a name she didn't catch had called and told her, in broken English, that the main requirement for their position would be to edit a book for free so they could see whether she was any good at it.

"For free?" she'd asked, not sure she'd understood correctly.

"Yes, first book free."

"A whole book?"

"Just one. Very easy."

"What kind of book? How many pages?"

"Hot sexy book. Easy job! Not too long. Easy!"

Hot sexy book? "How much do you pay me if I get the job?"

"Percentage! Good money! But first book free."

"How do I know it's worth my time?"

"You want job or not?"

"But it's not a job!"

That had been the end of that interview.

But she had almost three months of severance left, and unemployment starting, too. Something would come along.

"This is really pretty country," she said Sunday afternoon as she transferred a boxed pie to Winslow's hands in the wide gravel driveway outside the Jennings' white farmhouse. It sprawled in three distinct architectural styles across a rise overlooking the Took River. Fields stretched off in every direction, some recently plowed and others already sporting rows of cut hay. Mary was wearing one of her rare dresses, having assumed that Winslow's father would expect her to look nice for Sunday dinner.

"Very pretty," he agreed, with a smile that suggested he was talking about her rather than the country. He leaned over the box to give her a quick kiss.

Their farm lay primarily on the floodplain, he explained, as he pointed out the distant limits of their land. The Took River occasionally swallowed half or more of their fields. This was a boon in fertility if it happened in late winter and dried out quickly, a curse if it happened when there was a crop in or needing to get in.

She nodded, distractedly following the progress of a small flock of hens as they hunted and pecked their way across the scraggly lawn. Winslow was dressed more casually than she had expected, in jeans and a woven shirt of the "imperfections are normal in this fabric" variety. "Did you go to church today?"

"Of course."

Perhaps he'd changed to feed chickens or something.

"Father Arthur asked about you, actually."

Her heart skipped. "Did he?"

"You must have mentioned to him that we had a date."

An odd sensation overtook her, as if her ears were ringing. "Yes, I think I did."

"You look a little tired. Come into the house."

As they came in through a mudroom on the side of the house, a large black dog of mixed breed ran up, wagging its tail. It sniffed Mary thoroughly.

"This is Abigail," Winslow said. "I'm going to put her out so she doesn't become a pest during dinner. Scoot, Abigail," he commanded, opening the door. The dog gave him a reproachful look, but left obediently.

Winslow drew her into a large, white farm kitchen. The room was steamy with the mingled smells of dog, man, roast chicken, and bleach, and Mary felt a twinge of something like nausea, or maybe it was panic.

"Mary, this is my dad, Bert. Dad, this is Mary Bellamy."

A wiry old man with brilliantly white hair looked up from a tray of pea pods on a large table and stood up. He cleaned his hands on his apron and extended the right one for a strong shake. He was missing his little finger.

"Pleased to meet ya, Mary." Mr. Jennings' accent was more pronounced than his son's.

"Likewise, Mr. Jennings." Mary nodded at Winslow. "I brought a pie."

"Did you now? What kind is it?"

"Rhubarb."

Bert smiled broadly, revealing a gold tooth. "Rhubahb! I love rhubahb. I'm looking forward to that." He glared at Winslow and said, "Don't say nothing, boy."

"Can I help?" she asked.

Bert looked shocked. "No, no, no. You go through to the parlor now. Winslow will get you something to drink."

Winslow escorted her back to the "parlor," a beamed, low-ceilinged room with a big fireplace that had left its mark in a wide grey circle of soot on the wall and ceiling above. A motley selection of furniture from various eras crowded around an old coffee table neatly piled with back issues of *Reader's Digest* and *Farm News*.

"Was the pie not such a good idea?"

"Dad's supposed to watch his cholesterol, but that's a losing battle. What would you like to drink? He doesn't partake, but I have a bottle of chardonnay in the fridge."

"Just water, please."

"Orange juice, soda, coffee?"

"Water's fine." She sat in an upholstered rocker and looked around. The white walls were decorated in a random gunshot pattern of cheaply framed 8x10's: a very young, nearly bald Winslow in his Marine uniform; his sister and brother, presumably, in graduation gowns; a couple of young children she took for grandchildren; an older military photograph of Bert; a couple of smaller, yellowed snapshots of dogs. On the mantel, there was a silver-framed photograph of young Bert and his bride, a strikingly tall and attractive blonde woman, and another of the same couple taken many years later — Mrs. Jennings had grown quite fat. Oval portraits of ancestors glared from the back wall, where they hung over an uncomfortable looking Victorian settee. Lace doilies and runners carpeted virtually every surface, and a busy floral rug betrayed deep patterns of wear that suggested the furniture had not been rearranged in decades.

Winslow brought her a glass of ice water and sat down on the sagging plaid sofa, looking a bit awkward. "It's really worn in here. I've had to concentrate first on the roof and the boiler and the kitchen appliances. And we don't really spend that much time in this room."

"It's fine," she said, though the clutter of warring patterns felt oppressive.

"The older Dad gets the more he hates change. He used to complain about all these doilies, but after Mom died he became their biggest champion."

"That's so sweet." She felt unaccountably weepy at the thought.

"Or stubborn. Hey, are you okay?"

She wasn't. Maybe it was the atmosphere of the house, but she was also feeling exhausted. Her period had started with all the attendant cramps, but was sputtering along as if unsure it was really time yet, as occasionally happened in times of stress. "I'm kind of tired," she admitted.

"How's the job hunt going?"

She told him about the outrageous interview.

"Guess you won't be moving soon for that position."

"No."

"I'm going to get you some crackers," he said abruptly, and left.

She leaned back in the rocker. She felt wiped out.

"Here, eat." Winslow put a plate of wheat crackers and cheddar in front of her.

She obeyed, embarrassed. "I guess I am hungry." She nibbled on a cracker and took deep, even breaths. Maybe she was having a panic attack.

"Father Arthur told me I should make sure you eat."

"Yeah, he's big on that."

Winslow gave her an uncertain look, perhaps detecting a note of disdain he would have no reason to expect. She resolved to attempt perfect neutrality if Arthur came up again. The cracker was helping, and she reached for another with genuine appetite.

"There, you look better. You might want to get your blood sugar checked."

"I haven't gotten a doctor here yet. I probably just need to eat a better breakfast."

"Potter is good; you met him when Father Arthur was sick."

"I suppose I probably should get a check-up before the insurance runs out."

"What do you mean?"

"It ends when my severance ends."

"No COBRA?"

She shook her head. "It's very expensive."

"You could get in a jam if you drop it. I've seen it happen."

"And I might lose the house if I have to pay COBRA. I think that would qualify as more of a jam."

He leaned back. "Lawson Police Department employees have excellent family health coverage."

She raised her eyebrows. "Is there a job opening I should know about?"

"I just thought you should know." He smiled.

Was this what passed for flirting nowadays? *Look, baby, I've got great health insurance.*

A bell that sounded like it belonged on a fire truck tolled outside the house. "Dinnertime," Winslow announced, standing up.

She followed him into the dining room through a set of French doors. Bert was already seated at the head of the table, which was covered with an old lace tablecloth, and food steamed from an array of old china bowls and platters. A glass vase was arranged with clusters of roses and sprigs of ivy. "This is lovely!" Mary said.

"My dear late wife Priscilla believed in proper Sunday dinner," Bert said. "You sit here, on my good side. I don't hear so well out of the other ear, and Winslow never says much of account." He smiled and unfurled his cloth napkin with a dramatic snap. His remaining fingers, she noticed, were gnarled, scarred, and age-spotted, the nails and cuticles outlined by thin dark lines apparently beyond the reach of any soap.

"You must miss her," Mary said.

"Like it was yesterday," Bert said fervently. "Would you say grace, Mary?"

Winslow frowned. "Why don't you do the honors, Dad?"

"Priscilla was particularly gifted at saying grace," Bert confided to Mary. "All right then. Dear Lord Jesus Christ in Heaven, thank you for this food, and thank you for the company of this lovely young woman who has bestowed her presence on us today, and thank you for all the great and various blessings you have showered upon us, not least of which is your Father's eternal grace — our solace and strength in good times and bad. Amen."

Mary wasn't sure whether she'd just been editorially addressed.

"Chicken?" Bert asked.

The meal was quiet. Both men seemed content to focus on the food, which was quite good, except that the vegetables had been boiled to the point of disintegration. The bread, sliced and piled on a plate, went quickly. Bert shook appalling amounts of salt over everything he ate and lathered butter on his bread like a brick mason laying down mortar.

"You know that's not good for you," Winslow said.

"Our Winslow is quite the worrywart," Bert said to Mary.

"Well, leave room for pie," she said, trying to help.

"Never fear! I wouldn't miss that pie for all the tea in China." He turned to Winslow. "Not much of an eater, is she?"

"Mary is right there, Dad, if you'd like to address any comments to her."

Bert turned to Mary. "You don't eat much, do ya?"

"No, not that much."

"Not like my Priscilla. Good Gawd, that woman could put it away. She must've put on a hundred pounds over the fifty years we were married."

"Fifty years! That's quite an accomplishment."

"I hear you were married yourself."

"Dad," Winslow said warningly.

"Yes, I was married for eight years."

"Then you know what an accomplishment it is, don't ya!" he chortled. Then he sobered. "Although I must say it sounds to me like your husband was a man of little faith."

"Dad," Winslow said again, rather loudly.

"Now, Winslow tells me you're not a church-going woman."

Winslow put down his knife and fork.

"That's true, I'm not." She met Bert's gaze without flinching.

"I do feel sorry for that," he said. He shrugged. "But you're young. You may yet discover what it means to be born again in the love of our Lord Jesus Christ. Just as I still have hope that our Winslow will return to the bosom of the church he grew up in."

"Hope springs eternal," Winslow said sourly.

"Still, I suppose some church is better than none," Bert said, with a sly glance back at Mary.

She smiled and refused to take the bait.

"Now, did you attend church as a child?" Bert asked.

"Oh yes. I was raised Catholic."

"Well, there's your problem," Bert said earnestly. "No wonder that didn't grab ya. You come to prayer meeting with me sometime. I've seen many a lost soul transformed by the spirit of God and born again in the love of Christ, right in front of all of us!"

Winslow sighed and asked Mary, "You want some coffee with your pie?"

"Yes, please. May I help?"

"But you are a good girl, aren't you?" Bert said. "You stay put, we'll do it."

Bert's voice was loud, typical of a man whose hearing was impaired, so Mary hardly missed a word in the kitchen.

"Bit delicate looking, don't you think?"

"She's just not feeling that well today."

"Hardly ate a thing."

"She doesn't need to eat as much as we do."

"Your mother wouldn't have left this much food."

"Mom was morbidly obese."

"That's an awful mean thing to say about your mother."

"Sorry."

"She is pretty, in a horsy kind of way."

"Dad!"

"Bit skittish, too. But she seems nice enough."

"She is."

"All right, then."

They came out the swinging door of the kitchen bearing pie, plates, cutlery, and a tray with coffee, cream, sugar, and mugs on it, all arranged on another doily. What was it with these two farm men and lacey things?

Mary was a little surprised that she didn't feel more uncomfortable. Bert wasn't bothering her at all — save perhaps that comment about looking horsy. Compared to enduring her mother and maternal grandmother's biting commentary at the dining room table, this was a cakewalk — Bert actually mixed in the occasional nice comment and a few jokes.

"Good Gawd, I love this pie!" Bert said.

"I see they've decided it's okay to take the Lord's name in vain up at the chapel," Winslow said.

"Don't you get high and mighty on me, Winslow Albert Jennings!" He turned to Mary. "Sometimes an old man forgets his tongue, but I believe the good Lord understands and forgives."

She smiled. The pie and the coffee were good. But what she really wanted was to go home and take a nap.

Winslow walked her out to her car later, after a tour of the vegetable and flower gardens and a peek at the barn and the henhouse.

"It's all lovely," she said, although the henhouse had definitely required some mouth-breathing.

"Dad can be a bit much."

"Oh, he's fine."

"Not very shy about his beliefs, I'm afraid."

"No," Mary agreed.

He cleared his throat and turned to face her. "So. Mary. Would you like to go out again?"

"Sure," she said, surprised at his formal tone.

"Dad hasn't scared you off?"

She regarded him, and he regarded her. His face was unreadable. "I like your dad. But, Winslow, please understand, it's just going out. If you're looking for more than that...." She trailed off as she noticed tiny lines of disappointment creep into his expression. Not so impossible to read, then, she thought and felt somehow reassured. "I don't want to mislead you."

The slight traces of pain disappeared as if they were never there. "I'll call when I get my schedule, then." He walked her to the car. "Drive carefully. You look like you need some rest."

She nodded, and leaned forward to give him a kiss. He returned it formally, and his face was impassive as she backed the car out.

CHAPTER NINETEEN

MARY CONTINUED TO feel out of sorts through the week, and had to push herself to get her daily walk. Her period was trailing along without really amounting to anything. One of the fertility doctors had warned her menopause would come early. Maybe this was it.

When the period ended, but her other symptoms didn't go away, she wondered if she might have picked up an infection (surely not from Arthur?). She called Dr. Potter's office to make an appointment. They couldn't fit her in until the following week, and she took the appointment, not feeling poorly enough to endure the hassle of a clinic or emergency room.

Eventually she realized that Winslow had never called. It was a revelation how disappointed she felt. She had probably discouraged him. How could she not have, though? He seemed to have already made up his mind, on the strength of no more than a few conversations, that she was the woman for him. It was an extreme example of the man who decides it's time to get married, looks around and goes, *ah — she'll do*. And even though she had begun, despite herself, to weigh Winslow as a possible companion, she'd become highly skeptical of her own judgment. Roger, then Arthur? How could she know Winslow wouldn't be just another terrible mistake?

But life in Lawson seemed bleaker without Winslow to talk to, and nobody else she could call a friend. Mary was so lonely she actually called her mother.

"Found a job yet?" her mother asked.

"No, but I have a lot of resumes out."

"You should come out to Arizona. Lots of jobs out here."

"Publishing jobs?"

"Well, I don't know about that. But I see 'Help Wanted' everywhere I go."

Mary began to pace with the phone in her hand. "How's the weather?"

"Oh, the grass is completely brown, but this is a desert climate, you know. So good for my sinuses. I'm thinking of tearing out the lawn and putting in stones instead. It's all the rage."

It sounded like living on the moon. "Did I tell you my garden is full of peonies?"

"That's lovely, dear. Did I tell you that none of Patricia's children remember who their Aunt Mary is? Have you called Patricia at all?"

"No, not recently, but she hasn't called me either."

"Well, she's a busy woman, with a husband and family and her work, too. You don't even have a job right now."

Mary cursed her impulse to pick up the phone. She supposed, in some deep recess of her mind, she had been hoping her mother would say, "Don't worry, dear, you'll always have a home with me." It was still on the tip of her tongue to ask, but instead she just held the phone silently.

Her mother didn't slow down. "It's a pity you're not in the church, dear; that would keep you grounded right now, give you activities to get involved in."

"But I'm divorced."

"Heavens, it would be that easy to get an annulment. You've had the perfect argument for one ever since you found out you couldn't get pregnant."

She should have known better than to call her mother when she was already feeling down.

"So, is there anyone I should know about?" Her mother didn't sound optimistic.

For sheer shock value, Mary considered telling her mother she had screwed a priest, but she figured she might need to borrow food money someday. "Nobody serious."

"But you've been dating?"

"A bit."

"How lovely! A nice man? He knows you can't have children?"

"Yes, but I don't want to jinx it by talking about it." Mary knew she was being disingenuous. Judging from the lack of a phone call, any potential relationship with Winslow was already dead.

After speaking to her mom, Mary considered calling Winslow to invite him somewhere, but decided she had better not. Why keep him dangling, if his feelings really were involved? It would be cruel.

She got her first serious response to a resume, but the job was only proofreading, located in Boston, and paid less than her old one. Although she was a capable proofreader, she considered it a tedious way to pass the day, so she endured traffic and a ride on the T to go into the interview with less enthusiasm than she knew she should have.

The interviewer probably didn't miss this. "Tell me why you want this job."

Mary hesitated, unable or unwilling to launch into the expected panegyric to the joy of fixing errors before they got into print. "I very much enjoyed my job at Shanley, and I'd really like to stay in publishing."

"And proofreading would be your ideal position?"

"Well, no. But I'm very good at it."

"I appreciate your honesty. And there's no doubt you're qualified. But I'm thinking perhaps it would be best if we could call you when we have a position better suited to your level of expertise."

"But if you hired me now, you'd have the use of my expertise, and I'd already be here when that position opens."

"Yes," the interviewer said stiffly, already shuffling papers. "I take your point, but I'm afraid you're not the only candidate for this position."

"I see." Mary was disappointed, but also a little relieved.

When she woke up tired yet again Friday morning, she imagined that she was growing a deadly tumor at the worst possible moment in her life, and wished she didn't have to wait so long for her appointment. She drove to the grocery store and bought a bottle of multivitamins and more food than usual, resolving to fix herself a proper dinner of steak, baked potato, and green salad. Maybe trail mix, apples, peanut butter, and microwave popcorn just weren't enough to keep a body going forever.

As she was broiling the steak that evening, there was a knock at the door. She opened it to Winslow, standing awkwardly on her front stoop in his civvies.

"Hi," she said.

"I was wondering if you'd like to join me for dinner."

"Actually, I'm already cooking. But you can split my steak with me, if you'd like."

"That's okay." He seemed flustered. "I'll come back another time."

"Don't go," she said. He was already backing away. "I have enough for two. I was planning on having leftovers."

He hesitated, obviously uncomfortable. "Well. Okay." When he walked in she was struck by how big he seemed in her little kitchen. Was she nuts, thinking she could actually feed him from what she had cooking?

"Can I do something?" he asked.

"Pour yourself a drink." She got him a glass. "How's your dad?"

"He's fine."

"And how are you?"

He shrugged. "Fine."

Unhappy. "I missed you this week."

"Did you?" He sounded as if he didn't quite believe her. "I'm sorry I didn't call."

She checked the steak. "How do you like it done?"

"Whatever you're doing is fine."

That was fortunate, because this was the first time she'd broiled anything in this oven. When she judged the steak done but not too done, she divided it into two relatively small portions, giving Winslow the greater part. Then she split the baked potato in half, and used extra salad she had put away to fill up the otherwise skimpy plates. "This isn't really going to be enough after all, I'm afraid," she muttered, grabbing the sliced bread and putting it on the table with a stick of butter.

"It's fine."

They ate. He kept his eyes mostly on the food. "How's the job hunt?" he asked.

"I had an interview in Boston yesterday."

His head came up.

"I didn't get it."

"Oh." He stabbed a cherry tomato out of the salad and stuck it in his mouth. Silence drew out.

"What's the matter, Winslow?"

He didn't answer immediately, but she waited.

"I guess I was thinking about what you said just before you left." His voice was soft and low. "Have you ever reached a point where you realize you're in water over your head, and the shore is pretty far away? That's what this feels like."

Oh dear.

"In as much as you keep warning me off."

"I didn't say it to hurt you."

"I realize that." He pushed a scrap across the plate. "Anyway, that's why I didn't call you this week. But then I felt bad about it, because I said I would."

Mary watched him play with his scraps and felt sorry for him, but also for herself. Why was she being presented with a man this lovely at the exact point in her life when she couldn't trust that he was what he appeared to be — or believe that she would be any good for him?

"Are you really ruling out any possibility that you'll get serious?"

She sighed. "I really like you, Winslow. It's just — I've been so stupid. I feel like I just can't rely on my own judgment."

Or his, for he was surely moving too fast.

"If you had more time?"

She stared down at her lap, trying to read her own heart. "I don't know. All I know for sure right now is that I really need to find a job. But I did miss you this week."

"Well, that's nice to hear." He still sounded discouraged.

"I almost called to ask you out, actually. But then I thought I probably shouldn't."

He smiled for the first time that evening. "You can always call me. How about we go get some dessert?"

"I'd love that."

After the dishes, which he insisted on drying, they walked down to the diner. As they passed the church, Mary was relieved to see no sign of Arthur.

"This church is important to you?" she asked.

He looked wary. "Yes."

"I mean, this particular church as opposed to any other Episcopal Church?"

"Yes."

"Why?"

"It's my home parish. I know the congregation, and they know me. It's like family."

"And Father Arthur? If he left, would you feel the same way?"

"I like Father Arthur, but I won't be surprised if he moves on before too long. I don't think he's particularly happy here."

No, she didn't either.

"I take it you haven't run into him lately?" he asked.

"No."

Having arrived at the bridge, they paused briefly to look at the water. "Something's bothering him right now, I think," he said. "Not surprising, with his life."

"Mm."

"Do you get depressed?"

"Depressed? Why do you ask?"

"Well, lately, you seem kind of... tired."

"I'm a little stressed out, I guess. I've never been laid off before."

"Or recently divorced and living in a new town where a strange guy keeps pestering you."

She smiled. "That last part doesn't bother me as much as you might think."

To her surprise, she managed to eat an entire ice cream sundae right down to the banana and the cherry.

"Maybe you just need to eat more."

"Could be." She hid a yawn behind her hand.

"You're tired. Let's go."

He shepherded her out. She was conscious of the curious looks they were drawing. "This is going to be all over town," she said.

He shrugged. "It's common knowledge that we're sleeping together, thanks to your neighbor there."

Mary sighed. She had predicted that, but it still annoyed

her. It hardly seemed fair to get the reputation without having first had the pleasure of earning it.

"My father even felt the need to warn me once again about the evils of sex outside the holy bonds of matrimony."

"Doesn't he know you've signed the pledge on that one?"

"He figures the flesh is weak, especially for those who lack a true appreciation of hellfire and damnation."

On the bridge they paused again to watch the river. The late evening sun was glinting off the ripples formed by its passage around rocks and boulders. A bird repeatedly flicked its tail from its perch on a reed and dove for insects.

"I love this spot," she said.

"I know a few other nice spots on this river that you probably haven't seen."

"You'll have to show me."

"I will."

After they started up Hill Street, he added, "My father does like you, actually."

"Despite my heathen nature and horsy looks?"

Winslow smiled. "You're not horsy. He just sees the world with farmer's eyes."

"I guess I should be thankful he didn't say I look like a cow." Now that they were climbing, the hill was taking her breath.

Winslow threaded her arm through his. "You really are tired."

She nodded.

"I think you should see a doctor."

"I have an appointment Monday."

"Good."

"It's all that ice cream," she said. Or she really had come down with some dread disease.

When they got back to the house, he asked, "Will you be okay?"

"Oh I'm fine," she said, hiding her own alarm on the subject. "Thank you for dessert."

"Thank you for dinner."

"I can do better if I actually know you're coming."

"I don't doubt it." He stepped forward and bent to kiss her, his tongue rich with hints of chocolate and caramel. This time one hand steadied her head as he plumbed her mouth, while another wandered further afield.

When he pulled back at last, she was panting. "Get a woman all riled up for nothing, why don't you."

His eyes were dark. "You have no idea how tempted I am."

She stepped back instinctively, though she was unsure why that idea bothered her so much. "I don't want to be the evil temptress."

"No? Why not?"

Because I thought you were the one man I've met who wouldn't throw away his beliefs to satisfy his dick. "I just don't."

"Why don't you just marry me, then?"

"Just so we can have sex?"

He leaned down and kissed her quickly. "Come for dinner Sunday?"

"Two Sundays in a row? What will your dad think?"

"That we're sleeping together, but he already thinks that."

"I don't want him thinking that!"

"Come on, Mary, live dangerously."

190

She only hesitated a moment, then grinned. He'd let that marriage thing go easily enough, thank God. "All right. I'll live dangerously."

CHAPTER TWENTY

THE NEXT MORNING she felt better. Maybe the steak had helped. Maybe she'd been low on iron. The cramps continued, however, and she finally broke out the Tylenol. She looked up horrid diseases on the Internet, wondering if Arthur could have had something contagious after all. However, according to her symptoms she didn't seem to be suffering from anything except perhaps an ovarian cyst or a bout of pelvic inflammatory disease. Neither alarmed her greatly since the most serious potential consequence was infertility.

Sunday afternoon when she turned onto the Jennings' farm road, Abigail met her car and escorted it up the hill, barking and dancing the whole way. Winslow came out and yelled at the creature to shut up, his face red and his manner unusually flustered.

"You can expect a lecture on sexual responsibility from Dad," he warned her. "I'll understand if you prefer to turn around right now and go home."

"I can handle it." She gave him a quick kiss. She was hungry, and she could already smell dinner.

Bert's greeting was reserved. He accepted Mary's gift of an apple pie from the market stiffly.

The meal was quiet. Mary was uncomfortably aware that Bert was narrowing his eyes and assessing her in a less subtle version of what his son did all the time. The food was good, however — meatloaf, mashed potatoes, cabbage, and carrots, though the latter two were, as before, boiled into an almost liquid state.

When they were done, Bert asked Winslow to clear the table and get the coffee going, but remained at the table with Mary.

Once Winslow had left the room, Bert said, "Now, my girl, are you aware that the whole town believes you two are — let's say — getting ahead of yourselves?"

"Winslow did mention something about that."

"And what do you have to say for yourself?"

He was really quite worked up, she realized, noting his white face. "I find it very odd, since we haven't actually had sex." It was even odder to be discussing her sexual engagements, or lack thereof, with the father of a forty-year-old man.

Bert had flinched when she said "sex" and he was still staring darkly at her, clearly unconvinced.

She stared right back. "You do realize my neighbor is prone to drawing lurid conclusions every time a man steps in the door of my house?"

"Does that happen often?"

Mary flushed.

Bert's mouth was set in a grim line. "In my day, an unmarried woman would never allow an unescorted man

194

into her house unless he was related to her. It was the only way she could protect her reputation."

Mary folded her arms, aware that her face was still red.

"Now, I do understand how these things can go." Bert turned pink himself. "We all of us, when young, have a natural attraction to the opposite sex, which God gave all His creatures that they might see fit to procreate and fill the earth. I can see that my boy is smitten. And I value honesty even more than good behavior. Now, are you still going to tell me you're not sleeping with my son?"

"I'm not sleeping with your son, Mr. Jennings. He doesn't believe in sex before marriage."

Bert looked pleased, but not entirely satisfied. "And you?"

"I don't think it's anyone's business what two consenting adults get up to, as long as they're not hurting anybody."

Winslow swung through the kitchen door bearing the coffee and pie on a platter. "How's the interrogation going?"

"Your girl here has a disturbing lack of outrage for the sin of fornication," Bert reported sadly.

"I'm just thankful she hasn't run screaming from the house." Winslow cut Mary a piece of pie twice as large as she would have cut herself.

"This is nothing," Mary said. "I grew up getting daily lectures on this same topic from my mother."

"She wanted what was best for you," Bert said.

"She wanted to make sure I wouldn't embarrass her by getting pregnant before I was properly married off."

Bert shrugged. "Children deserve to be raised in a

loving and stable family." He swallowed a forkful of pie and said, "Not half bad."

"Sometimes I look back and wish I had gotten knocked up," Mary said.

Both men stopped their forks in mid-air and stared at her.

"While I still could," she explained.

Bert frowned, disapproving, but Winslow's grimace was more understanding.

This time Mary helped Winslow clean up in the kitchen. Bert left for the garden, grumbling about sending Mary home with some snow peas, especially since he didn't know why he'd grown the danged weird things in the first place.

"You're a trooper," Winslow said, as he scrubbed.

"I think he's pretty harmless." She stood ready with a faded linen tea towel.

"I don't know. Laura is sure he'd cut her off."

"What do you think?"

"I really don't know. But I have a theory that when Mom died he stopped feeling the need to thunder at us quite so much."

"Did your mother know about Laura?"

"She suspected. She once asked me about it."

"You didn't tell her?"

Winslow was a thorough dishwasher, she noticed, inspecting each piece as he finished it to make sure it was really clean. "I told her she had to ask Laura herself. But she never did."

"Did Laura ever see your mom before she died?"

"Oh, sure. She was here when she passed. She visits at least once a year. But without Carla."

"Does your brother know?"

Winslow shook his head. "He and his wife are born again."

Mary realized again how out of her element she was in this family. No wonder Laura lived about as far away as a person possibly could.

"Winslow, I like your dad, but there's never going to be much common ground. I'm sure he thinks I'm the whore of Babylon or something."

"Actually he's quite keen on me marrying you. I told him I was working on it."

She sighed.

He gave her a bleak glance. "You'd tell me if I was working for nothing, wouldn't you?"

"Right now I feel like I just don't know and I don't see how you can either. What have we had, three dates and two Sunday dinners?"

"And two coffees," Winslow said promptly; apparently he was keeping track. "Besides, people say you just know when you know."

"Well, I thought I just knew with Roger. Now I think it was just timing. We happened to both want the same things at the same time. Then when we couldn't get everything we wanted, it fell apart. So here you are, you've just turned forty, and you're looking to marry. How do you know it really has anything to do with who we really are?"

Winslow frowned, carefully rinsing the flowered china gravy boat and handing it to her. "I *am* forty. I *am* ready to get married. So, yes, maybe it is timing. But it's also choosing someone I want to be with, whatever happens. Someone I can trust."

But how much would Winslow trust her if he knew about Arthur?

He asked, "Would you have left *him* because he couldn't have children?"

She grimaced. "I hope not."

"Because you're a good person."

She shook her head. "It's not that simple." *Tell him,* she thought, but she couldn't bring herself to do it. She was afraid of what he might say. That, and she was sure Arthur trusted her not to.

The afternoon was lovely and she was feeling better than she had the week before, so Winslow walked her down a deeply rutted tractor run to the Took River, which was broad and shallow as it meandered past the Jennings' cornfields. They picked their way from rock to rock, finally settling down together on a large, nearly flat boulder. Hot from the walk down, Mary pulled off her sandals and dipped her feet into the clear, cold current. Winslow removed his beat-up loafers and did the same. Such lovely feet, she thought again. Minnows nibbled at their toes.

"You fish in here?"

"Not in a long time."

"Where does it go, anyway?"

"About twelve miles up, it turns east and eventually meets up with the Merrimack."

"So it's not completely perverse." The northern flow of the Took had surprised and charmed her on her first visit to Lawson.

"It flows downhill like any other river. It's just not always an obvious slope."

She thought about Winslow's sister. "Maybe that's what we all do," she said. "We just flow downhill. Sometimes the slope isn't obvious to others, or even to us, but sooner or later, down we go. If we're lucky, other people feel we're going in the right direction, which is usually the same direction they are. But if it looks like we're not, they freak."

"I'm more comfortable with the idea of free will. That you could swim upstream if you believed that was the better direction."

"But how long can you really fight a current? It's your life; you can't just pull up on shore and rest whenever you feel like it."

He cocked his head at her. "Can't you?"

"What do you mean?"

"Isn't that what you're trying to do?"

Mary frowned. She hadn't expected her river metaphor for homosexuality to be used on her own heterosexual self.

"You're trying to stay out of the river. You think you've had enough."

"While you feel like you're in over your head," she said slowly.

Winslow nudged her and nodded at her white feet submerged in the water. "I can't help noticing that you keep poking your toes back in."

She felt outmaneuvered. "It's just a metaphor. I could say, yes, but this water's too rocky for swimming."

"Maybe, but I know a great swimming hole right around the bend. I could say come on in, the water's great."

He was sitting right next to her, right in her space.

"Is it?" She was suddenly aware of the heat rising off his body.

"Uh huh." He picked up her right hand and brought it to his mouth. He turned it over and kissed her palm and then slowly kissed his way up her arm.

At first, this was almost ticklish, and so quaintly romantic as to seem a little silly, but she didn't pull her arm back, mesmerized by the sight of this lovely golden-haired man making love to her skinny, freckled arm. By the time he was kissing the tender inside of her elbow, she had turned towards him in expectation of those delicious lips getting to her mouth. He lay her back on the warm, sun-baked rock and kissed her deeply, accepting her kisses back, then explored her neck and collar bone, cupped her breasts in his hands, nuzzled her nipples through the thin cotton of her shirt. Lying on the warm rock, with her feet still trailing in the cold water, the babbling of the river all around them, her own hands exploring new territory of their own, Mary felt caught up in an intense sensory overload. She wanted him. Badly.

They rubbed and thrust at each other through their clothing like a couple of teenagers. They kissed and moaned and dimly in the back of her mind she began to think the logistics here were a little challenging, really, and what was that noise?

"Shit!" Winslow said, and rolled off her. She realized the noise was Abigail, barking furiously as she ran down the tractor run and then splashed through the water towards them. Coming more slowly behind her was Bert, a half-pained, half-amused expression on his face.

"Maybe you want to jus' jump in, boy! Looks like you could use a cold dip!"

Winslow was focused on discouraging a soaked Abigail from coming joyfully up to greet them on the rock. Mary stood up, shaking out her wet feet and getting back into her sandals.

"No sex before marriage my *ass*," Bert said from the bank. "What kind of idiot do you take me for?"

"A goddamned self-righteous interfering idiot!" Winslow muttered. He shoved his feet back into his loafers and yelled furiously at Abigail to scoot. Abigail's ears lay back and she splashed back to Bert with a whimper.

Mary picked her way back to shore, where Bert still waited. Abigail promptly shook out her coat, showering them with water.

"Picked you some snow peas," Bert said, and handed Mary a paper bag.

"Thanks," she said, with as much dignity as she could muster.

"You had to come down here to tell her that?" Winslow said.

"No, I had to come down here to save you from yourself," Bert snapped. "Jeezum crow, you almost had me falling for it, too, all your protestations about the sanctity of marriage. I should have known an *Episcopalian* wouldn't have the wherewithal to resist the temptations of the flesh."

"You are pissing me off, Dad," Winslow said in a dangerous voice.

"I suggest you stop pissing around and get married if you want to taste the fruit of the vine."

"I'm working on it!" Winslow yelled.

"Oh ho!"

"I'm going to head back to the house," Mary said, without any great expectation that the two arguing men would actually hear her, and started walking up the tractor run. Abigail joined her, looking up companionably from time to time.

As she approached the driveway, Mary heard feet pounding up towards her and turned to watch Winslow, panting, catch her up.

"Everything all right?" she asked.

"Just another Sunday afternoon on the Jennings farm. Sorry."

"At least he keeps me in snow peas." She held up the bag.

"I guess I *was* acting like an overheated teenager."

"We both were. You know, since your reputation is already ruined, maybe you'd like to just come over and enjoy the benefits of my nice new mattress in relative comfort."

He shifted from foot to foot, self-consciously peeking back down the run.

"Or not." She reached into her pocket for her car keys.

He stepped forward and kissed her again. "Marry me," he said.

She paused, aware somehow that this time he had tendered something more formal, which meant that no became a real rejection. "I'm just not there yet, Winslow."

His face fell, and he stepped back.

"Don't you think that being desperate to have sex is a very bad reason to rush into marriage?"

"Sex isn't the main reason. And timing isn't the main reason either. I love you."

Her breath caught as she felt a flutter of something — happiness? — gratitude? — strong enough to take her by surprise. She couldn't help smiling.

He smiled back. "You do feel something for me, don't you?"

She nodded, not trusting herself to speak.

He smiled and bent down to kiss her again. "I guess that'll do for now."

That night, Mary walked around her little house, from room to room, thinking of all the reasons why marrying Winslow was crazy and all the reasons why it felt like the most natural thing in the world.

She barely knew him. Objectively, they had little in common except that each was alone and approaching middle age. How could she know she was not just bowled over by his considerable physical attractions and his regard for her, as she had been in the early days with Roger? But this was different, too, she told herself. Both Winslow and Roger were attractive and educated, but Winslow appeared to be that rare creature, a true adult. And she could be fairly sure it was Winslow she liked, rather than the life he represented. Roger and his wealthy parents had promised an entrée to the good life in the suburbs, good schools for the children, a life of security and accomplishment — in short, upward mobility. She was embarrassed to realize how powerfully this had worked as an incentive for her to ignore some of her early concerns about his character. Winslow, on the other hand, could deliver only a creaky Norman

Rockwell existence: Bert as a father-in-law, religion at the dinner table, living as a cop's wife in a town that was far too small, raising chickens instead of children. It was nothing she had ever wanted, yet it didn't stop her from wanting to be with him.

What stopped her was Arthur. However much she told herself that what she had done there was old news, it felt like an insurmountable hurdle. Eventually she realized it was because Winslow believed in a lie — in her own honesty and virtue — something he would have to seriously temper with reality if he ever found out about her dalliance with his priest.

She didn't want any more unpleasant surprises to pop up in the middle of a marriage, no more deal breakers. He was going to have to know about it, at least in some form. She knew she was risking Winslow's love and respect for her, but better now, before either of them got in deeper. Unfortunately, if he didn't take it well, or if Winslow realized who it was, it might also have terrible repercussions for Arthur.

Did she have the right to do that?

CHAPTER TWENTY-ONE

IN THE EXAMINING room on Monday morning, the nurse asked, "Date of your last period?"

Mary hated this question. After years of obsessive attention to her reproductive cycle, she refused to keep track anymore. But this time she remembered. "Last Sunday."

"Are you sexually active?"

She hesitated, suddenly very conscious of living in a small town. "Yes."

The nurse handed her a cup. "Let's get a urine sample, and then you can come back in and take off everything, robe open in the front."

Mary peed into her cup and took it gingerly back to the examining room, where she changed into the flimsy paper robe and sat on the end of the examining table. She had spent far too much of her life sitting half-naked in rooms like this.

The nurse came back in with a smile and dropped urine from her cup into various test items on the counter, then took Mary's temperature and blood pressure. "Your temperature is slightly elevated. What are you using for birth control?"

"Nothing. I'm infertile."

The nurse went back to the counter. "I don't think so, hon."

"Excuse me?"

The nurse showed her the pregnancy test module. "See that plus?"

Mary stared at the little pink plus sign. "That must be a mistake. I just had a period."

"This is definitely your urine?"

"Yes."

"Well, this is a strong positive. I'll run a second strip, though. Have you been taking any hormones?"

"No, not recently." She felt clammy.

"Hey," the nurse said, turning back from dropping more urine in a second test. "Put your head down on your knees. Come on. Deep breaths."

"It's not possible," she mumbled.

"You didn't want to be pregnant?"

There was no easy reply to that.

"Where do I know you from?" Potter asked, after he had examined her and asked her to get dressed and join him in his office.

"The hospital. When we brought Arthur Tennant in."

"Oh, right. The pneumonia. So, tell me about this history of infertility."

She described her failed struggle to get pregnant during her marriage: the temperature charting, the ovulation predictors, the post-coital test, the x-rays of her fallopian tubes, the ultrasounds and blood tests, the treatments with Clomid and Pergonal.

"But you never did insemination or in vitro?"

"My ex-husband didn't feel comfortable with those procedures."

"And your husband's sperm count was ruled out as a problem?"

She hesitated. "He didn't feel comfortable with that procedure either."

The doctor looked nonplussed. "Really."

"He's since found out there was an issue there. But they told me I had poor ovulation and low hormone levels and suggested I was a poor candidate for IVF unless we could obtain donor eggs."

"Well, these things can be a bit mysterious sometimes. We'll have to wait for the blood work to see what your levels are, but this looks like a perfectly viable pregnancy to me. Your iron's a little low."

"I just started taking vitamins."

"Good. Here are some samples of prenatal vitamins and a prescription for more. Start those today, with a meal." He slid a copy of *What to Expect When You're Expecting* across his desk, from a stack on the floor.

Mary swallowed. She'd had a copy of her own years before, when she'd still been optimistic. She'd read the chapter on signs of early pregnancy at least a dozen times, hoping against hope. Eventually she had grown to hate it.

"I can see you've got a lot to adjust to here," he said.

She nodded, blinking back tears.

He cleared his throat. "Do you have an idea when this child was conceived?"

"Do you have a calendar?" She looked for the day she had learned about the layoffs. "There," she said, pointing.

He raised an eyebrow, then counted off weeks. "That makes your due date February 22."

February. Unbelievable.

"Is the father likely to be... supportive?"

She shook her head.

Potter frowned. "There are Planned Parenthood offices in Keene and Manchester, if you need counseling or information about abortion or adoption services — it's free." He pulled a flyer out of his desk drawer and handed it over to her. He waited for Mary to say something. When she didn't, he continued, "And here's a folder of information about our practice and our pregnancy services. I don't handle obstetrics myself these days, but we have two very capable obstetricians on staff. Look it over and give me a call if you have any questions. We'll need to see you again in about a month."

"I feel so stupid."

He looked uncomfortable. "You're going to be fine." He stood up, dismissing her.

"Is this going to get around?"

He looked indignant. "Not from this office."

She looked down at the book and folder in her hands.

"Here," he said, emptying out a large manila envelope on his desk. "Slip that in here. You're entitled to your privacy."

For the next two days, Mary hid in her house, trying to process the seismic shift in her existence. She was pregnant. In February, if all went well, she would have a baby.

And she was delighted. Finally, her body was doing what it was designed to do.

At the same time, she was terrified. She had no job. She had less than $5,000 in the bank, with severance due to run out in two months and unemployment due to run out not long after. The practice, she had discovered in reading over her information, wanted $3,000 by the fifth month for the delivery. Meanwhile, the COBRA payments required to keep her health insurance going after severance would take most of her unemployment. She needed a job now, and not just any job either, but one with decent health insurance. But she'd received no more responses to the resumes she already had out. She couldn't afford to wait for fall now. She would start to show by then, and who would want to hire a pregnant woman?

She'd never been so conscious of being on her own before. Nobody was going to want to be this child's father. Arthur would see it as his ruination. Winslow would have to be a saint to want this child, or her, once he knew she was pregnant. Roger had already made it clear how he felt about other men's children, and anyway she'd rather go on welfare than live with him again. Her mother would take her in, she assumed, though the cost in disapproving comments was bound to be high. Still, if that was what it would take to keep her baby fed, that was what she would do.

She screened her calls, unable to talk to anyone yet, letting Winslow leave two messages on her machine. The first affectionately suggested dinner out; the second sounded uncertain. She was going to break his heart. She would hurt, too, but at least she had the baby to look forward to. And she hadn't really gotten into the deep water yet.

If they had made love, she supposed, it might be different. She'd feel more connected to him, perhaps. He would want to believe it was his, perhaps. Could perhaps even be led to think it was his. But that was an evil thought. She knew she could make some other excuse — stall, buy herself time. It was early. She could still lose the baby, and almost no one would ever know. But she couldn't imagine holding this news back.

She had intended to tell Arthur first, but before she could screw up her courage, Winslow showed up at the door.

"Hi," he said, standing there in his police uniform. He bent down to kiss her, but she dodged him. He looked so hurt that she wondered why she had ever thought it was hard to read him.

"Can I come in?" he asked, persevering.

She stood back to let him in and wondered if he could hear her heart pounding.

"Why haven't you returned my calls?"

"I've had some disturbing news."

"Are you okay? Did you go to the doctor?"

"Yes, I went."

"And?"

She sat down at the kitchen table and gestured at the other seat.

He took a seat and waited.

She licked her lips. Here went nothing. "I'm pregnant."

He shook his head slightly, as if he hadn't heard right. "I thought that was impossible."

"So did I."

She watched realization sink in.

"I don't understand." He looked at her as if there had to be some explanation.

She swallowed. Her heart was still pounding. "There was someone just before you. We had this very short..." She cast around for a word. "Thing."

"Thing? Who was it?"

"I can't tell you that."

Some color returned to his face. "What do you mean, you can't tell me that?"

"He doesn't even know about it yet."

"Was it your ex?"

"No!" She wrinkled her face in disgust, then realized she'd better watch herself or he'd get the answer out of her by default.

"Who, then? Do I know him?"

"Someone who had no idea what he was getting into."

"No?" Winslow was turning red now, getting angry.

She willed her heart to slow, willed herself to focus on the child inside.

"What are you planning to do about it?"

"To have it. I've wanted a child for years."

"But you haven't told him yet? What if he doesn't feel the same way?"

"It's not up to him."

"No, of course not. It never is." He got up and stalked around the room. "I suppose you expect him to marry you?"

"No. Not at all." She took a deep breath. "He's already married."

Winslow's mouth dropped open. "And you knew that?"

Mary bowed her head and nodded.

"You knowingly had sex with a married man?"

"Yes, I knowingly had sex with a married man. I knew it was wrong, but I did it anyway!" The moral stance she had found so attractive in him suddenly enraged her. "I guess because I'm just so really, really bad."

"And you got pregnant, just like that." He sounded dubious. He stalked around some more. "I can't believe this," he said, and then, "So stupid!"

"I realize that."

"I meant me."

She closed her eyes against a rising tide of tears. Her anger had drained away. "I'm sorry, Winslow." She could not meet his eyes. "I know you deserve better than this."

"Do you realize that everyone in town is going to assume I'm the father?"

She'd been so absorbed in her own problems, this hadn't occurred to her at all. She looked up, and watched him read the answer in her face. He turned away, but not before she saw a flash of pure disgust overlay his grief. It felt like being kicked in the stomach.

"I'm trying to get out of town," she said in small voice. "Maybe I'll be gone before it gets around. If anyone asks I'll tell them it wasn't you. I know it's not enough, but it's the best I can do."

"When is the baby due?" he asked. He sounded strangely calm.

"February 22nd."

"February. Well," he said softly, "Congratulations."

Undone, she burst into tears and hid her face in her hands.

After a moment, she heard his footsteps, then the door opening and shutting. She was alone.

Chapter Twenty-Two

S HE KNEW SHE should tell Arthur quickly. What if Winslow went to him? But when she thought about Winslow she got weepy and incoherent, and she couldn't imagine talking to Arthur in that state. Maybe it was the hormones, she thought, as she sniffled helplessly.

After a couple of days of being continually ambushed by her own emotions, she finally felt dried out and leaden, capable of facing the business at hand if only because she wanted it over with. She called the rectory first, reasoning that Sharon never picked up the phone. When a girl's high voice answered, she hung up. Lucy. She must be home from school for the summer.

The next day she tried the church office, but she got the secretary. Already having decided to persevere even if someone else picked up, she asked if Father Arthur was available. He was with a parishioner. Could she leave a message?

No, she said, she'd just call back. When would he be available?

"Is the matter urgent?"

"Well, no." Technically, she had about eight months to get it all figured out.

She mailed another dozen resumes and posted on every Internet job site she could find, even though she'd been warned it would put her private information in questionable hands. She was moving soon; what did she care if strange men knew her address? How many of them were likely to know how to find Lawson, or feel the need to prey on an unemployed editor? Editors were probably the least sexually appealing demographic on the planet, in the same league as librarians and English teachers — women with near-sighted squints, who read too much and gloried in finding faults. Perhaps that's why she'd been swept off her feet by Roger years ago, and by the male attention she'd received since moving to Lawson; it was just not something she'd ever been used to.

She'd been in the wrong place at the wrong time, that was all: Arthur had been lonely enough to fall for any woman who could string two words together. And Winslow had been ready to fall in love with any woman who could tolerate his dad.

Wiping away more annoying tears and resolutely putting both men out of her mind, she called her new, expanded, everybody-but-complete-Nazis list of old friends and colleagues with renewed purpose, trying to stir up something. After five hours on the phone, she had learned about two divorces, four layoffs, three new children, a criminal indictment, and two career changes — both out of publishing. She hadn't learned about any jobs. She could possibly pick up freelance work, though, a couple of old friends told her, so she emailed them her resume.

But freelance work wouldn't keep her insured. She almost hoped she didn't get any; it would just get in the way of finding a real job.

The next morning she tried the church office again. "Father Arthur has just stepped out," she was told.

Four days had passed without a walk, and Mary was getting stir-crazy. She stood in front of the mirror in her usual clothing, which fit just fine, getting used to the idea that people couldn't yet tell she was pregnant just by looking at her. Even to her the signs were subtle: a slight darkening of the nipples, slightly fuller breasts — still nothing to write home about — a rosy flush on her face. The cramps weren't bothering her now that she knew what was causing them.

Winslow could just ignore her if they accidentally crossed paths, couldn't he? After two days of mourning she was relatively sure she wouldn't burst into tears just because she caught a glimpse of him. So she put on her walking shoes and headed down Hill Street.

She paused at the river and stared at the rectory office window, wondering whether, if she stayed there long enough, Arthur would come out and talk to her. She nearly shrieked when instead he appeared from the town side and said, "What's up?"

"Where'd you come from?"

He gestured back at the town. "I was just taking a walk." He looked so cheerful, so unburdened — it wasn't fair. Of course, she was about to change all that.

"We need to talk."

"I'm not surprised." He sounded chipper.

"No?"

"I ran into Winslow at the market last night. That is one unhappy fellow."

"Did he tell you why?"

Arthur peered at her. "I assumed you broke it off with him."

"Then he didn't tell you."

Now he was beginning to look properly concerned. "Why, what happened?"

Mary took a deep breath. This ought to be the easier conversation, she thought. She was quite sure she didn't love Arthur and that he didn't really love her, and that they were never going to be together anyway. But it wasn't easier. One didn't casually blast another person's existence into chaos.

"Mary?"

"We need to find a private place to talk about this."

"You want to come to my office?"

"I mean really private."

"Okay, now you're scaring me."

She looked around. The town was quiet in the cool of the morning. There were no pedestrians in sight and little traffic.

"I'm pregnant."

His mouth opened, but no sound came out.

She stared down at the river, glumly remembering how she and Winslow had groped each other on that rock in the middle of it just a few miles downstream, just a lifetime ago.

"We need to find a private place to talk about it," she said.

His mouth was still hanging open. "You mean...?"

"Yes."

"Oh God."

She gave him a moment, while she watched the river flow with utter indifference under their feet. Then she said, "So, where can we talk?"

They met later that morning at a quiet coffee shop in the town where they had met for lunch. She got there first and ordered milk and a muffin, grateful that she still felt that protective leaden heaviness. Arthur was still in the thick of shock, and she was a little worried about him driving this far out. It had been his suggestion, though, and she figured she'd allow him any control over the situation that she could at this point, which wasn't much.

When he arrived, he'd shed his collar. Good idea, she thought, still not sure a coffee shop was the best place for a discussion of this nature. But it turned out he merely wanted to meet there before driving up to a wooded shrine nearby.

"A shrine? You want us to pray for guidance or something?"

He looked surprised. "Would you be willing to do that? I chose it because it's a nice quiet spot for a talk."

"Oh." She studied him, wondering if he was at all likely to want to murder her and leave her body in the woods. He looked a bit pale and shaken, but he was still Arthur. Not the murdering kind. Of course, she hadn't pegged him for the adulterous kind, either. Just to be safe, she suggested that she drive.

"Does my driving scare you for some reason?" he asked, after they were on their way.

"You just look a bit rattled," she said, honestly enough.

"Well, I am rattled." He pointed ahead. "There it is."

Arthur passed her some money to pay at the gate and they drove into the nearly empty parking lot. Tall pines surrounded it and the smell was intense and soothing.

"Nice," she said, breathing deeply.

"How are you feeling, anyway?"

She could tell he was looking her over for signs. "Good."

"You're happy to be pregnant." His tone was flat.

"Well, yes. I wish it wasn't such a mess for everyone, but I'm happy."

He pointed out a path into the woods, and she fell in next to him on the soft path of pine needles. Tall pines formed a cathedral-like canopy over them and quickly blocked out the sounds of the highway.

"So you're having it."

She stopped and looked at him. "You don't think I should?" This shocked her a bit. He was a priest, after all. While she'd never been against abortion on principle, after so many years of hopeless longing for a child the idea had come to appall her at some primal level. She'd often wished she could say, "No, give it to me!" to the troubled women choosing that option.

Arthur looked sick. "It's not up to me, is it?"

She stared past him at a marker which said "Our Lady of Lourdes Trail." Was it possible the Blessed Virgin had needed to keep a secret that didn't have anything to do with God? "I'm really sorry, Arthur."

"It's okay. I'm not sure that ruining my life might not be a good thing, in the long run."

"I don't want or expect you to ruin your life over this."

"No?" They came to a bench and he lowered himself onto it, looking spent.

She sat down next to him, smoothing her shirt over her belly and its imperceptible passenger. "As you once said, this isn't *The Scarlet Letter*. I'm quite content to be a single mother."

He gave her a sharp look. "You have no idea what you're getting into, do you?"

"What do you mean?"

"All that responsibility, all on you. And even if there's not nearly the stigma there used to be, I assure you that not all the good people of Lawson are going to think this is a good idea."

"But I'll be leaving town soon."

"Leaving? To go where?"

"Anywhere I find a job. That's the main priority. Find a job, sell the house, get on with my life."

He looked confused. "But you still have the old job for now, don't you?"

So much had changed in such a short time. "No, I was laid off."

"I didn't know that. Oh boy."

Mary leaned her head back and stared into the interlaced pine boughs overhead.

"What about your family?"

"I haven't told my mother yet. I will. I'm just not ready."

"Would she take you in?"

"Probably. But I'd rather do almost anything else first."

Arthur leaned forward, resting his head in his hands for a moment before tilting it over to look at her. "So what do you want from me?"

"Preferably nothing. But if it takes me longer than I hope to find a job, if things start getting a little tight...."

"I'm willing to help, of course. Hell, it's part of my job, helping unwed mothers in the community. But you're going to want to establish child support."

"Child support? Wouldn't child support be something Sharon would notice?"

"Well, I'm going to have to tell Sharon about this, obviously."

"You are?"

He nodded and blew a breath out slowly, apparently resigned to his fate.

"So this is the part where it ruins your life?"

"Presumably."

"Do you think she'll leave you?"

His face darkened. "I don't know. That might require too much energy."

Mary couldn't think of anything to say to that, so they sat quietly for a moment. A ray of sun angled down through the pines, illuminating a circle of forest floor ahead of them. As a child she had taken that sort of thing as a sign of God's presence.

"It's more the part where I lose my livelihood that I'm not looking forward to. That and the look on Lucy's face."

"You'd get defrocked for this?"

He gave a startled laugh. "You must think our standards for the clergy are extraordinarily low."

"Priests have been getting away with stuff like this for centuries. They just hush it up and move them along."

"It's Catholic bishops who can move people around at will. It's not the same in the Episcopal Church. And this is a rather obvious transgression. For one thing, if you need any kind of public assistance, the state of New Hampshire is going to insist you name a father."

"I don't understand why you have to tell Sharon or anybody. I'm prepared to handle this on my own. I don't expect to require public assistance. Nobody knows you're the father, and nobody has to know."

"Don't you think the child will want to know?"

Mary faltered. "Single parents aren't unusual these days." She hadn't thought that far ahead, and didn't want to start now. "If I just knew I could rely on you to pitch in if things got really tight, like with the doctor."

"Have you already lost your health insurance?"

"No, not yet. But they want the delivery fee up front."

"Who is it?"

"Dr. Potter confirmed the pregnancy."

"Oh, you can talk to him about things being tight."

Mary shook her head. "It won't be him. I'll have moved by then."

"And Winslow's really out of the picture?"

A lump formed in her throat. "Yes. But as he pointed out, everybody will assume he's the father. That's another reason I need to leave."

"He's a big boy," Arthur said dismissively. "He can handle it."

"I think I've done enough harm there already."

He cocked his head. "You like him."

Was that a trace of jealousy in his voice, or surprise? "Hardly matters now."

Arthur regarded her for a moment. "You ready for that prayer yet?"

She laughed, which collided with barely contained tears and formed a hiccup.

He laid a hand on her belly. "So we have a kid in there, huh?"

She was taken aback that he was touching her so intimately — although it was, of course, a little late for her to be worried about that now. His use of "we" alarmed her a bit, too. All things considered, he was not nearly as upset as she felt he ought to be.

Arthur closed his eyes and, startling Mary, really did launch into prayer. "Merciful Lord, look with favor upon this new life coming into the world. Protect it from all manner of harm, and grant all of us the strength and courage to do what is right, to bring this child into the world in joyful obedience to your will, in the name of the Father, and of the Son, and of the Holy Spirit, Amen."

"Don't you think it's a little late for joyful obedience?"

Arthur shrugged. "Better late than never."

"Well, don't count me in on that." Just where was all his religious fervor when they were making this baby? She got up and put more distance between them.

He sighed. "I don't expect you to understand."

"Good." But then he looked so sad, sitting there hunched over on the bench with the heathen mother of his bastard child sneering at him. "I'm sorry, Arthur. I'm sorry it messes up your life."

He gave her a tight, unhappy smile. "I brought it on myself, didn't I? I just hope it happened for a reason."

Mary stood there in the pines and thought it must be comforting to be able to think that way — to believe that things happen for a reason, and that you were not simply careening through a short life shaped by biology and the unpredictable swoops of fate.

Chapter Twenty-Three

WHEN THE PHONE rang the next day, Mary expected it to be Arthur, but instead it was a former colleague who offered her some freelance editing under a tight deadline. She accepted and, the next afternoon, received a heavy overnight package containing a huge manuscript heavily tagged with Post-it notes that appeared to bear only a tangential relationship to the current electronic version.

After assessing what she had in hand, Mary called her old colleague, Paul. "When did you say you needed this?"

"Two weeks?"

"This thing needs a lot of work."

"I know. How long do you think it will take?"

Mary hesitated. She recognized editorial desperation when she heard it, and she didn't want to lose the job. "I might be able to make it in two weeks — I guess my question is just how long a book do you want here? And will I get paid enough to make it worth it?"

It arose that Paul's company was desperate for this book, which had been due out almost a year earlier; they preferred it not run longer than 600 manuscript pages, and Paul was willing to pay an hourly rate Mary had only dreamed about.

She hung up the phone feeling slightly giddy. Maybe she could make a living freelancing after all.

The giddiness passed after she had spent the next couple of days hunched over her desk, laboring to make sense of a desperately disorganized, bloated manuscript scarred by illegible corrections and warring notes from an author and editor who had clearly begun to loathe each other. Not used to keeping track of her hours, she spent a morning trying to reconstruct the previous days' labor and get a handle on just how to accomplish the monumental job. Eventually she stopped because she was faint with hunger. Remembering that she really needed to eat more than trail mix now that she was eating for two, she downed a slice of cantaloupe — and promptly threw it up. She wasn't sure if this was morning sickness or simply a commentary on the cantaloupe.

After a recovery period of cracker-eating, she realized her larder was bare and she could use a walk before she turned into a hunchback. She made herself presentable for town, and opened her door. A small, crinkled brown paper bag sat on her front stoop. Puzzled, she picked it up and peered inside: it held a pound or so of warm, slightly wilted snow peas.

Bert? *Winslow?*

She took them into the house to douse in cold water, hopeful they could be brought back to crunchiness, and noticed a scrawl on the side of the bag: John 3:16.

Bert, then. Still trying to save her soul. Although John 3:16 was something she had seen on bumper stickers, football fans' signs, and front yards, she hadn't a clue what the exact verse was. Curious, she pulled out an old paperback Bible she had kept as an editorial reference and looked it up:

> *Yes, God loved the world so much*
> *That he gave his only Son,*
> *So that everyone who believes in him may not be lost*
> *But may have eternal life.*

Apparently Bert had felt that a concise restatement of the central tenet of Christianity might somehow steer her back onto the path of righteousness. Or perhaps he felt guilty passing along snow peas to an adulteress without witnessing to God's redeeming love.

The snow peas, which she'd put to soak in a bowl of cold water in the refrigerator, inspired her as she walked down the hill. Some sliced steak marinated in soy sauce, some onion, garlic, carrots, all stir-fried together with the snow peas, should make a nice healthy dinner that she wouldn't want to throw up. Bert was a good man in his simple way.

Her cheer faltered when she realized the Lawson Police Department's SUV was parked in front of the market. But there was no point in trying to avoid a man who might merely have gone into the neighboring pharmacy, so she walked in and started collecting groceries. Feeling reassured when she didn't see any sign of Winslow, she got in line. However, just as the cashier was starting her order, he stepped down from the market's front office, in uniform, bidding goodbye to another man. Mary felt herself flush scarlet. She kept her head down and hoped he wouldn't notice her.

"Hey, Winslow," the cashier called out, dashing Mary's hopes. "How's it going?"

"Keeping busy, Peggy," he said, and came over. He stopped dead when he saw Mary.

Peggy looked from one to the other, chewing gum.

"Hi," Mary said.

"Hi," Winslow echoed.

Peggy grinned. "I heard Winslow was going out with the woman who moved into Miss Lacey's house. That's you, isn't it?"

Mary exchanged a quick, pained glance with Winslow. "Yes, that's me, but I'm afraid it didn't work out."

"It didn't? Oh, Jeezum crow, I'm sorry." Peggy cringed apologetically at Mary and then at Winslow, who just stood there, looking awkward. "I didn't mean to embarrass you, Miss —"

"Mary Bellamy," Winslow broke in. "Mary, this is Peggy Cantwell. Peggy and her husband Dave own the farm north of ours. He's my cousin."

This had to be one of the stranger introductions in her life. "Pleased to meet you, Peggy."

"Likewise, I'm sure." Peggy, wide-eyed, handed Mary her groceries.

"You need a ride up the hill?" Winslow asked.

"A ride? Um. No, not really. Thanks, though." Apparently Winslow was going to be civilized about it all. But this was perhaps a necessity in a small town.

He nodded and moved out of her way.

She remembered and turned back. "Could you thank your father for me?"

He looked confused. "My dad?"

"Yes, he left some snow peas for me. Please, tell him I'm looking forward to eating them tonight." She smiled and walked out.

At least that first meeting was past. It had been painful for both of them, obviously, but it was reassuring that he was handling his disappointment like a grown-up. He would be fine. Of course, it might be harder when she was showing, but she would be gone by then.

Mary enjoyed her steak and snow pea feast, which stayed put, then spent the weekend struggling with the manuscript. By late Sunday night, as she stretched and headed for bed, she realized she had forgotten to get the Sunday papers, search the Internet, send out any resumes, or do anything else to find a job. But she wouldn't have time for any of this if she meant to meet her deadline.

Monday morning she woke up queasy and her breakfast went into the toilet. She was profoundly annoyed to be having morning sickness, since she had read that Japanese women never got it and decided she was going to be just like them. She started to work while nibbling on saltines. She'd have to get some ginger ale or something like that, she supposed. She hoped the nausea would pass quickly so she could focus on the task at hand. It did, but by lunch time she was nauseated again and the chicken soup she forced down forced its way back up.

Okay, this was getting tedious. And wouldn't a diet of

nothing but saltine crackers harm a developing fetus? She drove into town for ginger ale, more saltines, and other comfort foods like instant oatmeal. Peggy was at the register and asked her if she was feeling okay, because she didn't look too good.

"I think I have a stomach bug."

"Oh." She took Mary's money gingerly. "I'm awfully sorry about the other day. I hope you won't mind me butting in — but you know, Winslow's a great guy. You just couldn't ask for better."

"I know."

"You're definitely looking a bit green, there." Peggy handed Mary her change and quickly wiped her hands on a rag. "My kids picked up one of those bugs in school last winter and we all came down with it at once. Jeezum crow, what a horror show!"

Mary smiled faintly and ran for the car, but ended up retching into the weeds around the corner of the storefront.

"You okay, honey?" an old lady asked her, patting her on her back.

Mary nodded, trembling.

"I was wicked sick with all of mine. Try not to let yourself get hungry — that makes it worse."

Mary spit one last time to clear her mouth. "Must have been something I ate."

The old lady smiled kindly at her. "Just about anything will set it off."

How could the old lady know? Was it that obvious? Mary drove back up the hill and took a package of crackers and a glass of ginger ale into her office, along with a large bowl. She didn't have time to be sick.

*

The next two weeks passed in a blur of manuscript, saltine crackers, and nausea. The old lady was right about getting hungry — she began to keep food at hand everywhere, even next to the bed to eat before she got up. But it seemed that most of it still ended up in the toilet. Terribly aware of her deadline, she edited more ruthlessly than she ever had in her life, slashing out whole pages and three entire chapters, until a publishable manuscript began to form. At night she dreamed of manuscripts that got larger instead of smaller. She woke up exhausted, and was disturbed one morning to realize she was losing weight. That couldn't be a good thing. But according to the book, this common concern would probably be temporary, and anyway she didn't have time to go to the doctor if she was going to meet her deadline.

The day finally came when she felt her project was done. She repaginated furiously, created a clean new file for emailing, and drove the now only 589-page manuscript and its predecessor down to the stationery store to be sent off. Then she ran into the neighboring park, site of John Underwood's Folly, and vomited into a clump of black-eyed-susans. Bees droned off in disgust.

"Is that some new way of fertilizing the rudbeckia?"

Arthur. She spit a few times and turned around. "Long time no see."

He gestured to a bench. "You look terrible."

She sat down. "Thank you. I feel terrible."

"I'm sorry about that."

"You sure as hell ought to feel sorry." Now that the assignment was over she could afford to sit and take stock of just how miserable she felt.

"Have you been to the doctor?"

"I have an appointment in a few days."

"Maybe you should move it up."

She didn't answer, just sat and enjoyed the idea that she didn't have to go back and edit anything. She examined Arthur. He was as gaunt as ever. "You've been awfully quiet."

"I know. I told Sharon. I suggested divorce, actually."

Mary was surprised. "Did she agree?"

He grimaced. "She insisted we go for counseling. I suspect she wants to avoid any really significant changes in her lifestyle."

It was hard to imagine Sharon getting in the car, let alone going for counseling. "Wasn't she upset?"

"Oh, she accused me of being the worst sort of hypocrite, but she doesn't seem excessively offended by the infidelity itself. She does think it was unforgivably stupid of me to get you pregnant." He grabbed a daisy that overhung the bench and methodically plucked the petals from it.

"And she knows it's me?"

"I told her. I'm not sure she really remembers who you are. There's just one thing she insists on, and the therapist agrees: complete secrecy."

She sighed. That was convenient for them, wasn't it? Neither of them would be pregnant. They wouldn't have to deal with the looks and questions.

Or the nausea. She swallowed, already strategizing her next hurl.

"To be honest," he said, "I think I could happily chuck it all. The problem is that I'd need to support Sharon somehow, even more so if we get divorced, as well as the baby. Lucy, thank God, is already provided for."

"What if I don't want secrecy?"

He looked stunned. "But I thought —"

"I'd just like to be able to tell Winslow." Not that Winslow would even care at this point, but she figured she owed him that much.

"Don't you realize he's a member of my congregation? And a policeman? You'd honestly expect him to just sit on something like this?"

"I don't know. If he didn't, you'd be forced to chuck it all, but that seems like something you won't necessarily mind."

Arthur turned red. "I was willing to do it at first, thinking that it would get me free of Sharon. But she's not letting me go, is she? And I can't help wondering, how am I supposed to afford all of this?"

Mary stiffened. It was probably a good thing she had just made a big chunk of money. "Are you saying I shouldn't count on any help?"

"No, not at all. Sharon realizes I'm going to have to help provide for the baby. She just wants to make sure it's off the record. We'll work something out."

Mary was definitely feeling queasy again.

Arthur coughed uncomfortably. "The other thing is that I'm not supposed to see you. At least, not during the counseling process."

"But...."

"You can write me if you need anything. Mail it to the church, and mark the envelope confidential. Or call, if you really need to."

Nausea building, Mary focused on taking short, shallow breaths.

Arthur stared into the distance. "I don't know how long this will take. Maybe the counselor will help us realize that this marriage is over, and I'll be free to move on."

He wasn't hoping he'd end up with her, was he?

A young couple passed in front of them, wheeling a toddler in a complicated stroller with mountain bike wheels. Before she could speak, nausea overcame her. She dashed back to her clump of black-eyed susans to gag repeatedly, although at this point very little was coming up.

And when she returned, he was gone.

CHAPTER TWENTY-FOUR

THE OBSTETRICIAN, AN exotic looking young woman named Dr. Gupta, was not pleased. "You've lost weight."

"I just keep throwing up." Mary already had her eye on the little sink in the room in case she needed it.

"If this keeps up, you're going to have to go into the hospital so we can get your fluids back up. Are you having any fever, chills, headache?"

"No. I just spit up all day long. Can't you give me something?"

"Are you taking your prenatal vitamins?"

Mary shook her head. "I can't even look at them."

The doctor sighed, and handed her a sample. "These are folate pills. They're very small, try to just take them until you can stomach your regular vitamins again. And take as many liquids as you can. Dry toast might help."

"There's nothing I can take for this?"

"It really should clear up soon. Shall we see if we can pick up a heartbeat?"

Mary lay back, annoyed that she wouldn't give her some magical anti-nausea pill.

Dr. Gupta placed an instrument on her abdomen and suddenly the room was alive with the loud, fast *swish-swish* of life.

The doctor looked up and smiled. "This is a very healthy fetal heartbeat."

Mary burst into tears.

Dr. Gupta handed her a tissue.

"Sorry," Mary sniffed. "I'm actually happy, you know."

"Oh, lots of women cry. Crying is very easy with all these hormones floating around."

"Do you have children?"

Gupta drew back. "I'm not even married."

Neither am I, Mary thought. But unmarried women her age sometimes went out and got themselves inseminated. They realized the biological clock was winding down and decided not to wait. If she had known she could get pregnant, she might have chosen to, rather than just stupidly blundering into it. Maybe not at the very moment she'd lost her job, maybe not at the very moment it would cost her a promising relationship, but still. The fact that she was pregnant was practically a miracle. So she was happy, really.

When she was not throwing up.

"I'm supposed to get married next year," the doctor said.

Mary was surprised to be offered information so intimate. "Supposed to?"

"My parents are trying to arrange it. They have found a nice young professional for me." She smiled half-mockingly.

"I didn't know people still did that."

"Oh, yes, certainly they do. We younger people don't

always go along, though. Thankfully they do try to match us up with someone we'll like, though."

"Have you met him?"

"He seems very nice. Well educated, handsome. To tell you the truth, I'm leaning towards going through with it. I haven't noticed a huge difference in success between arranged marriages and love matches, and I don't have much time for dating."

"I'm divorced myself. And I married for love. Or so I thought."

Dr. Gupta's smiled. "You're going to feel better soon. You'll see."

Mary called up Paul and confirmed that he'd received the manuscript.

"It looks great," he said. "You did a great job."

"And you got the invoice."

"Yep, signed it and sent it on its way. You should get the check within the month."

She was relieved. She'd half expected a protest at the amount. "Do you have any more for me to do?"

"Not at the moment, but I'll definitely keep you in mind."

She hung up the phone and forced herself to sip a bright blue sports drink she didn't much like, but which a web site for pregnant women had recommended for morning sickness. Ten minutes later, after a bright blue bout of vomiting, she decided to ignore her list of things to do and take a nap.

When she got up, after carefully munching saltines she kept

next to her bed, it was almost dark out. She vomited almost perfunctorily, brushed her teeth, went out to get the mail, and nearly tripped over another paper bag, this one much larger. Inside she found a generous supply of green beans, a head of lettuce, a bunch of scallions, and a loaf of home-baked bread wrapped in a dish towel. On the bag was written John 8:3-11 and a little happy face. Underneath it was written no more peas with a little unhappy face.

Did Winslow know where his bread was ending up? She sliced off one end and chewed slowly while she looked up the passage. Ah, but of course. She might have expected this one.

The scribes and Pharisees brought a woman along who had been caught committing adultery; and making her stand there in full view of everybody, they said to Jesus, "Master, this woman was caught in the very act of committing adultery, and Moses has ordered us in the Law to condemn women like this to death by stoning. What have you to say?" They asked him this as a test, looking for something to use against him. But Jesus bent down and started writing on the ground with his finger. As they persisted with their question, he looked up and said, "If there is one of you who has not sinned, let him be the first to throw a stone at her." Then he bent down and wrote on the ground again. When they heard this they went away one by one, beginning with the eldest, until Jesus was left alone with the woman, who remained standing there. He looked up and said, "Woman, where are they? Has no one condemned you?" "No one, sir," she replied. "Neither do I condemn you," said Jesus, "go away and don't sin any more."

Actually, this was a Jesus whose fan club she would be

willing to join. Too bad he hadn't stopped there but had also made all those claims about being the son of God.

However, the part in which Jesus told the woman to go away and sin no more reminded her to call up the real estate agent who had sold her the house to discuss putting it back on the market.

Dr. Gupta is a lying bitch, Mary thought later that evening as she vomited up her lovely salad. She retreated to the bread, which she toasted until dry. She chewed it between tiny sips of the hated sports drink and thought nostalgically of Winslow and his beautiful forearms. It was just as well he couldn't see her now, with her existence reduced to a track between the kitchen and the toilet. Throwing up, while it was becoming routine, always raised a sweat on her; the late July weather was hot and humid; and she was already warm with pregnancy. Her teeth and gums were bothering her, despite frequent brushing, and she was sure her breath stank. She took a shower and sat in front of the fan and told herself that this, too, must pass — hopefully before she or the baby died of malnutrition.

The real estate agent, Lisa, arrived the next morning looking completely put together. Mary had just cleaned the evidence of her last attempt at a meal from the toilet and knew she looked haggard. She probably should have put the meeting off.

"Why do you want to sell?" Lisa asked. She looked around with a more skeptical expression than when she had showed it to Mary the first time. Perhaps she had expected greater things of her — a transformation from creaky little New England house into comfy country cottage, perhaps.

"I lost my job."

"Oh dear. Is the mortgage in arrears?"

"No, that's fine for now. But I don't anticipate finding a job locally that pays me what I need, and I'd rather not risk the equity I have in the house." She remembered Lisa advising her back in December that she didn't need to put so much down, and could probably negotiate a lower price. She wished she'd listened.

"Well, it's in somewhat better shape than when you bought it. And you've definitely improved the curb appeal. But the housing market is a little soft right now, and fall is not a great time to sell a house. You do realize this is going to be a losing proposition for you, considering you just paid closing costs, and this time you'll get hit with a sales commission? Are you sure you can't just get a home equity loan to tide you over until you get another job?"

"Don't they expect you to have some source of income?"

Lisa shrugged. "Depends."

Did she know some secret way of filling out loan forms that Mary had naively missed all these years? "I'm okay losing a little money on the deal. It's better than losing everything. And I'd really like to be able to move as soon as possible."

Lisa walked from room to room. Mary followed her, suddenly realizing that she hadn't even thought about vacuuming up the dust bunnies and spider webs.

"So where are you going?"

"Probably closer to Boston."

"You'll pay more in rent out there than you pay for your house here. And in a house you're building equity."

Mary felt another bout of nausea on the way. "Are you saying you don't want to list it?"

"Not at all. I have the contract right here." Lisa patted her bag.

Mary followed her into the bedroom, realizing too late that the crackers next to the bed might be incriminating.

Lisa turned in a circle. "I like what you've done in here, Mary. We need to talk about some simple fix-ups for the rest of the house, though."

"Um, if you'll just excuse me…." Mary ran for the bathroom and vomited up bile, dropping to her knees because of the trembling in her legs.

She rinsed her mouth out as quickly as she could, washed the sweat off her face, and tracked Lisa back to the kitchen, where she had spread materials out across the table.

"You're not feeling at all well, are you?" Lisa said.

Mary sank into the nearest kitchen chair.

"When are you due?"

"Excuse me?"

"If you don't want this to get around while we're showing the house, you need to hide the prenatal vitamins. And the pregnancy literature. And not just in the drawers or cabinets, because women always open the drawers and cabinets. I'd put those bedside crackers in a tin under the bed or something. Are you really sure about moving right now?"

"Yes, the sooner the better."

"It's up to you. You do understand that I won't say a

word to a soul. I represent you, so ethically speaking your secrets are my secrets — as long as we're not hiding any serious conditions in the house, of course."

Mary smiled uncomfortably. Lisa seemed entirely too pleased about having a secret she was ethically required to keep.

"Is there somewhere you can go when the house is being shown?"

Mary hadn't thought about that, but it made sense. People were likely to be turned off by a house if there was a woman vomiting in the bathroom while they looked at it. "I guess the library."

"Good." Lisa smiled. "Then let's just go over those fix-ups, shall we?"

Chapter Twenty-Five

WHEN THE PHONE rang later, Mary thought it might be Lisa calling with more suggestions, but it was Dr. Gupta.

"How are you feeling?"

Mary hesitated. She'd never had a doctor call her before.

"Still vomiting frequently?"

"Yes."

"Why don't you come on down to the hospital."

"The hospital?"

"Your blood work suggests your electrolytes are getting out of balance. When that happens, you can end up dangerously dehydrated. So let's get an IV on you before it gets out of hand. Just bring a small bag of overnight things. They'll be expecting you."

Mary just stood there, holding the phone. "But I have a cat."

There was a pause on the other end. "So give the cat plenty of food and water, and then come down. Or ask a neighbor to look after it. This shouldn't take more than one night, two at most."

"Someone might call...."

"Mary, you need to do this."

The hospital air conditioning was almost worth the humiliation of explaining that she didn't have an emergency contact. "Nobody at all?" the clerk said. "No neighbor, no parents, no siblings?"

"My family is in Arizona."

"Don't you think they'd want to know you're in the hospital?"

"I didn't bring any of their phone numbers with me." Mary hadn't even told her mother she was pregnant yet.

"What town is it? Maybe we can call information."

"I don't know," Mary said miserably, nauseated again. "Yuma Linda, Luna Vista, something like that."

The woman said, "What if something happens? Who do we call?"

Mary took shallow breaths and tried to avoid gagging into the bowl she had already used and emptied once in the parking lot. She considered providing Roger's phone number, or his parents', but that was too pathetic. Winslow's was out of the question, too. "You could try Arthur Tennant at St. Andrew's, I guess."

"Oh, Father Arthur. Then I should also put you down Episcopal? Do you want a pastoral visit?"

"No, no. But if I drop dead or lapse into a coma or something, go ahead and tell him. In fact, if you don't mind, put a note in there that he should find someone to feed my cat."

The clerk stared at her.

Mary tried to stare back, but ended up gagging into her bowl instead.

"You know what, dear, let's get you upstairs," the clerk said hastily.

It was possible they had a few concerns about her state of mind up on the third floor. The nurses were attentive, and more than one doctor came in and warily asked her how she was feeling. Dr. Potter came along too, eventually. "Dr. Gupta asked me to check in on you. She said you were concerned about your cat?"

Mary shrugged. They'd given her something in her IV to reduce the nausea and it was so calming to be able to just lie there without the desire to throw up that she expected to fall asleep any minute. Maybe it was actually a sedative. A sedative for the crazy pregnant woman. "He'll be okay until tomorrow night."

"Ah. Glad to hear it. So how's your stress level these days?"

Mary laughed, which hurt her stomach, the muscles sore from so much retching.

"That good, huh?" Potter checked her vitals on the machines she was plugged into then moved into a quick examination. "Well, don't let this stress you out too much. One night of good fluids, good rest, and you'll be good as new."

"Okay."

"Art's here on his chaplaincy rounds. I'll tell him you're here, okay?"

She sighed, half-asleep. "Okay."

Later, after dark, she opened her eyes and discovered

Arthur, looking very clerical in his dark suit and collar, sitting in the visitor's chair next to the bed.

"Hey, sleepyhead," he said.

"Hey." She felt like a stone. A stone that really needed to pee.

"Not feeling so good, huh?"

"I'm okay." She had her mind on more pressing matters. Experimentally, she raised her head. Yes, it moved. Not such a stone. She scooted up in bed, eyeing the IV apparatus.

"What are you doing?"

"I need to use the bathroom."

"Are you allowed to get up?"

"Do they want me to pee on the bed?"

He buzzed the nurse. She bustled in. "She needs to use the bathroom," Arthur said, which Mary thought was taking a bit much on himself.

"Feel like getting up?" the nurse asked her.

"Yes." Mary waited impatiently while the nurse helped her disengage from various instruments and get out of bed, rolling her IV alongside her on a pole.

The nurse walked her to the bathroom and handed her a glorified measuring cup. "Empty your bladder into this and leave it on the counter for me."

"Okay." Mary was happy to cooperate if she would just let her pee.

When she came back out, Arthur had left the chair and was slowly pacing in front of the window. There was nobody in the other bed. Perhaps they thought she was too deranged to be around other patients.

The nurse reattached her to everything, took her temperature, wrote some notes, and left.

Mary sighed. She didn't understand what Arthur was doing here, but he might as well make himself useful. "Would you mind feeding Bob if I don't get out tomorrow?" she asked.

"Potter says you'll almost certainly be discharged in the morning."

"Oh. Good."

A lab tech bustled in and took tubes of blood out of Mary's arm. Arthur paced.

After the tech left, Arthur came back to his earlier seat, with every appearance of settling in. "He told me you were here."

Mary placidly adjusted her blankets. It was so nice to be not even the slightest bit nauseated.

Arthur leaned in. "Did you tell him?"

"Tell who?"

"Potter."

"Oh. No, of course not."

"I think he's figured it out."

"I don't see how he could."

"It doesn't matter. He's very discreet."

"And the nurses? Are they discreet?" How long had he been sitting there?

"I visit a lot of patients here."

"Yeah, but isn't this against the rules?"

He shrugged. *Fuck the rules* echoed in her mind. "So how's the marriage counseling going?"

Arthur scowled. "It's going."

"She leaves the house and everything?"

"Oh yes. She got her hair cut yesterday, and she went out for lunch with Lucy, too."

Mary sighed. "Maybe she just needed a kick in the backside."

"I think she's savoring this opportunity to torture me with my many failings."

"What does the counselor say?"

"Oh, Sharon does most of the talking. Who knew she had so many grievances? Every once in a while, he turns to me and says 'What do you think about that, Arthur?' and I try to come up with something that sounds like I actually give a damn."

Mary was struggling to keep her eyes open. "Don't you give even a little bit of a damn?"

"You're tired. I'll check in on you tomorrow." He squeezed her hand.

She didn't squeeze back, already sliding into sleep.

The next time she awoke it was the middle of the night and she struggled for a moment to remember where she was. Once again needing to pee, she started wrestling with her IV and detaching the leads that tied her to the machines.

A different nurse rushed in. "What do you think you're doing?"

"I need to go to the bathroom."

"You should call for assistance!" The nurse turned on the overhead light, half-blinding Mary. "You don't need these anymore anyway," she said, clearing away everything except the IV. "Come on, then."

"How much did you get?" the nurse asked, when she came out.

Oh, the cup. "Sorry. I forgot."

The nurse scowled. "Next time, remember."

"Is there anything to eat?"

"In the pantry."

"Where's that?"

"Nurse's station, then turn left."

"Thanks." Mary followed the nurse out, though she couldn't match her pace while rolling along her IV. Dr. Gupta was seated at a computer behind the nurses' station, looking sleepy.

"Hello," Mary said, with a little wave.

Dr. Gupta smiled. "Hello. You're looking better. What are you doing up?"

"I'm hungry."

"Excellent. By all means, eat. I'd suggest you start with something bland, but that applies to everything here."

The two nurses at the desk looked over as if Gupta had somehow impugned the honor of the hospital.

"Let me just finish what I'm doing here, and I'll come see you. Doesn't pay to get behind on the paperwork."

This time a nurse distinctly rolled her eyes at the other one. Mary shuffled along, wondering what their problem was. Did they despise all doctors, or were they offended by Dr. Gupta's efficiency or sex or beauty or youth or ethnicity? Was it possible she treated the nurses badly? It was none of her business, really, though she felt immensely grateful that she was no longer throwing up.

The pantry was stocked with saltines, gelatin, sunshine cups, apple juice, and other necessities of the sick life. Mary decided to start with red Jell-O and enjoyed every spoon-ful, wondering why she hadn't thought of it over the last couple of weeks, for red Jell-O was simply magnificent.

"You were asleep the last time I checked on you," Dr. Gupta said, coming in after Mary had shuffled back to her room. "Your blood work looks much better. They'll discharge you in the morning. When you get home, call the office to schedule a follow-up visit in a week. In the meantime: frequent, small meals, bland foods, plenty of liquids. If you throw up more than two or three times a day, call us."

"And the baby?"

"The baby's fine. No worries there. Is anyone helping you out at home?"

"No, but that's okay."

Gupta eyed her. "You have a car, a way to get around?"

"Yes."

"Is money a problem?"

"Not yet. I mean, no."

"Don't be ashamed to ask for help if you need it."

"I don't need it."

Gupta sighed and yawned behind her hand. "Is the father of this baby helping you out at all?"

"There's no father."

Gupta raised an eyebrow. "That's not what they taught us in med school."

Mary smiled. "That just shows you can't learn everything you need to know in school."

CHAPTER TWENTY-SIX

THE NEXT MORNING, Mary woke up hungry and enjoyed her hospital breakfast. The nurse removed her IV, which allowed her to get a shower and dress in her own clothes. Then it was just a matter of waiting for paperwork.

Arthur stopped in just as Mary had gotten so bored she'd clicked on the TV. "They're sending you home?"

"Yes."

"You should probably know that I've talked to a lawyer."

Mary eyed him warily.

"He's drawing up a support agreement."

"Oh." Just support. No divorce. "Okay."

"I also told him I wanted a divorce."

Damn. Yes, she had advised him that he should get one, but somehow she feared this one would come with obligations on her part.

"He said I have to go to someone else for that, since he represents Sharon's interests, too."

"That makes sense." Mary tried to sound as neutral as possible.

"He did suggest to me that I was going to get thoroughly cleaned out if I went through with it."

Mary nodded, thinking the lawyer was probably right.

"And after all that, you aren't even going to want to get together, are you?"

She swallowed. He sounded so aggrieved. "I'm really sorry, Arthur, but I don't love you. I like you, but that's not enough, is it? I think we were just two lonely people in the wrong place at the wrong time. I mean, what do we really have in common?"

"You seem quite fond of Winslow, but what do you have in common with him? Was that just loneliness, too?"

She shook her head, misery welling up in her. "I don't know. Maybe."

"Besides, I can think of something very important we now have in common." He gave her belly a significant look.

He had a point there, but she was not eager to take it.

Arthur got up and went to the window, pulling the vertical blinds aside to peer out. "He came to talk to me, you know. Winslow."

Her stomach lurched. "What did he say?"

Arthur didn't turn around. "It was a pastoral counseling session, Mary. I'm under an ethical requirement for confidentiality."

Whatever happened to *fuck the rules?* "Is he okay?"

Arthur turned around. He looked surprised by her concern. "I'm sure he'll be fine. He's going out to California to visit his sister. I've noticed he tends to do that when he wants to clear his head."

California! So far away. What if he didn't come home?

Of course, once he did, with his head cleared, she'd no longer be in it.

But of course, she wasn't going to be here much longer herself.

"I will tell you that he's perplexed his father has taken such a shine to you."

Mary smiled. "Bert leaves bags of food on my front stoop. With Bible verses."

Arthur snorted. "That sounds like Bert all right." He fingered the blinds. "*Do* you need help with food?"

"Just keeping it down, not getting it." But the whole morning had passed without any nausea.

A nurse knocked on the door and came in with the paperwork Mary needed to sign to get out of there. "I'll call you a wheelchair."

"I don't need one."

"Hospital policy," the nurse said. "Just enjoy the ride." She glanced curiously at Arthur before leaving.

"I guess I'd better go," Arthur said. "Look, call me if you need anything."

"Thanks, but I should be gone soon. I just put the house on the market."

"Are you sure that's a good thing to do right now?"

"Yes, I'm sure," Mary said, as a teenager pushed in a wheelchair.

"Are you ready to go, ma'am?" the boy asked.

"Yes, I'm ready."

Rejuvenated, Mary went home and sent out another batch of resumes and started cleaning the house, protecting the baby and her appetite by using only innocuous chemicals like baking soda and salt. She avoided letting herself get hungry and that worked well, although she still had the occasional bout.

Lisa had suggested that certain items of furniture should go and recommended two local boys who could move stuff out to the curb for a nominal price. Jake and Mike turned out to be cheerful and industrious, so Mary also put them to work washing down the exterior of the house and mowing the lawn while she got back to the garden. Lisa was pleased with the results and planted a "For Sale" sign in her front yard that Friday.

Mary was weeding the front garden late that afternoon when she realized a car had pulled up behind her. She straightened up to discover Winslow idling in the town's SUV. He nodded at her.

"I thought you were in California," she said.

"I leave tomorrow."

"Oh." Should she wish him good luck clearing his head? "Have a good trip."

"Thanks."

Why had he stopped? Was it possible he was pissed off at the way his dad kept bringing her food? "Your dad gave me a loaf of your bread the other day. It was delicious. I hope you didn't miss it too much."

"No, not at all."

"Actually, I have something to return to him." She'd been planning to drive the dish towel back to the farm while Winslow was safely away, but this would save her that awkwardness. "If you could wait a minute?" He nodded, so she ran in, washed off as much dirt as she could without breaking out the fingernail brush, and grabbed the freshly laundered towel. Then she ran back out, afraid he might have left, feeling ridiculous. "Please give him my thanks. But tell him he doesn't need to worry about me. I'm not starving or anything."

Winslow eyed her as if he wasn't sure whether to believe that. "You're moving?" he asked, and it suddenly occurred to her that maybe this is why he had stopped. Perhaps this was even why he looked upset. The thought made her heart swell.

"Yes."

He didn't say anything, just looked at her as if she'd somehow managed to screw up yet another thing, so she added, "I told you I would."

He flushed. "Don't do it on my account."

Why not, she wanted to ask. But what was the point? "I have to sell anyway. You don't need to feel bad about it."

He blinked at her as if what she was saying made no sense. "You got a job?"

"No, not yet."

"I see." His expression drew in. "Well, I'd better go. I'm on duty."

"Okay," Mary said softly, and watched him drive off down the hill.

The next morning the doorbell rang. *Not already people to see the house,* she thought, in a panic. But when she opened the door, there was Cici.

"Hello," Mary said.

Cici was dressed to impress, with a flowered scarf tied rakishly over her polyester tunic and white sandals under apple green pants. "Hello, dear. I heard you were ill and I thought I would bring you some cookies. I always find Social Teas so comforting, don't you?"

"My grandmother always liked them." Mary remembered carefully arranged cookies on a flowered china plate on a treasured tea cart. "But I'm all better, thank you."

"I can't tell you how sorry I am that you're moving."

Ah, so this was a fact-finding expedition. Still, civility required the proper response. "Would you like to come in?"

"Oh, if you're sure you don't mind." Cici was already stepping in the door. "You've done a lot of work this week, haven't you? Were those boys helpful?"

"Yes, very."

"I suppose they expected to be paid."

"Well, yes, of course."

"Kids these days. In my day, we helped out our neighbors without expecting anything in return. Where are you moving, dear?"

"I'm not sure yet." Mary placed cookies on a plate and set it on the kitchen table. "Would you like a cup of tea?"

"That would be lovely." Cici sat down primly at the kitchen table. "One of my friends has a daughter who's a nurse down at the hospital, you know. That's how I heard you were ill."

"Yes, I got a little dehydrated. Some kind of stomach flu, I guess."

"I heard it was morning sickness."

"Imagine, and with all those new privacy laws. What's your friend's daughter's name?"

Cici smiled thinly. "No one you know, I'm sure. Besides, you know things like that are bound to get around."

The kettle whistled, and Mary quickly brewed a weak cup of tea and set the mug, sugar bowl and creamer in front of Cici.

"Aren't you having any, dear?"

"I had a cup earlier," she lied, sitting down. Cici might already know, but she was damned if she was going to confirm it. Besides, she might just be fishing.

"Well, you must have a cookie. You need to keep your strength up."

Mary just sat there and watched her.

"How's that Winslow doing?" Cici drank with her pinkie out, even though Mary had served her tea in a mug.

"He's off on vacation, I believe."

"I've seen his father here a couple of times."

Mary smiled. "Yes. He brought me vegetables from the farm."

"I wish someone would bring me vegetables. The prices lately!"

Mary just sat, a half smile fixed on her face. She would outlast the old bat if it killed her.

"Well, this has been lovely, dear," Cici said, grabbing a couple of cookies for the road. "Now, you will be eating these? They won't just go to waste? Because I could—"

"Oh, don't worry, I'm looking forward to eating them."

"I'm so glad," Cici said, bereft. Mary saw her out and closed the door firmly.

Cici made her own mother look like an angel of mercy. True, Margaret Mary McMahon could make quite the cutting personal judgment right to one's face, but she probably also, by now, would have started organizing a collection of used baby furniture and clothing.

Which reminded her that she had been putting off an important phone call.

"You've found a new job?" her mother said.

"No, not yet. But I did just put the house on the market."

"So soon? Well, and why not? You know, I really think you should come out here. As I think I mentioned before, it's quite a good job market. Though the traffic's getting a bit much."

"Mom, what happened to Grandma's tea cart?"

"Grandma's tea cart?" her mother echoed, faintly. "Why, I don't know. We didn't bring much furniture out. Why?"

"I just remembered how she used to serve tea and cookies to her guests."

"Quite the proper hostess, your grandmother." Her tone was clipped. Mother and daughter had lived together for years, but not for the sheer joy of each other's company.

"So, Mom — "

"I suppose you've heard about my friendship with Mr. Donnelly across the street?"

Mary paused. "I think Patty mentioned something." She and her sister had agreed it might have saved Mary from a maternal mission to Save The Marriage.

"Would you believe it, he's asked me to marry him!"

"He has?" Mary realized her news might have to wait for another day.

"Yes, I was so surprised!"

"What did you say?"

"I haven't made up my mind. Would it upset you terribly, dear?"

"Me? Why would it upset me?"

Her mother lowered her voice. "Well, just between you and me, Charlie seems kind of huffy about it."

"I can't imagine why. Dad died a long time ago."

"I think maybe it's the money."

"Really?" Her mother was comfortable, but hardly wealthy. She couldn't imagine her brother Charlie, who pulled down an executive salary, caring in the slightest.

"Well, that must be it, don't you think? Otherwise, why would he object?"

Maybe he couldn't bear the thought of his sainted mother and a strange old man going at it in the bedroom. Mary was trying hard not to visualize it herself. "I have no idea." She was going to have to call her sister to get the scoop on Mr. Donnelly. "Do you love him?"

Her mother giggled, an odd sound that reminded Mary of her mother's old bridge parties, after the women had broken out the sherry. "Oh, he's a doll. And he treats me like a lady."

"Well, I'm happy for you, Mom."

"And we could save some money if we moved in together, you know, dear, though we'd have to give up some other benefits. I'm afraid a lot of the old folks around here just partner up without getting married, but Mr. Donnelly doesn't think that's the right thing to do. Living in sin at our age! Imagine. And both of us so involved in the church. Mr. Donnelly says if it's wrong when you're young, how can it suddenly be right just because of social security?"

"But since the purpose of marriage is procreation, wouldn't your priest counsel you to avoid romantic entanglements like this at your time of life?"

There was silence on the other end.

"I'm just teasing, Mom." Mary decided she might as well get it over with. "Actually, I called to give you some news. I'm pregnant."

There was another silence, this one longer.

"Mom?"

"Are you teasing me about that, too?"

"No."

"But how? And I prayed for it for so long. Well, until recently."

"Apparently your prayers were just answered a little late."

"And it's Roger's?" Her mother sounded perplexed.

"No. Roger was the reason I didn't get pregnant before."

There was a pause. "Then who's the father?"

"I can't tell you that."

"My God, don't you know?"

"Of course I know! It's just that it's no one you know. I'm not marrying him, and I need to protect his privacy."

Her mother's voice rose. "You need to protect his privacy? Who is he, the President? And what do you mean you're not marrying him?"

"It was an accident, Mom. We're not in love. So we're not getting married." She didn't have the stamina to reveal that he was already married, let alone that he was a priest.

Her mother didn't reply, but disapproval radiated out of the receiver.

"It's not the ideal way to raise a child, I know. But I'm still happy about it. I hope you can be happy for me, too."

"You were such a good little girl, Mary Elizabeth, until you turned your back on the church. And now look at you."

A slut for all the world to see.

"When are you due?"

"February 22nd."

"February! How can you shovel snow with a newborn baby in the house? And just how do you expect to support this child if you don't have a husband or a job?"

"I'll get a job. And he's going to help with support. And by then I'll probably be in an apartment. The landlord can deal with the snow." *But you could invite me to stay with you.*

Her mother just sniffed. "That's no way to raise a child."

"You'd prefer I get an abortion?"

That earned her a horrified gasp. "Heaven forbid!"

"Mom, it will be fine. Women raise children on their own all the time these days."

"That doesn't make it right! You know, here's an idea. Maybe your brother could raise the child. Charlie's been nagging Karen about having another one."

Mary was speechless. Had her mother not the slightest idea of how she had felt, all these years, watching her brother and sister effortlessly conceive again and again while she looked on, childless? "I'm going to go now," she said, voice choking.

"Mary —"

She hung up and disconnected the phone. That was it. She'd rather starve to death than move to Arizona.

Chapter Twenty-Seven

A NUMBER OF PEOPLE trooped through the house over the weekend, but no offers were tendered. Lisa assured her it was early yet. She also suggested that Mary move the litter box out of the bathroom to a less noticeable spot.

"All right, I'll put it in the cellar." Mary generally avoided that dark hole. She was sure the ancient boiler coated in asbestos and the low ceilings were scaring buyers away; it would have done the same to her if she had been able to find anything better in her price range.

"Should you even be dealing with cat litter in your condition?"

Mary hoped Lisa wasn't sitting in the middle of a busy office. "I'm careful."

"So you're definitely attached to that animal."

"Yes, I am." Bob was her only reliable companion these days.

On Monday afternoon, after she had sent out another batch of resumes, she returned from a quick walk to find an old pick-up truck in her driveway.

"Well hullo there, missy!" Bert was coming down her front walk. "I just left ya some squash and tomatoes!"

"That's so sweet of you. Which verse did I get?"

Bert brushed what was left of his hair back rather sheepishly. "The prodigal son. Are you familiar with that one?"

"Actually, I am." It had been a favorite of her mother's, who liked to emphasize that the prodigal son had still lost his inheritance, even if he did get treated to the fatted lamb when he came slinking back home, penniless and starving. Mary's phone had been plugged back in for days now, but her mother hadn't tried again. Mary was her prodigal daughter, no doubt, though not yet so desperate as to go home and beg for the crumbs under the table. If she did, would her mom throw her a party? Perhaps a baby shower.

Bert looked disappointed, perhaps thinking that if Mary remembered the passage she was unlikely to have a conversion experience upon reading it.

"You must be missing Winslow," she said.

"I suppose you could call him my prodigal son. I confess I'm terrible ashamed of him right now."

"What for?"

"Well, you know. I never would believe he'd get a girl in this condition and run away. He didn't do it the first time, and he wasn't nearly as gone on her as he was on you."

"Didn't he tell you it isn't his?"

Bert gave her a reproachful look. "I have eyes in my head, girl."

"Then your eyes have deceived you."

"Look, I don't intend to judge. Let he who is without sin cast the first stone. I just don't want to miss seeing my grandchild grow up. My daughter's all the way in

California and my youngest goes to his in-laws for every holiday. Only Winslow sticks by me, and that boy can go days without putting two sentences together, especially lately. Family is precious, Mary, and I hate to miss out on it."

"I wish this were your grandchild, Bert, but it's not. You can't blame Winslow for not wanting to take on something like this."

Bert stared hard at her for a minute before visibly deflating. "You're telling me I failed to believe my own son when he spoke the truth."

She patted him on the arm. "He'll forgive you."

"Jeezum crow, no wonder he ain't saying much."

She wished Winslow would forgive her, although she knew that wasn't exactly fair. After that first discussion Winslow hadn't seemed so much resentful as sad. But it was Bert who looked sad now, slumped against his truck.

"Would you like a cup of tea? I have a nice box of cookies my neighbor brought over."

"Not old Cici? You'd better check they're not expired."

"No, they're fresh. I believe it pained her greatly to part with them. Come on in."

Bert shuffled his feet. "Well, now, I don't know that I should, though."

Mary suddenly realized that Bert was probably embarrassed to keep company with her now that she had confirmed the worst about her. "Oh, I see," she said softly. "Well, thank you for all the food. You're sure you don't want this batch back, now?"

"Want it back?" Bert looked shocked. "Don't be silly, woman."

But there wouldn't be any more scriptural vegetables, Mary guessed. "Well. Thank you, Bert. You take care now, okay?" She stiffly collected the bag and unlocked the door, then took it into the kitchen, where she unpacked tomato after tomato, and another loaf of bread, too.

Embarrassed tears stung her eyes. Why did the small humiliations like these seem so much harder to bear than the larger one?

There was a quick knock on the screen door, and Bert opened it and leaned in. "Is it too late to say yes?"

"No," she said, sniffing.

"There now, sweetheart, don't cry." Bert patted her awkwardly on her back. "I thought maybe you were taking it the wrong way."

She filled the kettle and set it on the stove, then grabbed a paper towel and blew her nose.

"I just don't want Winslow thinking I'm stepping on his toes," Bert said. "I felt it was my righteous duty before, but now — I guess he could definitely look at this as interfering in his business."

"You don't have to explain."

"This just feels all messed up."

"It is all messed up. I messed it up."

"So what happened to the fella who did this, anyway? He ran off?"

Winslow apparently hadn't told his father the worst about her. "We broke it off before I found out." Mary ducked the more obvious reason her relationship with Arthur had never progressed. "He says he's going to help me financially, but he'd be a fool to do any more than that."

"A real man doesn't run away from his responsibilities."

"He's going to help. I don't want more than that."

Bert still looked put out. "Do I know him?"

"No," she lied.

"And just why do you think you should protect him from his share of shame?"

"Oh, I imagine he's suffering more than I am. For me, there's a baby at the end of it. So I'm content enough."

Bert harrumphed. "That baby deserves a father."

Mary felt a twinge of guilt. Her baby wasn't even born yet and already she was a deficient mother. The water boiled and she brewed the tea and set out the cookies, everything a repeat of what she had done just a few days before with Cici, except that this time she made a better cup of tea, and sat down with a glass of milk and had a cookie herself.

"Why don't ya come up to chapel sometime?"

"Because I'm not religious."

"Do it for the baby, then."

Mary wrinkled her nose. Her child would grow up free from the guilt and boredom of rote piety.

"And for yourself," Bert said. "To feel the soothing balm of God's forgiveness."

Mary took another cookie and hoped he'd drop the subject.

"Winslow told me the house was up for sale. Where are you going?"

"I'll know that when I find a job."

Bert gave her an appraising look. "Won't be long before you're showing."

"I know." Already her pants were tight, her blouses gapped, and her bras were beginning to feel like instruments of slow torture. "Maybe they'll just think I'm fat."

Bert snorted. "And what are you doing with yourself these days?"

"Hunting up job leads and sending out resumes. And working on the house. I had some freelance keeping me busy a while back, but nothing at the moment."

"You need to find a way to keep busy."

"That's not busy enough?"

"No, I mean, ya need a reason to see people. That was what my Priscilla had trouble with. She was a little shy, you know, like you, and sitting out there on that farm, she'd get lonely and bored. As long as she kept herself involved in the chapel or the community, she'd be fine. But if she didn't, she'd start eating and she'd get sad, or she'd get sad and she'd start eating. Winters were the worst, because she never wanted to drive."

"I did okay last winter." Mary remembered the delicious peace of it after the pain of divorce. "And I don't want to go to church just to be with people."

"I'm not talking about church. We have a food pantry in this town that's always looking for volunteers. I volunteer there myself. I know for a fact they're looking for some help in the office."

Mary folded her arms. "That's got to be a church thing."

"Nope. It's just a community group, with representatives from all the churches and other groups too, like the Kiwanis. But we don't tend to have quite enough people all the time we need them. And seeing as how they don't pay you a cent, they're pretty flexible with hours. The girl who runs it, Annie, she's a peach."

Maybe it wasn't a bad idea. She might as well get a handle on what it was like to live in poverty, in case that was where she was going to end up. "I suppose I could help out a bit, until I get closer to moving. You don't think they'll object to the presence of someone in my condition?"

"Heck, no. The ladies down there, they just love a pregnant woman. They actually run a little side operation that collects used baby furniture and stuff for mothers who need it."

Was that why he'd brought it up? Bert struck her as shrewd enough to realize she'd have a much easier time accepting help if she was giving something in exchange. "Where is it?"

"Couldn't be more convenient. It's run out of St. Andrew's, right down the street."

That stopped her.

"Something the matter with that?"

She foundered for an excuse. "That sure sounds like church to me."

"But it isn't. We have our own separate office, next to the kitchen."

She'd need to warn Arthur, wouldn't she?

"Winslow had given me to understand you're friends with Art Tennant."

She smiled faintly. "Yes."

His eyes narrowed. "So that shouldn't be a problem at all, should it?"

"No, of course not." She could feel that her face was hot. She got up quickly and took the tea things to the sink.

"The man who got you in trouble, does he belong to that church?"

"I would appreciate it if you'd respect my privacy in this matter, Bert." She didn't dare turn around.

There was a short silence. "Well, I'd best be moving on." He groaned a little as he got out of the chair. "Maybe I'll see you down at the food pantry one of these days."

"You might just. You take care, Bert. And thank you — for everything."

"Thank you for the tea. And God bless you, dear." He kissed her on the cheek.

That was definitely the end of the vegetables, she thought, watching him leave. Bert was a sweetheart, but he had — very appropriately — just handed her off.

CHAPTER TWENTY-EIGHT

MARY WENT ON five interviews in August, requiring a looser suit, which she found used at a thrift store. She was told she was over-qualified for one job, under-qualified for another, and never heard a single word about the other three, despite calling and leaving repeated messages.

Her phone seldom rang, but when it did it was usually someone looking for Roger over a delinquent account. This puzzled Mary. Roger had never hurt for money — he made a hefty salary, and his parents had never been reluctant to pitch in. Yet some callers still tried to insist that it was her obligation to pay. She explained that they were divorced and gave them his parents' phone number.

A few times Roger himself called, usually late at night. He was so obviously drunk that he probably didn't even remember that she'd hung up on him.

One night just before she turned in she looked out the front window and there was his BMW parked in front of her house. When the phone rang a minute later, she ignored it, her heart hammering. What if he came to the door? Should she call 911? She was sure everyone in the police department knew about her and Winslow. Eventually Roger saved her the dilemma by driving off.

Her face plumped up, her belly rounded, her butt spread, and she finally gave in and bought a couple of maternity bras. She took to wearing baggy shirts and alternating between her three pairs of drawstring shorts, hoping her bare legs might draw attention from the growing mound in her middle, but women often gave her appraising looks. She assumed the news was already all over town anyway. Cici would have seen to that.

No longer optimistic she'd get a good job before the baby came, she did a careful budget and decided she should be able to make it through to the middle of spring if she was careful and her boiler didn't die. After that, she would be in trouble, especially since the only offer that had come in on the house was untenably low.

Lisa suggested taking it off the market until spring.

"But I'll have an infant to take care of then." Suddenly it seemed like no time at all. With her situation so uncertain, Mary hadn't even planned where the baby would sleep. She was also superstitiously afraid of making too many plans. It was enough simply to be pregnant. Why push her luck by dreaming about a child she didn't have yet?

"Can we reduce the price by $10,000?"

"Yes." She'd lose even more money on the deal, but at least she'd be free to go.

"If that doesn't do it by Thanksgiving, you've got to take it off. Houses don't sell well over the holidays. If you stay on the market all winter, people will assume there's something wrong with the place."

"It's only September. I bought it in November."

"You were not the typical homebuyer. If I were you, I'd try setting up a home equity line of credit. They may not require any proof of income because of all the equity you put in with your down payment. You'll get a higher rate, but you can pay it all off when you sell."

"Maybe I'll do that. But you are going to keep trying, aren't you?"

"Of course I will. I'd like this commission before next spring too, you know."

Mary bit her lip. Liking was just not the same thing as needing.

As she had anticipated, no more scriptural vegetables appeared on her doorstep. After another flurry of interviews yielded no offers, she thought again about the food pantry. She felt like a hypocrite volunteering at just the point in her life when she stood a good chance of becoming a beneficiary. But for years she had supported the United Way and the Red Cross, and she had helped out elderly neighbors with car trips and snow shoveling. She had not spent an entirely self-involved existence. And at least she'd be starting out as a volunteer.

She'd need to warn Arthur, though. She called, but was told that Arthur and his family had gone on vacation for a couple of weeks. Would she like to leave a message?

Well, no. At least now she could check it out in the safety of his absence.

She found the building nearly deserted, and peeked into the sanctuary. It was prettier on the inside with the sun illuminating the stained glass windows. She backtracked down a dismal hallway, then tried another corridor, which opened into a large, empty hall.

"Can I help you?"

Mary turned. The young woman who had spoken was as wide as she was tall. Her hair was a giant mane of frizzy henna red, and she was dressed in a giant tie-dyed sack of a dress. She held a cardboard box in her arms.

"Looking for the food pantry?"

"Yes."

"It's Mary, isn't it?"

"Yes." Did everybody in town know who she was?

"I'm Annie Soper. Bert mentioned you might come by. Need some food?"

"No! I'm here to volunteer."

"Oh, that's wonderful! Follow me."

Mary followed to where Annie unlocked a door into a cramped store room.

"Mac and cheese goes there," Annie said, quickly slicing open the box she'd been carrying, and pointed at nearly empty shelf space. She started handing boxes to Mary. "Older stuff comes up, newer stuff goes back." She pointed out the other shelves for canned goods, cereals, juices. "Weird shit goes over there," she said, and pointed to a shelf crammed with a motley collection of dusty Jell-O boxes, bake mixes, and exotic canned foods. "You know, the stuff we get when people clean out their pantries of stuff they've never brought themselves to eat."

Mary guiltily remembered her last contribution to a food drive at work, especially that can of celery hearts she'd avoided opening for her entire marriage and the leftover bags of microwave popcorn that had somehow always

SANDRA HUTCHISON

smelled like cigarette butts when they were finished popping. She unpacked and stocked while Annie worked on a neighboring shelf.

"Bert told me you were trying to find a job."

"Yes."

"Any luck so far?"

"Not yet."

"Well, I'm sorry about that, but we can sure use you."

"I guess my big question is whether I have to do it here."

Annie looked at her. "What do you mean?"

"I thought maybe I could do stuff on my computer at home."

"I was hoping you could help answer the phone and stock food. But beggars can't be choosers. Bert said you were an editor. So you can spell and stuff?"

"Yes."

"That's great. I hate writing, and I can't spell. We'll figure something out. I'd appreciate it if you could spend some time learning what we do, though."

"I can be here for the next week or so," Mary said. Until Arthur got back.

Mary was surprised to discover how much she'd missed working, though she found the jury-rigged arrangements of the tiny food pantry office trying. Senior citizens and busy matrons dropped by regularly with bags of food or just to chat. Annie always introduced Mary. She usually got a friendly greeting as well as a careful examination. Sometimes she felt like just saying, "Yes, I'm pregnant! No, I'm not married!"

275

The clients were only allowed to pick up food on Fridays and Saturdays, but new clients had to register ahead of time, a process that Mary watched with her own possible future in mind. One rasping woman came in with an elaborate tale of disability and bad luck that Annie listened to without the slightest sympathy, refusing half the dependents she'd listed because she had brought no identification for them. A recently unemployed man was embarrassed and quiet; Annie was gentler with him, reminding him that he should not put off applying for food stamps. One young woman reeked of alcohol at ten in the morning. Annie took her information and set her up without much comment.

"That woman was drunk," Mary observed after she left.

"Yep," Annie said. "But her kids still need to eat."

Wednesday, Bert showed up with crates of sweet corn and poked his head into the office. "There you are!" he said, and squeezed between the desks to give Mary a hug. "I hoped I'd see you here. How's life treating ya?"

"Fine."

"Yes? Any luck with the job or the house?"

"Not yet. Did Winslow get home safe?"

Bert shook his head. "He took an extra week. I just hope he's not thinking of moving out there."

Mary felt a stab of abandonment. Apparently she hadn't cleared Winslow completely from her own mind, although by now he'd surely cleared her from his. He might even have met somebody — he'd shown a propensity to move quickly in these matters.

"Take some sweet corn home with ya," Bert said.

"Oh no. That's for the clients. I can get it at the market."

"That's Cantwell corn," he sniffed. "Ours is better." He scratched his head and looked at his feet. "I figured Winslow might not appreciate me dropping food off anymore, poking into his business, you know."

"I know, Bert. Don't worry about it."

"You're looking better than you did."

"I feel better."

"And the baby's doing well?"

"Yes, very well." She knocked wood on Annie's desk to be safe.

"Feels good to get out of the house, don't it?" He tilted his head. "Seen Art Tennant about?" he asked, just as Annie lumbered into the room.

"Hey, Bert! Art's in North Carolina on vacation. The big news is that Sharon actually went with them this year."

"Did she now? That's nigh unto a miracle, ain't it?"

"I guess so," Annie said. "The way I hear it, she looks like a new woman, and he looks like death warmed over."

Mary looked over, startled.

"Marriage is a bizarre institution," Annie declared. "God save me from ever doing anything that stupid again."

"Now you don't mean that, Annie," Bert said.

"Oh yes I do. You're divorced, aren't you, Mary? Don't you agree that single life beats married, any day?"

Mary gave Bert a wary glance. "I'm sure it beats a bad married life."

Bert waved his hand dismissively. "Obviously neither of you has yet to experience the balm of good Christian marriage, and that's all I'm going to say."

"And a good thing, too, Bert," Annie said, "Or I might have to whup your ass."

Bert laughed. "I'll be back later to do the shut-ins."

"Thank you, Bert," Annie said. "He's a peach," she said to Mary, after he left.

"That's what he says about you."

"You know him pretty well, then?"

"Not that well."

"Ah, well, maybe if he were about twenty years younger and not so damned religious. Of course, that son of his can write me a ticket anytime he wants."

Mary kept silent.

"Most eligible bachelor in town. I heard you and he were an item for a while there."

Mary held her ground.

"And I guess I'll shut up now," Annie said.

At the end of the week, Mary packed up a bag of food cupboard correspondence to take home to her own computer. So far she had mostly typed up and sent thank-you letters, though she had also answered the phone, providing information and passing along various inquiries, such as whether the food cupboard would welcome a large donation of frozen organic alpaca meat.

As she stuffed envelopes with thank-you letters she had already finished, she asked Annie, "Have you ever thought about using this opportunity to ask people for another donation?"

Annie raised her eyebrows. "You don't think that might seem a little pushy?"

This had never stopped any of the causes Mary had contributed to from immediately hitting her up for more. "If they were willing to donate the first time, how annoyed can they be about us asking again? I could just add a low-pressure postscript about how to contribute again if they want."

Annie looked interested. "We'd have to ask the board. Why don't you come to the meeting Tuesday night? I'll put it on the agenda."

"Who will be there?"

"Just the board members. If someone actually showed up for public comment I think we'd all fall out of our seats."

Mary squinted down at the stationery on her desk. It listed board members in tiny print. Yes, there it was: *The Rev. Arthur Tennant, St. Andrew's Episcopal Church.* "Let me check my schedule and get back to you," she said. She would come up with some reason why Tuesday wouldn't work.

Chapter Twenty-Nine

LABOR DAY WEEKEND was too quiet. After only a week of mornings devoted to the food pantry, Mary missed the routine. Half days felt like perfect workdays, but half days without pay couldn't continue forever. She took advantage of the lovely weather to do some work in the yard. She was going to miss mucking about in the garden once she was in an apartment, but probably she'd have no time once the baby came anyway.

On Labor Day she got up early and treated herself to breakfast in the diner. Jeanette greeted her warmly. "Go ahead and take a booth, hon," she said, after Mary plopped herself down on one of the stools.

"But I'm by myself."

"We're not busy yet. You'll be more comfortable."

Mary ducked into the booth and blinked back tears. These days unexpected kindness made her very emotional.

The eggs and sausage and toast were steadying, however, and she was at work on them and her glass of milk when she heard the door jangle and the waitress greet the newcomer. "Winslow! Long time no see. We were afraid you weren't coming back!"

Mary's heart began to thump. She peeked back. Damn. He was as handsome as ever. She turned back and slouched down in her seat.

"Well, I'm here now." He yawned. "I need a big cup of coffee to go."

"Coming right up. Donut?"

"Just coffee."

"How was California?"

"Good."

"How's Laura?"

"Good."

"Got herself a man yet?"

He didn't reply. Mary heard the register drawer open and close, and Jeanette mumble something.

"What?"

More mumbling.

"Oh." He sounded less than thrilled.

Mary realized with dismay that those must be his footsteps headed her way. She kept her eyes on the cooling remains of her breakfast until he was standing there, a large blue presence.

"Hey," he said.

She looked up. "Hey. Good trip?"

"Yep."

"Good."

"So how are you?" he asked.

She tried to smile and the corners of her mouth definitely turned up, though it felt more like a grimace than anything else. "I'm fine."

"You look better."

"Thanks. I am doing better."

He shifted the hot cup of coffee from hand to hand. There were deep circles under his eyes. Perhaps it was just jet lag, but Winslow suddenly looked his age, or even older, and she felt a great wave of tenderness for him. What would he do if she asked him to join her?

"Well, I'm on duty."

She nodded, smiling stiffly.

"You take care," he said, and it felt just like a door slamming.

Jeanette stopped at her table not long after and caught Mary blowing her nose on a napkin. "You okay, hon?"

"It's nothing." Mary sniffed. "Hormones."

"Oh, tell me about it. When I was pregnant I would cry at anything. Once I cried because the ketchup wouldn't pour. Once I dropped a plate of French fries and I bawled so hard Dad told me to go out back before I scared away all the customers."

Mary smiled. "That sounds about right." It was a comfort, how nice people were to her these days. The sight of a pregnant woman apparently inspired so much good will that they forgot to worry about those pesky little details, like whether she'd gotten that way by sleeping around.

"But I really don't understand Winslow," Jeanette said. "Why isn't he doing the right thing by you? It's not like him."

So much for ignoring the pesky details. "This isn't his baby."

"It isn't? But if it isn't his…"

"You know, I really need to get going." Mary was afraid she might cry again.

*

After a difficult night, Mary resolved to forget about Winslow as anything more than a fellow citizen, and decided she might as well extend that resolution to Arthur. She called the church and was amazed when he picked up the phone himself.

"Hi. It's me. Mary."

"Mary." His voice changed immediately to something warmer, but also warier. "Is there a problem?"

"No. It's just that I have something to discuss with you."

"I still haven't gotten a draft from the lawyer. Sharon has gotten more involved, unfortunately."

"It sounds like she's feeling a lot better."

There was a pause. "You could say that."

"So how are you?"

"I feel like I'm being ground into the pavement by a giant high heel. But that's neither here nor there."

"It's not?"

"You might end up just having to sue me for proper support. You have my permission. I should never have told her."

"She might have found out anyway," Mary said, although she didn't see how. As an invalid Sharon had never talked to anybody.

"I made it too easy for her. She's diabolical, Mary. Honestly, if she ever offers you something to eat, don't take a bite."

Was he going around the bend? "You don't sound like yourself, Arthur."

"I don't think I am myself. Anyway, what did you want to discuss?"

"Um, I've started volunteering at the food pantry."

"Oh that's nice. They can always use the help."

"But the office is in your church hall. I'm trying to work it out so that I do most of it from home, but once in a while...."

"Oh, I see." There was a pause. "Well, frankly, I don't see a problem. That's not one of Sharon's things, even if she does sit right in the front pew these days."

"She does? She's recovered her faith?"

He snorted. "I doubt that."

What a bizarre couple they made. "So you really don't mind me being there?"

"No, not at all."

He sounded so offhand that she wondered if he'd really understood. "I was also invited to the board meeting tonight, but of course I won't be going."

"Why not?"

"Wouldn't that be breaking the rules?"

"No, not at all. I won't be there — our Outreach chair is going to handle it. I'm just not feeling up to it right now."

"Arthur, I'm a little worried about you."

"Are you? That's very sweet of you. It ought to be the other way round, don't you think?"

"But I'll be fine."

His little chuckle was slightly bitter. "Yes, I believe you will."

Mary dropped in to the food pantry office to tell Annie she could attend that night after all. Then, pleased that she was getting items crossed off her list, she stopped in to the bank in town that had financed her mortgage to ask about a home equity line of credit. She expected the answer would be a quick no after they heard she was unemployed. To her surprise, the loan officer, a young woman, told her it was quite possible she would qualify, since she had a solid amount of equity in the house. She took Mary's social security number and started an application. Then her face changed.

"I'm seeing problems on some joint accounts? With a Roger Bellamy?"

"We're divorced. Those aren't joint accounts anymore."

"You're still listed on them. And there's a mortgage from Shawmut Bank in foreclosure."

Mary stared at her. "In foreclosure? But my name isn't on that deed anymore. He bought out my interest."

"Your name is still on the mortgage."

"I don't understand." Her heart had begun to pound.

"You might want to take it up with your lawyer. Unfortunately, it makes it very difficult for us to loan you money right now, especially when taken with your employment situation."

"Can't I just prove that I'm not a party to those debts?"

The woman looked grim. "You can try."

Mary walked out of the bank feeling dazed. A foreclosure on her credit record? Roger's debts in her name? This meant she'd have trouble buying a house or a condo even if she did get a good job. It might make it harder to get the job. It might even keep her out of a decent apartment. And what the hell had that expensive lawyer been for? Could she sue him for not doing his damned job?

She marched back up the hill, not stopping at the river, not noticing the deep blue sky or the leaves just beginning to turn. Damn Roger. Damn the lawyer. And damn her, for not realizing that something like this could happen. No wonder she kept getting those phone calls. How could she have been so stupid?

When she got to her house she stood in front of it and glared at the "For Sale" sign. If she sold this house, she might never be able to get another. If she didn't sell this house, she might lose everything. No matter what she did, fall was coming, then winter, then a child who would need to be fed and clothed and sheltered.

She climbed into the middle of the front garden and took a deep breath, trying to calm down amid the flowers and the fat, droning bees. The annuals were at their full height and blooming furiously, as if they knew this was their last chance to set seed before the frost — just like her, really. She sank down onto a little boulder that jutted from the slope, surrounded by black-eyed susans and cosmos and great clumps of peony foliage, and went through what she was beginning to think of as her mantra: She wouldn't starve. The baby wouldn't starve. There was free food if she needed it. There was welfare. There were homeless shelters. She'd survive. In the end, she'd probably be stronger for having coped with adversity.

Yes, she'd be an incredibly wise, strong, horsy-looking old crone who dressed her kid in thrift store clothes and would never let any asshole man screw up her life ever again.

As she sat there brooding, Winslow's Toyota gunned up the road and turned into her driveway. He jumped out and carried a large wooden crate to the front door, where he all but threw it on the front stoop, then turned to leave.

Mary emerged from the flowers. "What the hell is that?"

He jumped. He must not have noticed her sulking there on her rock. "Dad told me he stopped bringing you vegetables."

"Yes. So?"

"So you also think just because I'm not the father, I'd want to withhold food from a pregnant woman!"

"I didn't think that at all. What makes you think I even need any?"

"I heard you were in the hospital, that you were losing weight!"

"For God's sake, that was weeks ago. Before you even went to California. It was just morning sickness. I'm fine now. You saw that yourself just yesterday, in the diner. What did you think, that I begged for my breakfast?"

"Jeanette feeds people all the time."

"She does?" Potentially useful tidbit, that.

His face had turned red. "So you're saying you're fine now."

"Yes, I'm fine."

"You have plenty of food."

"Yes, plenty. In fact, you can really take that back, because I don't need it."

He shook his head. "You must think I'm a very small man."

She hesitated, disarmed. "No."

He glared off at the flowers, or perhaps it was towards the road and his escape. "You probably think I never really loved you in the first place."

She hadn't expected him to ever use the word *love* again; she felt an involuntary thrill at the intimacy of it. "I think you were very much in love with the person you thought I was. That just wasn't exactly the person I turned out to be. You had no way of knowing." She meant it kindly, but she couldn't resist adding, "Once you did, you sure cleared off."

He shot her a look with more hurt in it than she expected.

"Which was perfectly understandable," she added quickly. "You made your standards clear early on."

He shook his head. "I thought..." He stopped. "It was a shock."

His feelings were still raw, clearly, even after the time away. "I'm sorry, Winslow. I really am. I screwed up. I made a mess of it. But I don't know what I can do about it now."

"You could tell me who the father is."

She took a step back. Had all this simply been a play for information? The cop trying to I.D. the perp? But he looked genuinely upset enough. She wished she could tell him, if only so she could feel that all was straight between them. But it wasn't up to her, and even if it was, she didn't see how telling this particular truth would help. "I've told you everything I can."

"Obviously not."

"I told you enough for you to know what kind of person I am. What more do you need?"

"Was it Arthur Tennant?"

Her mouth fell open. She turned away, hoping he couldn't read her well enough to know just from that first reaction.

"I'm not stupid. It is him, isn't it? And you're protecting him. Why?"

She closed her eyes.

After a moment, he stalked past her and got in his car. Their eyes met angrily for a moment, before he backed up and drove off.

Trembling, Mary turned to go into the house. The crate of vegetables he had left behind was heavier than a pregnant woman should carry, and more than she could possibly eat. She grabbed a paper bag from the kitchen and stuffed it full of ears of corn, onions, peppers, tomatoes, squash, and greens. Then she walked over to Cici's front door and rang the bell.

"Yes?" Cici looked distracted, her hair in curlers. A television soap was blasting in the background. Mary couldn't believe she'd actually missed the great scene next door.

"Have some vegetables," Mary said, and held the bag out.

Cici threw her hands up in surprise. "For me?"

"Yes. Sorry, I have to run." Mary set the bag down at Cici's feet.

"But, dear —"

"Got to go!" Mary insisted, and ran back to her house. She grabbed the now considerably lighter crate and dragged it through the door and into her kitchen. Then she sat down at the kitchen table and cried.

He *had* loved her.

Chapter Thirty

THE LAST THING Mary felt like doing that night was attending a board meeting full of church representatives, but she had told Annie she could make it after all, and she had come to the realization that a little structure and activity in life was a good thing, something a person could hang her day-to-day existence on when it might otherwise start to feel like one long dark tunnel.

So she ate some dinner and washed her face and went. She shared a quick, quiet hug with Bert, there representing God's Chapel on the Hill, and sat down at the long table on an uncomfortable folding chair. She recognized the representative from St. Andrew's as the woman who had given her a careful look on the bridge that day — Alma Whitaker, she was soon reminded, who smiled at her without warmth and watched her speculatively for much of the meeting.

Annie introduced Mary in glowing terms as a new volunteer with an idea they'd be considering under new business, and the meeting got underway, led with a prayer from the Baptist minister, Mike Carroll, who sat next to her. There was a great deal more joking and sarcasm than she'd expected. The proffered alpaca meat was cause for much hilarity, although the Unitarian, a thin woman in dangly earrings and natural fibers, looked impatient and suggested they might want to keep a more open mind about free sources of protein.

"You think our clients will know what to do with alpaca?" Alma asked. "What's it taste like, anyway?"

"Like chicken!" Bert chortled.

"Like sweaters!" someone else said.

"I don't think we have the freezer capacity we'd need to accept that gift, not with the Thanksgiving turkeys coming," Annie said. "I move we decline it with thanks, and give them the number of the soup kitchen in Keene. Do I have a second?"

And so the meeting went until it was Mary's turn to speak. She passed out a revised thank you letter with a demure postscript that suggested an additional donation would be welcome at any time, and waited for the inevitable nitpicking.

"Wow, this is amazing. Quite an improvement," Mike Carroll said. "You must be very talented — what did you say you did?"

"Editing."

"Well, this is truly remarkable." He gave her an alarmingly white smile.

Alma Whitaker said slowly, "You don't think people will feel we're hitting them up again too soon?"

"A polite request like this?" Bert said. "Heck, they can ignore it if they want to."

"And most of them will," sighed the Catholic representative.

"But if just one responds with another donation, then we're ahead of the game, aren't we? I move we adopt this as our new thank you," Mike said.

"Seconded," Bert said.

"All in favor? And the new thank you letter format is adopted." Annie looked pleased. "Thank you, Mary."

Mary wondered if she could slink away now, but the meeting immediately continued, eventually getting to an item listed on the agenda as "Web site????"

"Is this going to be listed under new business every month?" Alma asked.

"I really think we need one," Annie said.

"You know, maybe I could give it a try," Mary said.

Mike turned that smile on her again. "How did we get blessed with so much talent in one person?"

She addressed herself to Annie. "I just recently learned and I could use the practice."

"Excellent!" Annie said. "Do we need a vote on this one?"

"No!" someone else said quickly. "I move we adjourn and have some refreshments."

As they sipped punch, Bert pried Mary away from Mike Carroll's effusive welcome so he could introduce her to the Catholic representative. It turned out he was the vice president of her bank, and Mary blushed, wondering if he knew about her failed loan application. Then Alma Whitaker moved in. She recognized her from the bridge, conversing with Father Arthur that day. How well did she know Father Arthur? When was the baby due? Was it a boy or a girl? Mary answered or dodged questions until Bert interrupted. "Let this poor girl be," he told Alma. "She needs to go home and get some rest. Come on, Mary, I'll walk you out to the car."

"Thank you," she said, when they'd reached the cool night air.

"I'm awfully proud of you, my dear."

"Me? Whatever for?"

"You're making the best of a bad situation."

"I'm just trying to survive." She had wondered if Bert shared Winslow's suspicions, but that seemed unlikely when he was being so nice to her.

"Winslow and I got into one heck of an argument this morning. I thought he was annoyed I was taking you food. Come to find out he was angry I stopped. Wasn't really making much sense. He's got double shifts because of the extra leave, and I know that's hard on the boy, but he's beginning to worry me."

"Excuse me?" a clipped voice interrupted. Bert and Mary turned towards the woman who had approached them. "It's Mary, isn't it?" the woman said.

Mary stared, shocked to realize that this was Sharon Tennant, almost unrecognizable in a fashionable new hairstyle and flawlessly tailored suit.

"Hello, Bert," Sharon said, without actually looking at him. "Long time no see. Mary, may I have a word with you?"

Mary couldn't help a panicked look at Bert, who looked flummoxed, as Sharon half-pulled her back into the parish hall and then into a small classroom decorated with posters of Jesus with fluffy lambs and happy little ethnically diverse children.

Sharon closed the door firmly and turned to look hard

at Mary. She dwelled for a long moment on her belly, or perhaps it was her thrift store clothing. "Would you mind telling me what the hell you are doing here?"

"I was at the food pantry meeting. I'm a volunteer there. I checked with Arthur beforehand. He didn't think you'd have a problem with it."

Sharon narrowed her eyes as if assessing Mary's truthfulness. Then she scowled. "I can believe that. He's always so shocked and amazed when I have a problem with anything."

"I didn't mean to put you in an awkward situation."

"You do realize you're not the first, don't you?"

Mary went completely still.

"You don't suppose we came up here for the climate?"

A cold feeling settled in her stomach. "I never asked why."

"No?" Sharon had begun to pace energetically back and forth in her pumps. It was an amazing transformation from the pallid Sharon of March, and Mary watched warily. Was she was working herself up to throw a punch? Might she have a weapon concealed in that tailored jacket? "He claims you never actually spent that much time together."

"No, we didn't."

Sharon gave her a pointed look. "I guess that makes you an easy lay."

Mary flushed.

"The last one — the last one I knew about, anyway — had an abortion. Of course, she was a lot younger than you. She probably felt she still had her whole life ahead of her."

Although it registered that Sharon was insulting her in every way possible, Mary was too busy reeling at the revelation about Arthur's past to care. If it was true, she'd been quite taken in. Of course, she wasn't the only one.

"Why'd you stay with him, then?"

Sharon gave her a disgusted look. "He's my children's father. And he promised so faithfully that we would have a fresh start here." Her face twisted in bitterness, and she resumed her pacing.

"And then Matthew died."

"Yes."

"And you blamed him." It all made more sense now.

"Of course I blamed him. And myself."

"But why stay after that? And why stay now?"

Sharon's eyes flickered. "It's not that simple, you know. It isn't black and white. I was furious with him after Matthew died, but it was hardly something he'd intended. And my daughter adores him. She can't help it — he's her father. And then there's that little matter of keeping a roof over our heads. I never had a career. Our quality of life, pathetic as it is, depends on these morons continuing to believe that he's a worthy spiritual leader." Sharon stepped right into her space. "And you know that. So why you would you even think of showing your face in this building?"

She was all but growling. Mary was reminded of a she-wolf she'd once seen on a nature documentary. But Mary had trespassed into Sharon's territory. Among wolves that meant a little submission was in order.

"Thing is, the food pantry was recommended to me by Bert, who knows I lost my job, and he got suspicious when I hesitated about the location. If I drop out now, he might put two and two together. But I'll respect your wishes. I won't come if you don't want me to."

"Are you implying that money will keep you away?"

Mary was taken aback. "No."

"And you're saying that Bert doesn't already know?"

"I don't see how he could."

"Or his son? I hear you've been screwing him, too."

Mary blinked, momentarily derailed. "I haven't told anyone. I know Winslow suspects, but I don't see how he could know."

Sharon frowned. "I don't want you anywhere near my daughter," she said at last. "Or me. That's my bottom line."

"Then you want me off the food pantry?"

"No, you'd better keep on, if what you say is true. We're not involved in it. Just make sure you're nowhere to be seen during services."

"Believe me, I have no desire to be here during services."

Sharon gave her a toothy grin that was somehow more frightening than all her scowls. "I used to feel that way, too. But these days I find them quite entertaining."

Mary would have felt sorry for Arthur if she wasn't so disgusted with him.

"I believe we're done here," Sharon said, opening the classroom door and standing aside. Mary realized she was being dismissed. As Mary passed by Sharon murmured, "You do realize, don't you, that there are worse things in life than not having children?"

Mary stopped and stared at her uncertainly. Was this another insult, a threat, or just a commentary on life as Sharon saw it?

But Sharon just waved her hand as one might command a servant. "Off you go."

Mary went, and started her car with shaking hands. She had even more reason to get out of town now. Too bad she still had no idea how to manage it.

CHAPTER THIRTY-ONE

MARY TRIED AND failed to reach Roger. Apparently he had left his job. His home phone had been disconnected. Her lawyer wasn't very helpful, saying there was little remedy available against Roger for not following his side of the agreement since at this point he probably had no assets left worth recovering.

"Why didn't you warn me this could happen?"

"Your divorce wasn't contested. You divided everything up yourselves. There was no reason to anticipate a problem like this."

"But I was relying on your advice!"

"It's not my fault it didn't occur to you to close your joint accounts. In regards to the house, the mortgager might be persuaded to remove your name by a copy of the divorce decree and the records from the secondary transaction. It can't hurt to try, anyway. I don't suppose his parents were co-signers of the original loan?"

"No." They'd given Roger his half of the down payment; Mary had supplied the other half from her own savings.

"That's too bad. I bet they have plenty of money."

This was true. Furthermore, Roger's parents were nice people. Would they help? Surely they would at least tell her if there was any chance Roger would pay off his own debts.

It had been a long time since she'd walked into Mitchell Bellamy's beautifully appointed office in Framingham.

Mitchell gasped. "Mary! Goodness gracious, I see congratulations are in order!"

She smiled as he gave her a kiss on the cheek.

He looked perplexed. "But I thought...."

"Apparently the doctors were wrong."

"Oh dear." He looked embarrassed. He seemed as courtly as ever. She found it inexplicable that a man with such effortlessly good manners had a son who could utter the word *cunt* to a woman without blinking. She remembered late in their engagement, when she'd been disappointed by Roger's behavior at a party, reassuring herself that he came from a good family and couldn't possibly be too much of a lout. But what did she know? Perhaps Mitchell, after enough drinks with his buddies, or out at a job site, would be completely comfortable talking that way. This dark current in Roger had to come from somewhere. Was it in all men?

She took a deep breath. "Unfortunately, Mitchell, I'm getting a lot of calls from Roger's creditors. And I can't seem to find him."

Mitchell sighed. "I can't say that surprises me. He got into a mess with that woman, you know. She refused to move out. There was some sort of altercation and he got charged with assault."

"Assault?"

Mitchell looked at the door as if to ensure their conversation wasn't being overheard. "He claims it was self-defense. Who knows what really happened. We agreed to post bail for him if he went into rehab, but I'm afraid he didn't stay there very long. She got an order of protection against him, and he decided to let the house foreclose around her. Not a course we would have recommended. No doubt he is in some serious financial straits at the moment." Mitchell cleared his throat uncomfortably. "You can imagine my embarrassment, Mary, at having to fire my own son. I haven't seen him since. He calls his mother occasionally. Apparently he's working construction and staying with friends."

How quickly Roger had sunk from his comfortable middle-class existence. He certainly didn't sound like a man who was going to pay off his debts anytime soon.

"I blame the booze," Mitchell said. "They say you have to hit bottom. I would have thought he already has, but apparently he's still working on it."

She wasn't as inclined to blame the alcohol, but there was hardly any point in debating her ex-husband's character with his father. "Unfortunately, Mitchell, my name was still on that mortgage, and he has delinquent credit cards that were originally joint accounts. And they're trying to hold me responsible."

"Oh dear. Creditors can be so merciless. I know he claims she stole some of his credit cards."

"Well, then, can't the police...?"

"I don't think they even have a legal separation agreement yet. I suppose you might be able to do something."

"Oh, I've cancelled them. But that doesn't make the debt go away."

"I'm so sorry, my dear. It's very unfair, isn't it? Life can often be that way." He sat down, gave a little cough, and opened a folder on his desk. Mary stood there, shocked to realize she was being dismissed this quickly by the same man who'd affectionately hugged her hello and goodbye for eight years. Mitchell looked up as if surprised that she was still there and smiled. "Tell you what — if I can, I'll try to get the message to him that he should get in touch with you. Will that help?"

She faked a smile. "Oh, please, Mitchell, don't go to any trouble on my account. Give my best to Barbara, will you?" She turned and left, disgusted. She had really liked this man.

The evidence just kept mounting: She was no fit judge of *anybody*.

Chapter Thirty-Two

T HAT AFTERNOON DR. Gupta did an ultrasound, and Mary finally discerned the subtle outlines of the head, a little hand, the curve of back. Then the baby moved, just like that, right on the screen. Mary barely restrained herself from another bout of happy tears.

"Do you want to know the sex?"

"No, better not." She couldn't help feeling that the more she thought about her baby, the more she tempted fate to interfere. She couldn't help hunting for tell-tale signs in the print-out Gupta gave her, though: was that a finger or a penis?

Afterwards, Mary asked the billing clerk if she could talk to someone about the looming doctor's payment.

The woman looked at her computer and smiled. "You're all set, dear. The doctor has a note here to bill insurance upon delivery."

"But the contract…"

"It's been waived."

"How'd that happen?"

The woman frowned. "Do you *want* to pay it now?"

"No, thank you!" Mary said quickly. Outside the

doctor's office, the maples blazed with fierce autumn colors against a deep blue sky. Mary felt enormously heartened by the reprieve on the doctor's bill. Maybe she just had to lower her expectations, that was all. Forget publishing. Take any job that paid. Ignore Roger's debts. Get by.

She signed up with a temp agency and began to spend occasional days in Keene as a fill-in receptionist or administrative assistant. To her chagrin, no single assignment lasted more than a week. She hoped it wasn't because they were checking her credit history and deciding she was a bad risk. Other mornings she staffed the food pantry office or worked at her own computer, arduously relearning the art and science of putting together a web site. The principle of *graceful degradation* took on more practical meaning as she discovered what could occur to her web pages on different browsers and computers. She soon had every member of the board who was online reporting back how things looked from their end. Mike Carroll always said it looked absolutely amazing. She wondered whether this was a technique more designed for saving her soul or for getting in her pants.

She spent the rest of her time job-hunting and battling Roger's creditors. It appeared that the best she could do without finding Roger and getting him to pay was to negotiate costly repayment plans herself — that, or declare personal bankruptcy. Both options infuriated her, so she did nothing even as the phone calls became so threatening and so frequent that she had to unplug the phone every night. Her unemployment had run out, and her savings began to drop.

No serious offers were tendered on her house, though the new condos on the other side of town went at a good clip. When the last leaf had fallen, Lisa insisted they retire the sign until the holidays were over. Mary didn't argue. Keeping the house ready to show was exhausting.

She saw nothing of Arthur or Sharon. She now doubted any of the proffered child support would appear, but at least this would make it easier to claim public assistance if the need arose, even if it did mean naming the father. When she attended the November food pantry meeting, she didn't miss Alma Whitaker's roll of the eyes when Annie suggested that Arthur might be able to help out with a project.

"Is something the matter with Father Arthur?" Mary asked during refreshments.

"The man's falling apart. Seems like he's had bronchitis for months. He still gives a decent sermon, but that's about it. Personally, I think he needs to take a rest leave or something."

"Sharon looked pretty good the last time I saw her."

"Oh, she's a new woman. It's really too bad they can't both be well at the same time for once."

After the meeting Bert asked her what she was doing for Thanksgiving.

"I'm not sure yet." Patty had invited her out, but she couldn't risk the air fare and in any case was now big enough to find the idea of a long flight uncomfortable. She also hadn't heard another word from her mother, other than a thank-you note for the wedding present she'd sent.

"Laura's coming home," Bert said. "Says she has big news for me. I think she's met someone at last!"

Uh oh.

"How's Winslow?" she asked. On the rare occasion they crossed paths in town, he merely nodded and hurried away. She suspected he was actively avoiding her. Certainly no more vegetables had appeared on her doorstep, not that there was anything left to harvest.

Bert sighed. "Grumpy. When he has a day off he's always driving off somewhere."

Mary had half-expected a scandal to erupt, for Winslow to accuse Arthur, but nothing had happened. If people were still speculating about who the father was, they weren't addressing it to her. Nowadays they asked her if it was a girl or boy, had she done the nursery yet, would her mother be coming to help? Peggy, at the market, couldn't keep her hands off Mary's belly, but Mary didn't mind; she only got annoyed at the men who touched her, especially Mike Carroll.

She had no very high opinion of men in general at the moment. Roger hadn't called, though she didn't know if this was because he hadn't gotten the message or because he didn't want to discuss his debts. It was probably just as well — she'd wondered how he might react to the news she was pregnant. She also feared he might arrive on her doorstep one night and demand she take him in. She still admired Winslow, but he had disappointed her, too. And Arthur — well, Arthur didn't even bear thinking about.

So she was surprised, Friday morning, when he peered into the small food pantry office. She was alone; Annie had gone to Keene to buy supplies.

"Can I talk to you for a minute?" he asked.

She didn't answer, but he picked his way in. Mary was struck by how gaunt he looked.

He lowered himself into Annie's chair, adjacent to Mary's, and pulled a long envelope out of his suit jacket. "The lawyer finally gave me this. It's the support agreement. The money's not as pathetic as I feared, but the confidentiality clause may make you choke."

Mary opened it up and scanned it quickly. Indeed, the money was not pathetic. The confidentiality clause was written in legalese, but once she'd parsed it out it was what she had expected — nobody was to know about the paternity other than the parties themselves and their legal representatives — and the child only upon reaching maturity. "I'm surprised, Arthur. I didn't really think this was going to happen."

"I had my doubts, too. I guess she decided it was worth buying you off to keep me in indentured servitude for a few more years."

Mary folded it back up and put it in the envelope. "I'm told I'm not the first."

"I never claimed I was a saint." He coughed and then gave her an intense look. "Are you sure you can meet this confidentiality requirement?"

"I don't see why not."

"You didn't tell Winslow?"

"No. I know he suspects, though."

"Yes, he asked me point blank."

"What did you say?"

"I said I would never do such a thing. What did you say?"

"I didn't say anything. And he hasn't said one word to

me since." The loss of even those limited social greetings still grieved her.

"I can tell he didn't believe me," Arthur said, "but I assume he doesn't have any proof. He even stopped coming to church for awhile. Now he comes, but he sits and glares at me. So now every Sunday I've got Sharon sitting there in the front with that superior little smile on her face, and Winslow sitting in the back, looking like the wrath of God Himself."

Did he expect sympathy? "Well, Arthur, I guess you can always repent."

Arthur snorted. He patted her on her knee, then got up stiffly. "Oh, believe me, I do. Every damned day of my life."

CHAPTER THIRTY-THREE

A S THANKSGIVING APPROACHED, the food pantry got hectic. November was prime time for food collections and for new volunteers, who naturally expected to be given something to do. The generous Thanksgiving boxes, a point of pride and competition among the local churches and civic organizations, had to be organized so that frozen turkeys didn't defrost, stuffing mix didn't expire, pies didn't get squashed, and no one got lost trying to make deliveries.

Mary organized driving maps along sensible car routes for the approximate number of volunteers they expected to show up on delivery day, the Sunday afternoon before Thanksgiving. She and Annie supervised the distribution of lists and boxes. She had just finished checking off one set of boxes into the care of a couple of Catholics, when she turned to find herself facing Winslow.

"Oh, hi." She tried to ignore the rising heat on her face. "I didn't see you on the list. Are you here for St. Andrew's?"

"No, Chapel on the Hill." His blue eyes met hers for what seemed like the first time in months. "Dad's back is bothering him."

"I'm sorry to hear that. Here are their boxes" — she walked him over — "and this is where to deliver them." She handed over the packet with a tight smile. "Tell your Dad I hope he feels better." She stepped back, anxious to avoid further awkwardness.

He boosted a box into his arms. "You're not lifting these, I hope."

"No, not me." She patted her belly. If he had ever found her attractive, he must be safely past that now. Perhaps that explained the sudden willingness to talk to her again.

"My sister's arriving tomorrow," he said.

"Your dad told me she has big news."

"She's bringing Carla."

"Does he know?"

"No." He frowned and shifted the heavy box over to one hip.

"Don't you think it might be a good idea to give him a heads up?"

"She didn't want me to. She says if they have to leave, they will."

"Well that sounds like a fun holiday for everybody." Mary was annoyed on Bert's behalf. "Was this your sister's idea, or Carla's?"

"Probably Carla's. She can be a drama queen."

"I could tell him, if you want."

He looked astonished. "*You?*"

She suddenly realized how far she'd overstepped. There went her face, burning again. "Sorry," she said wretchedly. "Dumb suggestion." She turned away, blinking back tears of embarrassment, and stumbled over to another volunteer who looked like he needed direction. Out of the corner of her eye she could see Winslow staring after her. She turned her back and tried to focus on the man in front of her, who was geared out as if he were about to go climb Mount Monadnock.

"Hey, are you okay?" the man asked.

"Hormones," she said. The man looked alarmed. She tried to smile. "Which group are you?"

"Unitarian."

Thankfully, the Unitarian boxes were on the other side from the God's Chapel on the Hill boxes, over by the Kiwanis boxes. Perhaps Annie had mapped out the boxes by dogma, or lack thereof. Mary helped the Unitarian fellow and then hovered while he carried out one heavy box at a time. Winslow came in and out, too, loading his own boxes. She sensed him looking over at her, but carefully avoided making eye contact until his last box was gone and him with it. Then she checked both sets of boxes off her list and collapsed into a folding chair.

"You okay?" Annie asked, panting a bit herself.

"I'll be all right."

"Somebody say something mean to you? Tell me who it is, I'll fight 'im!"

Mary just shook her head.

"What are you doing for Thanksgiving?"

"I thought I might sign up to work the soup kitchen in Keene."

Annie scowled. "Why don't you let the once-a-year folks do that? I'm going to have a nice restaurant meal with my home girls. You want to come?"

"Home girls?" Lawson was not exactly a hub of hip urban street culture.

"Other divorced women from my support group. The few of us who don't have families we want to hang out with on Turkey Day, anyway."

Mary hesitated. "How expensive is it?"

"Pregnant unemployed food pantry volunteers get to eat free."

"I can still pay my way!"

Annie laughed. "No you can't. The restaurant is owned by one of the women in the group. She never lets us pay a dime for the food, just for the service."

"Well, that sounds lovely, actually. Thank you."

Annie did a little happy dance. "Excellent! Now everybody's taken care of."

Mary wished she had driven down to St. Andrew's or at least accepted Annie's offer of a ride home, once the parish hall had been cleared and locked up and she was standing on Hill Street. The afternoon had darkened with clouds, snow was spitting, and she was worn out.

As she trudged up the hill, she wondered what the weather was like in Arizona this time of year. She was not a very good daughter. She could never remember the name of the town her mother lived in, and had no idea how cold it got there or even whether it ever snowed.

Patty had offered to come out when the baby was born, but said she needed to request the time off and find reasonably priced tickets. Mary thought she'd probably take her up on it, and do her best to deliver the baby on Patty's schedule. From the way every woman kept asking her who was going to be helping her when the baby came, she got the idea this was important.

Eventually, she reached the house, where the front garden was now a twisted mass of dead flower stalks, and was startled to find a large paper bag on the front stoop. Bending down, she opened it up and discovered a large butternut squash, a bunch of carrots, a half dozen gourds and a folded piece of paper.

"I'm taking your advice," it read, in a hurried hand. Below that was scrawled a large "W," and then "P.S. Don't try to eat the gourds, they're just for looks."

Mary stared down at it, warmed by his gesture, but also confused. Was this a peace offering? An apology? Or did he just think she needed food? If she'd been home, would he have knocked and given it to her in person, or was it important that he could just dump it on the stoop and run?

It hardly mattered. Probably her larger belly had temporarily aroused enough sympathy to tamp down his contempt. She took the bag in and tried different arrangements of the oddly contorted gourds in a basket on her kitchen table, but none satisfied her. Finally she just sat there at the table as dusk fell, her right hand resting on the pebbled skin of a crookneck gourd.

One problem with a scribbled note left with a bag of produce on a front stoop was that there was no obvious way to respond. Mary was afraid to call Winslow on the phone, not sure he would really welcome that. She supposed she could scribble back, "How did he take it? M." and deliver it to the police station in a bag of donuts. But that was getting silly.

So she just went to do her usual work at the pantry Monday morning, and again on Wednesday. Wednesday was a day when the regional food bank often delivered, and she was hoping she'd see Bert there to help stock shelves with the usual crew of Kiwanis.

"Isn't Bert coming?" she asked Annie, as she lingered into lunch and he still hadn't appeared.

"No, he got Fred from St. Mary's to take it over."

"When did he tell you that?"

Annie looked at her curiously. "Last week. Why?"

"Winslow said he hurt his back. I just wanted to know if he was feeling better."

Annie raised an eyebrow. "I heard that Winslow is the father, but now I'm beginning to wonder if it's Bert's."

"Oh please."

"I sure wouldn't choose Bert over Winslow."

"No, you've made that quite clear." Mary got up stiffly. She was hungry, her butt was sore from sitting too long, and she no longer had any reason to wait around.

"I'm not pissing you off, am I?"

Mary shook her head, then yawned and put on her jacket.

"But you do like him, don't you? Winslow, I mean."

"I think he's the bee's knees, Annie. But he's not the father."

Normally, Mary walked home and fixed her own lunch; eating out was a sure way to go through money fast. But she was too hungry to face that hill without at least a snack to tide her over, so she walked over to the diner. Jeanette was now on good terms with her, partly because the diner frequently donated leftover food. "Hey, Mary!" she said. "What'll it be?"

"Hi, Jeanette. Chocolate malted to go, please."

"Coming right up." Jeanette tilted her head to the right and gave her a meaningful look.

Mary peered down the crowded counter and saw Winslow sitting at the end of it, in uniform, reading the paper while he chewed meditatively on a French fry.

"He's busy." She was hardly going to accost him in a crowded diner.

"Are you too busy to talk to this girl, Winslow?" Jeanette yelled.

Everybody looked up. Mary cringed.

Winslow looked up at Jeanette and followed her inclined head to Mary. He smiled.

Mary smiled back warily.

"Go on," Jeanette said.

Mary walked down the aisle, aware of heads turning, to where Winslow had spun around in his seat and appeared to be waiting expectantly.

"Thank you for the veggies. And the gourds. They look nice."

"Some people varnish them so they last longer. We don't. How long does anyone really want to have to look at the same gourds?"

He clearly had no idea how fond she had become of these particular gourds. It was a useful thought, a sobering thought. "Well, don't let me keep you from your lunch."

"You're not," he said, though he had at least half a plate of food left in front of him.

The burly man sitting next to Winslow patted her arm. "You want me to move down?"

"Oh, no," Mary said. "Thanks anyway. I'm just getting take-out."

The man shrugged and turned back to his food.

"How's your dad?" she asked Winslow.

Winslow rolled his eyes. "He'll survive."

"You told him."

"Yep."

"And they're still coming?"

"Yep."

"Should be an interesting Thanksgiving."

"Would you like to come?" He suddenly looked awkward.

She stared at him, surprised. "Um, thank you, but I already have plans."

He looked as if maybe he didn't believe her. "Dad wanted to invite you weeks ago. I should have let him."

Perhaps he wanted a neutral party at the table? Still felt a little guilty or something? He hadn't wanted her there before, she hadn't missed that.

Jeanette leaned over the counter and handed her the milk shake. Mary tried to hand over the money she had already counted out, but Jeanette waved it away. "Don't worry, it's his treat." She nodded at Winslow.

"Ha ha," Mary said, still holding out her money.

He smiled. "No, she's right, I've got it."

"No you don't," Mary said in a low voice.

"It's no big deal," Winslow said softly.

"Maybe not to you." Her face flushed hot and she looked back at the door. She needed to get out of here. "Look, I've got to go." She dropped the money on the counter next to his plate and turned away.

"Mary —"

She was all but running for the door, the faces of the people she passed a blur.

"Hormones," she heard Jeanette say as she ran out.

Climbing the hill at a furious pace, Mary tried to think rationally about what had just happened. She found it highly unlikely that Winslow, after months of distance, was suddenly warming to her again in any way that really mattered. Rather, she suspected there was now a conspiracy afoot, a quiet plan among the townspeople who made it their business to look after the vulnerable, to make sure she didn't starve to death or give birth all alone on the kitchen floor. "We look after our own" was a phrase she'd heard plenty of times in Lawson, and her work at the food pantry had apparently made her one of their own despite her ridiculously short tenure in town.

Well, she'd be damned if she was going to let Winslow feel like a good man just because he was inviting her to Thanksgiving dinner or paying for her chocolate malted. If he wanted to talk to her occasionally instead of just nodding, fine. She could make neighborly conversation with Cici, for God's sake, and even Arthur could call her tomorrow and she'd be civil. And she didn't mind admitting that she liked Winslow better than any of them. But that didn't mean she wanted his charity.

Bert understood her better than his son did. If Bert had asked her to dinner, it would be because he liked her, and not from feeling guilty that she'd be sitting all alone, poor pregnant Mary who couldn't find a job in her little house she couldn't sell.

Once home she sat on her front stoop, irritably sucking milk shake down and soaking the thin November sunshine in. As she calmed, the baby moved — still an amazing sensation. She hoped it wouldn't cause her to somehow damage her child, the intensity with which she was looking forward to having one person in her life who wouldn't judge, who wouldn't patronize, who wouldn't baffle her by alternating between warmth and coolness.

Bob meowed at her from the other side of the door, but she ignored him. He could be quite aloof, too, when it suited him, the little bastard.

Mary went inside and sorted through her paltry maternity wardrobe, looking for something that might be dressy enough for Thanksgiving dinner out. She held up a large red velour shirt that had already been showing signs of wear when she got it at Goodwill. Maybe with a string of fake pearls? She could always wear a suit, but she didn't want to waste dry cleaning on anything less than a paying job.

The phone rang while she was checking whether her black maternity pants required a wash.

Winslow. There went her heart, thumping away.

"Can I ask you something?" he said.

"What?"

"What did I do?"

She sighed. "Nothing." How to explain to a man that he shouldn't try to be nice?

"It must have been something."

"Look, I appreciate that people want to help me, I really

do. But in some situations, I guess I really just don't enjoy feeling like I've become the object of charity."

"You thought that was charity?"

"Yes. And thank you, but I really don't need it, at least not yet."

There was a longer pause, during which she heard an odd racket in the background. "Where are you calling from?"

"Work."

"Oh." That explained his lowered voice.

Winslow cleared his throat. "Do you think we could just get together and talk?"

"You can talk to me anytime. I just don't want you to…" she hesitated, unsure how to put it.

"What?"

"Do me any favors."

There was such a long pause after this that Mary began to think he'd hung up. But then he said, "Why do you have to make this so hard?"

"What am I making hard? What do you want from me?"

"I want to see you."

"So see me. I'm kind of hard to miss these days."

He huffed impatiently.

She decided to change the subject. "When does your sister get here?"

"They're already in Boston, with one of Laura's college friends. They're supposed to arrive around noon."

"Well, good luck with that."

"Where are you going to be?"

"Annie invited me to join her and some friends for dinner out."

"Oh." He sounded sour.

"What?"

"Are you aware her little group is known around town as the She-Woman Man-Hater's Club?"

"Really?" She smiled. Pretty cool name. "Look, I don't hate you, in case you're wondering."

"You don't?" His voice was unnaturally high.

"No," Mary said, blinking back sudden tears. "I don't."

"I don't hate you either."

She couldn't say anything; her heart was too full. How screwed up was her life that a statement like that sounded like a romantic declaration?

Chapter Thirty-Four

THE SHE-WOMAN MAN-HATER'S Club Thanksgiving dinner turned out to include only four other women, sitting around a table in the empty restaurant side of a sports tavern that sat just outside of town. They rolled their eyes when Mary asked them what they thought of their unofficial name.

"Typical," said Meg, a nurse who worked in a Keene senior facility. "They always think it's about them."

"When the whole point of our group is that it's about us," said another woman, Stella, who had a rose tattooed in her cleavage. She owned the place. Mary was surprised at the amount of business being done, and a little bemused that despite her divorce she was still spending Thanksgiving with football blasting in the background.

"So how come you're divorced?" the third woman, Missy, asked. Of the four, she seemed the most wistful.

"He left me because I couldn't have children."

Silence fell as they eyed her bulging maternity blouse.

"So I take it he's a freaking idiot?" Stella said.

They all laughed. Mary laughed, too, but she felt a

twinge of guilt. "Sometimes I feel a little bad for him. His life has gone to hell."

"You feel sorry for him?" Annie, who knew something about Mary's credit woes, looked appalled. "Are you kidding me?"

Mary sighed. "Okay, so he's a jerk, he's a drunk, he's a low-life — but it's just such a waste. He had a good life, he had every advantage — and now look at him. It's sad."

"Would you take him back?" Missy asked.

"Oh God, no."

Missy looked disappointed.

"Missy's still got a thing for her ex," Annie said.

"My sister stole him from me," Missy explained.

"He let himself get stolen, honey," Stella said.

"I didn't pay enough attention to him," Missy said. "I was working the night shift, he was working the day shift. I made it easy for her."

The other women just shook their heads.

"Your sister's the one you should feel sorry for," Meg said. "You'll see."

Voices rose over in the bar area. Stella said, "Excuse me, ladies," and stalked off.

"Stella is my hero," Annie said. "She's not afraid of anybody."

"She's a nut," Meg said.

Over in the bar, a loud and inebriated man with a booming voice was deeply offended about something. Other male voices were yelling at him to shut up.

"Stella's no fool," Annie said. "Those guys out there love her. If anyone tries to lay a hand on her, they'll immediately beat that guy to a pulp."

Mary sighed and focused on her turkey and cranberry sauce. How was dinner going in the Jennings house? Had peace been achieved between sinners and sermonizers? Was Winslow wondering how her dinner was going? Was he having second thoughts about the date they'd set up for Friday night?

The yelling in the bar got even louder. Stella bellowed, "You! Get the fuck out of this establishment — now! And don't come back!" A door slammed; there was a smattering of applause. "You tell him, babe!" somebody yelled. Eventually the game could be heard again.

Stella came back, shaking her head. "Sorry about that. Holidays can really bring out the worst in people — especially if they're assholes to begin with."

Annie lifted her beer in a toast to their hostess. "To Stella, warrior woman!"

Mary raised her seltzer. She could feel a bad case of heartburn coming on.

Meg didn't look happy. "One of these days one of these guys is going to have a gun or a knife and then what are you going to do?"

"You worry too much," Stella said. "There are at least three off-duty cops sitting out there drinking my beer. Plus I keep a gun behind the bar. No one's going to mess with me."

Mary glanced at Annie, who didn't look concerned by the existence of a gun behind the bar. Maybe it was a New Hampshire thing. *Live free or die.*

"Speaking of cops..." Stella said, and leaned towards Mary.

"What?" Mary felt herself beginning to blush.

"Most folks around here believe you're about to add to the local force," Stella said.

"Most folks are wrong," Mary said.

Missy leaned in. "Are you saying you never...?"

"We know you went out with him," Stella said. "We have multiple eyewitnesses."

"So I went out with him," Mary said. "He's not the father."

"Maybe he *is* gay," Stella said. "The guys say no, but what do they know?"

"He's not gay," Mary said. "He doesn't believe in sex before marriage."

"And you believed that?" Stella said. "Maybe he just acts straight around town so he doesn't freak everybody out. I mean, I wouldn't blame him. And it would explain why he's always taking off to places like San Francisco."

"He's not gay," Mary insisted.

"But how do you know?" Annie said. "I mean, if you didn't..."

"Look. Just because we didn't — you know — doesn't mean we didn't..."

"Ah ha!" Annie pointed at her, grinning. "I knew it."

"Ah ha nothing," Mary said. "Ah ha doesn't get you pregnant."

Missy piped up. "Actually, I heard about a girl who was just messing around with a guy pretty hot and heavy, and apparently his little guys could really swim. Come to find out she got pregnant when she was still a virgin."

Mary shook her head. "We never even took our clothes off."

"Gay," Stella said.

Meg said, "If Winslow's not the father, then who is?"

They all looked at Mary.

She shook her head, smiling. "Sorry, ladies. I'll never tell."

"Oh, come on," they whined.

Much to her surprise, Mary realized that she was having fun. "What's for dessert?" she asked.

Later that night she woke to furious pounding. Dazed, she noted that it was after one in the morning and flipped the light on, blinking against its brightness. She slid into a pair of slippers and shuffled to the kitchen just in time to see the door swing open. What the —?

A man stepped into her kitchen and she froze. It took her a moment to recognize Roger. He was bearded, bloody and bruised, far more disheveled than she had ever seen him.

He stared at her as if he didn't quite recognize her either. Then his lip curled. "So it's true," he said, and the sour tang of alcohol and sweat reached her from across the room.

Pretending to be calmer than she was, she walked past him to the door and held it open for him. "I don't want you here, Roger."

He punched her in the face.

Chapter Thirty-Five

MARY ROSE TO her hands and knees from where she'd fallen. Blood was dripping from her nose and splattering onto the worn vinyl. Roger was hopping around the kitchen, wincing in pain as he cradled his fist. Cold air poured in from outside; the front door still hung open.

"Get out of my house!" she screamed, hoping she'd wake her neighbor.

"Shut up, you freaking cunt!" he screamed back, coming at her again. She scrambled for the open door on her hands and knees, shrieking. He kicked her viciously between her legs and she curled up in pain.

He dragged her back from the door, then slammed and locked it. "You bitch! You just had to go see my dad, didn't you? Had to rub my face in it, had to make sure everybody knew!"

Undone by pain and fear, she vomited, then began to crawl towards the hall, away from him. If she could just make it to the back door, or any room that locked...

"Where do you think you're going?" he screamed, following her. She shrieked as he grabbed her hair and used it to drag her back into the kitchen.

"You stay right there!" he yelled, leaving her in a heap on the same place on the kitchen floor where she'd landed the first time. "We're going to talk."

She felt a hysterical laugh try to form, but swallowed it down. Roger opened her refrigerator, throwing items aside angrily. "Where's the beer?"

She didn't answer.

"BEER!" he yelled.

"Don't have any." Her voice had gone all nasal.

"Christ, don't you even have any fucking Coke?"

She didn't say anything, just watched him.

He settled for taking a swig from a carton of orange juice, then sat down at the kitchen table with it. "So who'd you fuck?"

She didn't answer.

"Who'd you FUCK!" he screamed.

When she didn't answer he jumped out of his chair and raised his hand.

"You don't know him," she moaned, then helplessly vomited again. She was trembling so hard she could barely keep herself from sinking down into the mess.

He kept that hand raised. "What's his NAME!"

"Arthur."

"Arthur? Arthur WHO?"

"Arthur Tennant."

Finally, his hand went down. Roger's mouth dropped open. "The priest? You fucked the priest?" He looked at her in disbelief for another moment, then walked over to her stove and threw her the dish towel she'd hung on its handle. "Clean up that mess. You're pathetic, you know that?"

Yes. She trembled against the wall, having dutifully

spit out Arthur's secret as well as her Thanksgiving meal. It was as if Roger knew she'd been laughing at him just a few hours ago.

"CLEAN IT UP!" he screamed, and she jumped, moving the towel around, trying not to gag again. Spots of blood kept blossoming on the floor and towel as her nose continued to drip. He sat and watched with a disgusted curl to his lip. "Jesus, he was an ugly son of a bitch. Don't you have any standards?"

Apparently not. She began to pray mindlessly to God to save her despite her conviction that God didn't exist. She moved the towel back and forth and glanced up at Roger. Could he be reasoned with? Why was he beating her up? What had she done to him?

"Look, I'm staying here tonight," Roger said, suddenly sounding almost normal.

In the quiet, a distant sound grew. Was that a siren?

Roger stood up and peered out the kitchen window. The siren grew louder.

Mary started inching her way back towards the hall again, praying that siren wouldn't just race past the house.

Roger looked back before she'd gotten far. "Oh no, you don't!" he muttered, and grabbed her by the hair again as the siren began to wail right in front of the house. He dragged her screaming to the cellar door and then shoved her down into darkness. She tumbled, thumping against stairs and walls until she came to rest on the landing near the bottom. "Not a word out of you and I MEAN IT!" he said, shutting the door and latching it.

She lay there in the dark, stunned and disbelieving.

Shouldn't she be dead? Most of her body lay twisted

across the landing, but her legs were sprawled above her on the steps above, and her head and one arm were hanging down towards the shorter, lower flight of steps to the cellar floor. The only light source in the cellar was the old boiler, glowing red like a demon.

Her head was hanging down from the edge of the landing, but she didn't have the strength or coordination to lift it up. She used the hand that still seemed under her control to feel for the baby. There was a tightening sensation across her belly. Was she going into labor? What if the baby was hurt? She tried to breathe deeply and calm herself, but there was a sharp pain in her chest every time she inhaled. She returned to mindless prayer: *Please God Please God Please God Please God...*

There was pounding at the front door, and she heard it open.

"Yes, officer?" Roger's voice was unnaturally friendly and cooperative.

"We've had a complaint," said a voice she didn't recognize.

"Ah, well, my wife and I had an argument, officer. I'm sorry about the noise."

"Your wife?" The officer sounded surprised. "Where is she?"

"She went to bed."

She tried to yell, but nothing came out of her mouth but a low moan.

"We'll need to see her."

"But she's really very tired, officer."

"I'm sure you won't mind if we search the premises," the voice said, and heavy footsteps pounded into the house.

"Actually — "

"Where is she?" yelled a second voice, followed by a loud thump, and Mary felt giddy with relief. Winslow.

Roger screeched in pain.

"Where's Ms. Bellamy?" the first voice demanded.

Mary couldn't hear Roger's answer, but it must have been accurate, because the cellar door opened and the light bulb right over her head flicked on. Mary slammed her eyes shut and went back to concentrating on her new-found, pain-inspired relationship with God.

"Oh fuck," the officer said, and yelled into his radio for an ambulance.

Upstairs, Roger yelled in pain again and men's voices were raised in argument. Mary began to drift. It was an enormous relief to leave the discomfort behind, and she watched curiously from a vantage point somewhere near the ceiling as Winslow pounded down the stairs, then stopped and picked his way carefully over her body. There was a dark stain spreading out on her sweats, not dark enough to be blood. She must have wet herself, but some-how she couldn't summon up enough concern about it to be embarrassed. It was her body itself that struck her as undignified — the comical bulk of her pregnancy, the way her arm was flung out with something not quite right about it, the way her head hung down over the next step, slowly dripping blood from the nose. Pick that poor woman's head up, she felt like saying, but Winslow merely brushed her hair back from her neck.

"Mary?" he asked, checking the pulse there. "Mary, can you hear me?"

"Is she alive?" the policeman upstairs yelled down.

"Throw me a blanket!" Winslow yelled back. He pulled up her eyelids, then leaned down to listen to her breathing.

The policeman upstairs yelled something back, but Mary didn't catch it.

"NOW!" Winslow screamed, and suddenly Mary was back on the stairs again, in pain again. There was a soft *whump* and she moaned as something was draped over her.

"Mary? Mary! Can you hear me?"

She moaned cooperatively.

"She's coming around!" Winslow yelled.

"Stop," she muttered.

"Stop? Stop what?"

"Yelling," she sighed, then moaned some more.

"Sorry. I'm sorry. I'm so sorry." Was he crying?

Then the EMTs arrived, and Winslow wasn't there anymore; other people started poking and prodding at her. Mary drifted in and out of awareness as they cut apart her sweats, put a collar around her neck, strapped her to a backboard, and babbled to each other. "More tilt," one said. She picked up the word "contraction" at one point and opened her eyes wide. "Baby?" she asked. "Try to relax," she was told.

The cold air outside the house was bracing. Little flecks of snow were drifting down out of a dark sky — the flashing lights made it otherworldly. "Is she going to be all right?" someone yelled, maybe Cici.

"Yes," Mary said, but the EMT, a puffing overweight woman, only smiled grimly.

"I'll see you at the hospital," Winslow's voice said. Then she was in the loud, rocking ambulance and it was too much, too much. The siren, the engine, the brakes, the people talking, the swinging equipment, they all got louder, until they built into one indistinguishable, overwhelming roar.

CHAPTER THIRTY-SIX

WHEN SHE WOKE it was to a cacophony of small beeps. She was lying propped up on her left side, hooked up to more instruments than she would have thought possible, including something strapped across her abdomen, a blood pressure cuff on her arm, a little clamp on her finger, a set of leads off her chest. There was something clamped to her nose and an IV tube taped to her left hand, supplying something clear. Her right arm was encased in some sort of thick pad and hanging in traction. She couldn't turn her head, just her eyes; her neck was immobilized. Her whole body ached. Through the swollen slits of her eyes she watched the fabric curtain that lay across her field of vision, noticing the subtle colors woven into it, the shadows delineated by the drape of it. She yawned. That hurt, too.

"She's awake," someone said. A young, pretty nurse in a bright tunic walked in front of the curtain and smiled at her. "How do you feel?"

This was surely the dumbest-ass question she'd ever heard in her entire life.

"Can you tell me your name?" the nurse asked, her smile faltering.

"Mary Bellamy," she muttered. It came out *Mawy Bewwamy*. Even her mouth was packed with something.

"Do you know what day it is, Mary?"

"Fi-ay?"

"Yes, very good," the nurse said, and ran through her questions.

"Baby?" Mary asked.

"So far so good. We're just monitoring him because you were having some contractions earlier."

"Him?"

The nurse made a little *oops* face. "I'm sorry. You didn't know?"

Huh. A boy. She was having a boy.

The neurologist had her look this way and that and move her toes and fingers and answer questions like "Who's the President of the United States?" and "Why are you here?" He praised her for remembering what happened, as if this was something she should be proud of. He explained that while she had suffered various hairline fractures of the vertebrae as well as a mild concussion, she was stable. There wasn't any compression of the spinal cord, no significant swelling or bleeding, no great risk of further harm. Rest and bracing for a few weeks, physical therapy for a couple of months, and she should be right as rain. Of course, she'd need to be extremely careful to avoid further injury. "You're very lucky," he said.

Lucky? Mary wanted to tell him to go to hell, but figured she didn't need any more enemies at this point in her life.

Dr. Gupta was next up. She performed a painful internal

exam, then smiled. "All good. The baby is doing well. The contractions you were having have stopped, and there are no signs of fetal distress. However, we do have to watch carefully because with trauma like this there's a risk of placental abruption."

"Wha?"

"Well, if that occurs, it means an emergency C-section. The good news is that the baby has an excellent chance of survival even if we have to go that route. But so far it all looks good, so we'll just monitor the situation and keep you on oxygen."

Mary couldn't help picturing tiny little broken bones, but Gupta — once she'd managed to decipher Mary's question — wasn't concerned. "I really don't think you have anything to worry about. If you're doing this well, the baby probably didn't feel a thing."

She thought Mary was doing well.

Well, granted, compared to being dead she was doing well. Compared to the baby being hurt, they were doing well. So apparently gratitude and good humor were expected of her.

Other doctors trooped in. One checked her front teeth and decided they were in satisfactory condition. He removed the packing from her mouth. This was a mercy — at least now if she started to curse they could understand what she was saying. Another explained that her right arm was fractured in two places and three of the fingers on that hand had also suffered hairline fractures; the arm would require a plaster cast once the swelling came down. Her nose and two ribs had minor fractures, too.

Hearing about all these injuries was bad enough, but the pain began to multiply the longer she lay there. When she complained, they gave her something that helped with the pain, but made her feel as if she was floating away. Not sure if she was awake or dreaming or somewhere in between, she saw her kitchen door at the foot of her bed, slowly opening, while she lay there immobile, staring at it in horror, knowing all too well what was going to happen next.

When she finally came back to herself, she lay there and began to replay the night before, along with as many variations as she could imagine that might have ended better. How could she have been stupid enough to leave the kitchen door unlocked, if that was what she'd done? For that matter, what if he came looking for her while she was strung up like this? And where was Winslow? Mary buzzed the nurse and asked, "Is Officer Jennings here?"

The nurse smiled. "He's just outside."

A moment later, Winslow stepped gingerly into the tiny curtained alcove. He winced sympathetically when he saw her and the smile that followed looked forced. "Hey," he said.

"Where's Roger?"

"On his way to the county jail. He couldn't make bail. He confessed, so it shouldn't be hard to get him put away for a while. We'll need a statement from you when you're up to it, though."

"What did he confess to? Trying to kill me?"

"Not exactly. He said he'd gone to see his family for Thanksgiving, but his father told him you were pregnant, and 'got on his case'. So he left, he got drunk, he got into a fight with the guy whose couch he'd been sleeping on. Then he decided he'd crash with you, that you owed him because you'd ruined his Thanksgiving. When you told him to leave he says he just lost it. He said he was afraid of another assault charge when we showed up, so he shoved you in a closet. Claimed he never realized that was the door to the stairs. Cried like a baby, said he never meant to hurt you, he has a drinking problem, he's very sorry, yadda yadda yadda."

"That bastard. I don't suppose there's any chance he'll get the death penalty?"

He smiled a little. "No. But he's in jail now, and since this is a second offense I expect he'll do some time." He pulled a chair over to her left side and sat down. "Tell me if this hurts," he said. Carefully avoiding the IV taped to the top of her hand, he worked his hand under hers.

She stretched her fingers over his, immeasurably soothed by the simple human contact. She looked at him more closely: his uniform was rumpled, his face unshaven, his eyes hooded. "Have you had any sleep?" she asked.

"I got a good nap in. Don't worry about it. I was hoping to see you today anyway, remember?"

She grunted. "I'm not at my best."

"You look damned good to me. You're not dead."

She felt the need to confess. "I think I forgot to lock the kitchen door."

"Yeah, you did. He said he was surprised to find it open."

"I can't believe I was so stupid!"

"Lots of people in this town never lock their doors."

"But I do, normally. He just walked right in! And

then… if I'd just run for it… if I hadn't tried to get him to leave…"

"Mary. He outweighs you, he woke you up in the middle of the night, and you're — what, six, seven months pregnant? Nobody would have put their money on you."

"I let him shove me down those stairs like… like I was the trash!"

"You didn't let him. You couldn't stop him."

"I know. I couldn't. So now what?"

"What do you mean?"

"How am I supposed to not be scared for the rest of my life?" Her voice had risen to a wail.

A nurse appeared at the end of the bed. "Is everything all right?" She gave Winslow a reproving look. "She needs her rest. Why don't you come back another time?"

"No!" Mary shrieked, clutching his hand.

"It's okay, I'm not going anywhere," he said, ignoring the nurse, who glared at him and left. "It's okay. You're safe now. I'll protect you."

She began to cry outright, overwhelmed by a jumbled combination of gratitude, shame, and skepticism. Nice as it was to hear, he couldn't stay here forever, even if he wanted to, which he surely didn't. Besides, she'd heard Roger's cries of pain. It was what the bastard deserved, but still — what it really meant was that Winslow could be dangerous, too.

But there was no way she was going to get into that right now.

"Everyone keeps telling me how lucky I am." She didn't hide her bitterness.

He sighed and began to smooth the hair back on her

forehead. Did he do this for other hysterical crime victims, or was this a sign of more personal affection? But it felt wonderful and eventually she gave up trying to figure anything out and just relaxed into it, as much as she could, which ultimately wasn't very much because crying did bad things to an already painfully swollen nose. "Pass me a tissue?"

He did and she dabbed under her nose, trying to avoid the oxygen. He took the bloody tissue and handed her another one. "The baby's okay?" he asked.

"They say he is. He's sure moving around. Do you want to feel him?"

He looked a little taken aback. But then he nodded, so she guided his hand to where the baby was kicking, and his eyes widened. "Praise God," he murmured.

"I prayed to God through that whole thing. Isn't that pathetic?"

He raised his eyebrows. "You expect me to think that's pathetic?"

"It's not because I suddenly believe in God. It's just because I'm a weenie who can't get through a crisis without groveling for help. I prayed to God and I peed my pants and I did whatever Roger said. I had no dignity at all."

He shook his head. "Dignity is overrated."

"Dignity was the only thing I had left."

"Let it go, Mary. You're going to have to let people help you now, whether you want it or not."

The fierceness with which he spoke surprised her a little. But as for letting go of any remaining shreds of her dignity — well, it wasn't like she had any choice, lying there with numerous foreign objects stuck into her body.

CHAPTER THIRTY-SEVEN

EVENTUALLY WINSLOW LEFT to get some sleep and Mary dozed again. Later in the afternoon the other policeman who had responded to the house, John Carmody, sat and took her statement. Mary's memory was precise, but she hesitated when she came to the part where Roger had demanded to know who she'd slept with.

"Is there any way to keep this private?"

Carmody looked uncomfortable. "He told us you said Arthur Tennant."

Why hadn't Winslow said anything? "So it's going to be public knowledge?"

"I couldn't say."

"Does Arthur know?"

"I have no idea." But Carmody didn't look at her.

Red-faced, she continued her story, but pulled up short at the part on the stairs. How could she possibly remember what she was remembering — her own body, sprawled on the stairs; Winslow picking his way down; the golden curls peeking out from under his hat as he bent over her? "You want my out of body experience in there, too?"

"Excuse me?" Carmody looked startled.

"Never mind." She skipped that part. She'd have to think about it later.

That night Mary was trying to get to sleep when she suddenly realized that she had bills she'd needed to get in the mail that day and no idea whether anybody was taking care of Bob.

Frantic, she persuaded a nurse to call Winslow for her. The nurse gave her the receiver and he reassured her that the cat was fine. Yes, he would be happy to bring in her checkbook and bills the next day. And yes, Roger was still in jail.

Mary wished she could ask him about Arthur, too, but the nurse was hovering.

Late the next morning Winslow arrived brisk and cheerful, with a large cup of coffee and a bag of crullers, as well as a folder of paperwork.

"Does Arthur know what I told Roger?" she asked, before he'd gotten his parka off.

He stopped. "Would you rather talk to Arthur?"

"No."

"I'll get him if you want him."

"I don't want him! I just want to know if he knows."

"Yes, he knows. He knows because I told him. I told him that this had become known in the course of a criminal investigation, and that this was very interesting to me, in as much as he had vigorously denied this very charge to my face on a previous occasion." He began to pace the small curtained area.

His anger was so palpable that Mary couldn't believe he was focusing all of it on Arthur and none of it on her. "I didn't tell you either."

"You didn't lie outright. Not only did he betray his marriage vows, he lied about it — and left you to shoulder all the responsibility."

"Not all of it." Though she supposed their support agreement was void now. She hadn't exactly maintained confidentiality.

"How can you defend him?"

"I'm not defending him," she said, thinking of his other infidelities. "But you knew what his life was like. The man was terribly lonely."

"Lots of people are lonely. He's a priest."

"So, what, he's supposed to be God?"

"I think it's reasonable to expect him to conform to a certain basic level of acceptable behavior. And not to lie about it when he doesn't."

"You could say just the same about me."

"You weren't married. You weren't a priest. And you didn't lie to my face."

No — she'd turned her back, and lied by omission.

Winslow's face had turned stony. "Do you love him?"

"No! That's what's so pathetic."

"Then why wouldn't you tell me? When it was the only—?" His voice cracked.

"Sharon wanted it kept secret."

"*Sharon?*"

"I wanted to tell you, but Arthur said you wouldn't be able to leave it alone — that it would mean the end of his career. And when he told her about it, Sharon didn't want a divorce. She insisted on counseling and secrecy. You've seen the rest."

He looked out of his depth. "He didn't say anything about her."

"What did he say?"

"That he would notify the bishop. That he would resign."

It was all unraveling. Arthur had lost his job. Sharon would be mortified. Poor Lucy, what could she possibly think? The whole town would be appalled. Even Winslow, sooner or later, must let disgust and embarrassment overtake his charitable impulses. He hadn't taken off his parka yet, she noticed.

"I thought his reaction was odd, actually," Winslow said. "He seemed relieved."

She could believe that, but it didn't make her feel any better.

"He was also concerned about you. I told him you were being well cared for."

This was true, even if it wouldn't last. "That's true. I am. Thank you."

It was a puzzle, how to sign the checks. Mary made her best approximation of her signature with her left hand, and agreed with Winslow — who had finally taken off his parka — that a call to the bank on Monday would be a good idea. "This is all the money you have left?" he asked, as he entered the checks into her register.

"No, I have almost $4,000 in savings."

"And that's it?"

"Yes, that's it."

"It's not enough."

"I know. But I was temping, and I was also going to start getting child support from Arthur once the baby was born."

"Oh." She watched it sink in. "Oh."

"Don't worry about it. There's always welfare."

"You're not going on welfare."

"I don't mind. This is why they invented it in the first place."

"You're not going on welfare."

"Whatever." She closed her eyes. She was too tired to argue about it.

Several doctors popped in to examine her through the day, a surprise to Mary who somehow hadn't imagined doctors working weekends. Dr. Gupta had a colorful sari on under her white coat.

"This baby is doing just fine," she said cheerfully.

"I know it's a boy."

"Well, yes, it is a boy. Are you pleased?"

"At least a boy can grow up to defend himself."

Gupta regarded her for a moment and then looked down at her chart. Probably she was searching for notes about her patient's state of mind. Without looking up, she said, "It would be considered quite normal to be feeling helpless or angry or depressed right now."

"Guess I'm pretty normal, then." Mary knew she probably ought to try harder to charm these people she was so utterly dependent on. But she was in no mood.

Gupta gave her a tight smile. "This says you didn't want more Demerol?"

"It felt like being trapped in a nightmare. Is there something else I can take?"

"Perhaps best to avoid other narcotics. I'll see what else we can do," she said. "Slow, deep breathing would help."

"I have broken ribs. Breathing hurts, too."

Gupta sighed and scribbled something in the chart. Probably something like "Patient is whining."

Winslow returned that evening and put Mary on the phone to her mother, who tearfully offered to come out right away. Mary asked her to wait. She'd seen what her face looked like now, bruised and swollen, with a cut lip and two impressive black eyes. She would just as soon heal a bit before giving her mother a look. She was also in no hurry to hear her mother's criticisms: somehow, inevitably, this would all be Mary's fault. Not that she could argue, with that unlocked door.

"You don't want your Mom to come?" Winslow looked puzzled.

"I don't have the energy for her right now." Mary grunted as another spasm in her back demanded attention.

"One of the doctors asked me who would be caring for you after discharge. He said they'd probably send you home in a few days."

They were mad. She couldn't even get up to pee.

"Should I talk to your sister?"

Patty had three kids of her own and a job to worry about, and Mary was still hoping she would be able to take time off to help her when the baby came. By then, Winslow would surely have tired of his current heroic exertions on her behalf. "Once I'm getting around, I can probably manage. Maybe you could you help me out with some errands?"

"Why don't you come out to the farm? Dad and I could take care of you."

"That's very sweet." She imagined lying immobile in that old parlor, doilies dripping onto her while the Jennings ancestors glared from the wall.

"Or I'll stay at your house with you. Dad could come over when I have to work."

"You don't have to do any of this. Why are you being so good to me?"

He gave her a look as if she were the slowest person in the world. "Because I love you?"

Her breath caught. But then again, he'd phrased it as a question. "Really?" she asked. But maybe — "Do you mean like Christian love?"

He looked exasperated. "No, I mean like love love. Like I'm in love. Like I, Winslow, am in love with you, Mary."

Okay, that seemed pretty definitive. She grinned, or she tried to. It hurt like hell because of her cracked lips, so it probably ended up looking more like a wince.

He took her hand and kissed it. "So is that clear enough now or do I need to draw a diagram?"

"I just can't believe that something finally went my way."

"Well, believe it," he said, and wrapped her free hand up in both of his.

"But how can you?"

"I don't know why, I just do. It's not like I haven't tried not to. And it's not like you've made it easy, either."

"I know. I'm sorry." As if to immediately prove his

point, doubt flood in. "But seriously. Are you sure you're not just suffering from an overwhelming urge to — you know — rescue the damsel in distress?"

Winslow groaned. "Oh, here we go...."

"Just think about it, that's all I'm saying! It's not like I don't also have the overwhelming urge to be rescued — especially by you. But what if this is mostly just because you're a really nice guy who likes to save people? What are you going to do when I'm back on my feet, and I'm still the same slut who screwed Arthur Tennant and is having his kid and everybody in this town knows it?"

He shook his head. "Do you honestly think of yourself as a slut?"

"No, but do real sluts ever really think they're sluts? Besides, it's what everybody else in this town is going to think. It's what you yourself thought. I saw it in your face. You were so disgusted." She would never forget that look.

"That was because it felt like Melissa all over again. I'm ninety percent sure she got pregnant just so I'd marry her. And she didn't love me — that became painfully obvious. So when you told me — well, I just thought I'd been a fool again. Even though it was really completely different. I mean, I fairly quickly realized that. But I still couldn't tell for certain whether you really cared for me." His voice dropped to a mumble. "Still can't."

"Oh. I do — I am — I —" But she couldn't make the words he wanted to hear come out of her mouth.

"What?" he said softly.

So she told him the truth. "I'm scared out of my wits."

He nodded tiredly and patted her on the arm. "Yeah, that's pretty much what I figured."

Chapter Thirty-Eight

SUNDAY THEY PRONOUNCED both her and the baby stable and moved Mary to the orthopedic ward, where she was allowed her first official visitors. Bert showed up with flowers and maple nut fudge in a brown paper bag with "Psalm 34 v. 4-8" written on it. She was not yet up to holding a Bible, let alone looking up something in it, but Bert was happy to find it in his own Bible and read it loudly for the benefit of her, her roommate, and the rest of the ward:

> *I sought the LORD, and he answered me*
> *and delivered me out of all my terror.*
>
> *Look upon him and be radiant,*
> *and let not your faces be ashamed.*
>
> *I called in my affliction and the LORD heard me*
> *and saved me from all my troubles.*
>
> *The angel of the LORD encompasses those who fear him,*
> *and he will deliver them.*
>
> *Taste and see that the LORD is good;*
> *happy are they who trust in him!*

"That last verse goes nicely with the fudge," he said.

She thought she wouldn't mind if Bert's Lord would deliver her from all her pain, or at least smite her roommate's television.

Bert offered to come and pray with her every afternoon. Winslow told him to lay off already, then excused himself. Mary listened to his footsteps recede. Her pain meds were due soon, and he made sure they were never late.

When she asked how Laura's visit was going, Bert turned pink. "Winslow told you, I expect, about the nature of his sister's relationship."

"Yes."

"I haven't changed my opinion that it's an abomination. However, as Winslow pointed out, we have had animals on the farm over the years who have exhibited similar tendencies, so I have to admit these things do seem to happen in God's world. Any rate, I'm aiming for forgiveness and humility. That, and keeping my daughter from avoiding me for the rest of my life. They're expecting a baby, too, you know."

"No." Why hadn't Winslow told her?

"Yep. Due in April."

"How'd they manage that?"

Bert twisted his Bible in his hands, clearly embarrassed. "Got them a sperm donor for insemination. Kind of like what we used to do with our cows. Carla told me she asked Winslow if he would supply the goods, but he declined. Actually, she said he was too 'weirded out,' that's how she put it, which is the least a brother would be in that situation if you ask me."

"How do you like Carla?"

He wrinkled his nose. "To be honest, I'm not sure I'd like her even if she was straight as a ruler. But Laura does, so we'll try."

"They're still here?"

"One more night." Bert sighed. "It's a mixed blessing."

After Bert left, she asked Winslow why he hadn't brought his sister by, and he said that he wanted to, but it would mean bringing Carla by, too, and Carla could be hard to take. "She lectures. Last night she was delivering this discourse on how men abuse women all over the globe. I know it's true, but after a while it feels like she's abusing *us*. And then she suggested to Dad that Mom's eating might have been her way of protecting herself from the pressure of never-ending male demands."

Mary couldn't imagine the sheer tactlessness required. "What did he do?"

"Turned white and left the room. Laura was pretty pissed at her, too."

"Why didn't you tell me they were expecting?"

He grimaced. "I was afraid you might lose the baby. Then that would just be one more... you know, baby shower."

She frowned. Were they telling him things they hadn't told her? Was it possible they were still downplaying the baby's condition? Anxiously, she replayed her most recent conversation with Dr. Gupta. "What about now? Do they really think he's fine?"

"If they had any concerns, you'd be in obstetrics, not orthopedics."

"You're sure?"

"Yeah, I'm sure."

She felt a surge of fury. "Privacy is a total joke at this hospital! How is it that you know more about my case than I do?"

He raised his eyebrows. "I don't think I do. But I am a cop and you're still a party in an open criminal investigation." He glanced towards her roommate's closed curtain. "On the other hand, yes, privacy is a total joke at this hospital."

She tried, gingerly, to shift her position in bed, but gave up. It hurt to lie still, but it hurt even more to move. Where was her next dose, anyway? "Why didn't you say yes to Laura and Carla's request? Your sister was probably hoping the baby would have a genetic relationship to her."

He eyed her roommate's curtain again. "I almost agreed. I even thought maybe this was going to be my only chance to have a kid in this life." He lowered his voice. "I just don't like Carla that much. What if she and Laura break up? Then I've got this relationship with a child whose mother I don't particularly like, while my sister has no direct biological relationship and only a questionable legal relationship. It was just too… weird."

"You want to talk weird." Mary rubbed her belly.

"You're not Carla. I like you."

"You have no biological relationship with this kid."

"So I'll have a legal relationship with him. You marry me, that's my kid. We either put my name on the birth certificate, or I adopt him."

"What if he looks just like Arthur?"

"If he looks just like Arthur the poor kid is going to need a good dad."

Mary laughed, then groaned, then gasped. It was late afternoon, she was tired, and the pain was spiking.

Winslow leaned in. "So is this an idea you're willing to consider?"

She tried to focus. "What?"

"Getting married?"

"Oh not *now*." She meant that she couldn't even think, but he drew back, obviously stung, and she realized he had taken this as yet another rejection. He got up and walked a circle around her half of the room and then stood at the door. She watched in a half-daze of pain and heard a low moan escape, not even realizing at first that she was the one making it, that it was the lower register of a howl of abandonment because Winslow was finally going to make his escape.

But he didn't. He sighed and returned, dropping back into the chair at her bedside.

She let loose with tears of mingled relief and frustration. "Please don't leave me. I couldn't bear it."

"Don't worry," he said, and took her hand. "You're not getting rid of me that easily."

By the middle of the week Mary was making her own way to the hospital bathroom and the idea of going home to her own bed no longer appalled her. When they discharged her, Winslow drove. The world outside his Toyota seemed excessively gray, almost ghost-like. But of course, it was early December, a grey time of year.

She was worried how she would feel, stepping into the kitchen again after what had happened there, but she barely recognized it. The worn vinyl floor was now refinished wood; the wall and cabinets had been painted soothing shades of taupe and cream; even the kitchen table had a new coat of paint and a small vase of cheerful flowers. The living room had been painted, too. "Oh my God," she said. "It's so beautiful!" She hobbled over to a pretty chintz sofa. "I can't believe it. You got me a new sofa?"

Winslow grinned. "No, that's your old sofa. Peggy replaced the cushions and slip-covered it. There's a rug from our attic coming, too, but we sent it out for cleaning first."

"But — how did you manage all this?" He'd been at her side or at work all week.

"Dave did most of it. You know, my cousin, Peggy's husband. He does home improvements in the off season. Laura and Carla picked out all the colors. And Annie and her friends came in last night and cleaned the place and stocked the kitchen."

Mary hobbled about, touching surfaces, feeling weepy at the effort they had put in for her. Then reality sank in. "Everyone's been so generous. But this must have cost quite a bit."

"It really didn't. Dave gave us the family rate. Don't worry about it. It's your coming-home present."

Suddenly exhausted, Mary shuffled over to a kitchen chair and lowered herself into it carefully. "I don't deserve all this. But thank you."

He looked pained. Probably her thank you had been too formal.

Bob padded in cautiously and meowed plaintively at her.

"Hello, stranger," Mary said, happy for the distraction. She held out her hand.

Bob sniffed it curiously, then went and rubbed against Winslow's legs, not hers.

"He knows who's more likely to feed him tonight," Winslow said. "You are going to let me stay, aren't you? You've got to have somebody." He sat down in the other chair. He looked worn out.

"Please. I'm counting on it." The thought of sleeping alone in this house was terrifying. She smiled, trying hard to appear jolly. "You're sure you don't mind ruining your reputation?"

"I still hope you'll make an honest man of me someday."

Mary smiled, but it was a strained smile. She didn't know why she couldn't just say *yes, Winslow, marry me tomorrow and we'll live happily ever after*. She just knew she wasn't ready. Was it because she was now so utterly dependent on him? Was it some deep-seated instinct for self-preservation that helplessly equated Winslow with Roger just because they were both men? Sometimes she wondered if the devil that drove her to deny him was pushing to see how much he would take before he hit her.

Or left her again, which any man with sense would have done by now.

Winslow got up and opened a kitchen cabinet.

"So does this have any effect on the no sex before marriage rule?" she asked.

He grunted. "Didn't you hear? I've changed it to the no sex before your bones heal rule. But only if you agree to marry me. Otherwise, forget it."

Mary raised her eyebrows. "All I have to do is agree to marry you?"

"And mean it."

"This is a pretty big shift for you."

"You think? We'd be engaged."

"You're not worried you'll burn in hell for the sin of fornication?"

"That was never my concern. I don't even believe in hell."

"You don't?"

"You know what hell is?" He closed the first cabinet and opened a second and stared into it. "Hell is finding the love of your life and then losing it. And then coming to the sick realization that you only really lost it because you threw it away in a fit of wounded pride."

She swallowed. She *had* felt thrown away. "I gave you ample reason."

He shook his head. "When I think that you could have died, or been paralyzed..." After a moment he added, "A point came when even Dad told me I was being too judgmental."

"Your *dad* said you were being too judgmental."

"Yep."

"That's pretty funny."

He frowned at her. "Maybe now. It wasn't at the time."

CHAPTER THIRTY-NINE

BERT OFTEN STAYED with her when Winslow was at work. He didn't approve of Winslow's decision to live with Mary, but appeared to be consoling himself with the idea that Mary was in an interesting state — one that might make her conducive to being steered onto the path of righteousness. He read her scripture at great length, including the entire gospels of Mark and Luke — the latter, he explained, was perfect for her because of all the healing going on.

Mary was content to indulge Bert, partly because she was afraid of being alone in the house, but also because she found it more interesting than she'd expected. She'd only gotten her gospels in little bits before, never in one sweep through. Jesus emerged as an intriguing and sympathetic figure with radical tendencies Mary would have considered incompatible with Bert's fervent political beliefs, though Bert certainly didn't see it that way.

If Jesus really were the son of God, Mary wished he would show up at the house, rub a little divine spit on her back and arm, and say "arise." However, it still seemed more likely to her that he was a particularly charismatic delusional who'd become the sad beneficiary of one of the greatest spin jobs of all time.

Arthur came to see her once before he left town. Bert, clearly rattled that he'd had the nerve to show up, only let him in reluctantly. Bert told Mary he was going to run a quick errand, all the while looking beseechingly at her as if she might be tempted to break his son's heart.

She made tea for Arthur and herself, a slow and deliberate procedure with one working arm and a back brace that kept her upright and facing resolutely forward. Arthur seemed oblivious, talking through all of it, updating her on his fast progress through the early stages of divorce. Sharon had left him as soon as he'd told her he was resigning. He was leaving for North Carolina and his brother's the next day. He had already loaded a U-Haul and wanted to be gone before Sharon returned to pack up everything else.

"Well, I hope you have a good trip," Mary said. She sat down carefully.

"Before I go, I believe we have a financial matter to discuss."

"I'm not sure we do, actually."

"No?" Arthur's eyebrows rose.

"Winslow wants to marry me and adopt the baby."

Arthur looked concerned. "And this is what you want?"

Mary smiled. "Yes, I think so."

"You *think* so? Do you love him?"

"Yes." Why was it so easy to tell Arthur this and so hard to tell Winslow?

Arthur came and kneeled in front of her. He put his

hand on her knee, but there was no thrill of contact this time. "For God's sake, Mary, don't rush into something as serious as marriage. How do you know you're not just acting out of fear? Or a sense of obligation? I know he's staying with you. You must feel very grateful for his help."

This was true. She felt so much safer when Winslow was in the house — not just physically safer, but better grounded to reality. These days she often felt oddly distanced from her own existence — except when she woke up from nightmares, heart thumping, sweat-soaked, the darkness hyper-real and ripe with menace.

"I fell in love with him before all this happened," she said. Arthur didn't need to know how thankful she was to have Winslow, who had somehow gotten out of all his night shifts, wake up with a grunt beside her to murmur reassurances. He had given up sleeping on the sofa after her first nightmare. Now they slept in the same bed like an old married couple — an old married couple that had never gotten around to having sex. She wasn't sure exactly what to make of this, but she was in no fit state to push the matter. Besides, he had that rule about getting engaged first.

She put down her tea. "Actually, Arthur, there's something I want to ask you."

Arthur looked eager. "Yes?"

"Is there any historical evidence for the divinity of Jesus?"

He nearly choked on his tea. "I'm sorry. Excuse me." He coughed. "That wasn't the kind of question I was expecting."

She explained that she'd been forced to spend part of each day with Bert being caught up on the Good News.

"And I guess I just wanted to know, how much of this stuff is even the least bit verifiable?"

"His divinity, not at all. That's a matter of faith. In terms of the events of his life, there is objective historical evidence of Jesus' ministry, trial, and crucifixion. There's not really a scrap of evidence about his early life, or his miraculous birth." He sipped his tea. "Frankly, I won't mind giving all that 'Away in a Manger' stuff a miss this year."

"I guess that's understandable."

"It's no reflection on our situation. I just don't believe for one minute that Mary was a virgin."

"Really?" This would make Jesus much less of a nut-case in Mary's eyes. "But wouldn't that make Christianity a total sham?"

Arthur drew back. "Excuse me?"

"If Jesus isn't really the son of God?" Hello?

"Just because he wasn't the literal son of God doesn't mean his teachings aren't worth following." He studied her. "Is it possible that Bert Jennings is converting you right under our noses?"

"Oh no. No. And he'd consider you a terrible heretic."

Arthur looked sour. "I guess he can just join the crowd."

"So what are you going to do for Christmas? Stay home and dodge all references to the virgin birth?"

He got up restlessly, moving to the sink to look out the kitchen window. "I'll do whatever my brother's family does. Lucy is coming down, too."

"How's she doing?"

He shrugged and turned to lean against the counter with his arms folded. Mary rotated in her seat so she could see him. "She's extremely angry at me, of course. At her mom, too. But she's curious about the baby. She wants to know if she'll be able to see it someday."

"Him. It's a boy."

"A boy?" Arthur sounded choked. He turned away to look out the window.

Mary was silent. She realized that a second son inevitably involved Arthur in painful memories of Matthew. But she also knew that one of Winslow's greatest fears was that Arthur would decide to pursue his paternity rights. "But he's not going to be her little brother. We can agree on that, can't we?"

Arthur looked over sharply. "I'm hardly in a position to argue, am I?"

Mary felt a surge of resentment. "No, you're not."

Arthur wasn't the only one to suggest to Mary that she shouldn't rush into marriage. Dr. Gupta had referred her to a therapist who told her that her symptoms were normal for a survivor of trauma and likely to dissipate significantly in a few months, especially if she continued working with him. This struck Mary as self-serving, but even she realized she might be having trust issues. He warned her not to rush into marriage just because the baby was coming, she was afraid to be alone, and Winslow wanted it. Dr. Gupta, on the other hand, confided to Mary that she had decided to accept her arranged marriage, because the man chosen for her struck her as a better choice than anyone she had met on her own. Mary felt her own case was not that different. The objective evidence was overwhelming that Winslow was as good a man as she was ever likely to meet. And he even loved her.

Of course, goodness wasn't everything. Their chaste sleeping arrangements had a sweet intimacy all their own, but they worried her. Did Winslow find her less attractive now, in her pregnant and crippled state? And if that were true, what would he make of her later, when she was the flabby, lactating mother of someone else's child?

That night she wanted a bath, so he helped her get out of her brace. She stayed in until the water cooled, debating whether what she was contemplating was awful or brilliant.

She got herself out of the tub and wrapped herself in a towel. "Winslow, could you help me?" she called. She knew he'd already settled into bed with *What to Expect When You're Expecting*. She only consulted it when she was feeling paranoid about some symptom, but Winslow dutifully read it at least a month ahead.

He arrived quickly, clad in his customary t-shirt and drawstring pajamas. "Yes?"

"Could you spread some oil on my back?"

"Oil?"

"Yeah, oil." She turned away from him and let the towel drop.

She didn't miss his quick intake of breath. They hadn't been trying for complete modesty — it was impossible, given the logistics of getting her bathed — but there had never been such flagrant nudity between them.

"It's right there." She pointed at the baby oil on the counter.

His breathing had quickened. "Are you trying to seduce me?"

"Yes." She peeked in the mirror — but he was squirting oil into his palm. At least he hadn't run for it. "Ow, that's cold!"

"You need something cold thrown on you. You're not ready for this yet."

"Yes I am. That's right, just rub it all over — ah — can you get my butt, too?"

He sighed and complied, taking his time, moving in closer. "Nice ass," he growled.

"You're sure the pregnancy isn't a turn-off?"

His answer sounded strangled. "A turn-off?" He smoothed his oiled hands around her butt and up her hips, over her round belly, up to her swollen breasts. He weighed one in each hand while bending to kiss her neck.

Apparently he wasn't totally appalled at the idea of being seduced, then. She felt almost lightheaded with relief. "You do know I love you, don't you?" But would he think this long overdue confession really counted in this context?

She felt him smile against her neck. "Sure you're really up to this?"

"We'll just have to be a little careful."

He turned her carefully around and kissed her thoroughly. "Go find a comfortable position in bed, okay? I need to wash."

She pulled the sheets on the bed down and lay on her side near the edge, goose bumps rising in the chill of the bedroom. When he walked out, she watched with appreciation; he was completely naked and impressively erect.

"You really sure about this?" he asked. He looked flushed, but apprehensive.

In answer, she reached out. "Come here."

"You don't have to —"

"If you could just get a little closer —"

He must have understood what she wanted; he moved to just the spot she needed and gasped in pleasure as she took him in her mouth. After a moment he leaned over and began to gently explore her folds with his finger, spreading her wetness with grunts of satisfaction while she worked on him. After what seemed like very little time, however, he pulled away.

"What?" she asked.

"Have mercy, Mary. It's been awhile, okay?"

"I don't expect perfection, you know, we're both — *ah! Ah!*" Winslow had gotten up on the bed and knelt between her legs and was doing things that made her forget all about the cold. She gasped and moaned. Clearly, it wasn't just ugly men who could make good lovers. Soon she was crying out as an orgasm rocked her. The relief was so intense, so overwhelming, that she burst into tears.

"Hey, are you okay?"

"Yes!" She sniffed and caught her breath as he pulled himself up alongside her and caressed her damp hair. She could feel his penis bob against her hip. "Oh yes."

"Is it okay if I try...?" He scrunched up behind her, his erection poking her clumsily.

"Please do."

"You say if it hurts."

"Okay." She felt so good at the moment, she couldn't imagine anything hurting.

"I mean it."

"Would you please just get in there?" She reached down with her good arm, trying to guide him, but he managed it on his own, slipping in and filling her up. She grunted in pleasure.

"You okay?"

He was probably afraid to move, she realized. "Fabulous. Go for it."

Cautiously, he began to thrust. It felt wonderful and she indulged the urge to arch against him. Her back instantly reminded her that this was not a good idea.

"That hurt?" He stopped abruptly.

"That was my fault, not yours. Please. I like it." He resumed cautiously. It probably wasn't good for him, she thought, this slow, careful pumping while she lay on her side doing an impression of a warm corpse. What kind of turn-on could that be? He must feel horribly restrained. Or perhaps she wasn't tight enough — maybe he was used to younger women. It would get even worse after she gave birth, wouldn't it? Desperate to contribute something, she bore down on him with her pelvic muscles, and thought there was a little moan of appreciation in response. She wished she were comfortable talking dirty — *come on baby, oh you know what I like, oh you're so big, baby* — but she couldn't bring herself to do it. For all she knew he'd be horrified. Instead, she searched for his hand, stuck his fingers in her mouth and sucked. He moaned and pumped faster. "I love you," she said, because it was the only thing she could say, and he cried out and came in an extended series of jerks.

They lay together in the bed, still joined. "Thank you," he sighed.

She lay there, basking in the intimacy, but feeling bleak about her own role in it. "I'll be better at this someday, I promise."

"Stop that. It was beautiful. You're beautiful."
"Even though I made you break your rule?"
"That's all right. I was already a lost man."

CHAPTER FORTY

A WEEK BEFORE CHRISTMAS, Roger was sentenced to eighteen months. He had pleaded guilty to assault to avoid facing more serious charges. With credit for time served and the realities of parole, he would probably be out in less than a year. Mary was incensed at first, but the district attorney suggested she might prefer to avoid a trial in which her own history could easily become as much the focus as Roger's, especially since she was now living with one of the arresting officers. At the hearing itself Roger's parents sat behind him. They looked grim and never met her eyes — they had already, through a lawyer, tried and failed to get her to drop the charges in exchange for a monetary settlement that would have more than covered his debts. This meant Mary was still stuck with the bills, but at least Roger would spend some real time in jail.

Roger tearfully explained that he knew that what he had done was wrong, that he was sorry, that he realized he had a serious drinking problem and needed help. He had in fact turned it over to a higher power. "Because of my alcohol addiction, I wronged someone I care about very deeply. I'm seeking God's help to make sure I never do anything like that ever again, and I can only hope that someday Mary will find it in her heart to forgive me." He turned and gave her a tearful smile.

Mary seethed.

Later that day she stood at the top of the cellar stairs, staring down at the landing and remembering the undignified heap her body had made lying there. Dave had carpeted the stairs and whitewashed the walls, but it was still a steep descent into a creepy hole in the ground.

Winslow watched her. "What do you think about selling this place in the spring?"

She continued staring down the steps. "I wouldn't mind."

"We could buy one of those condos. Or we could use the time we're still here to make some improvements at the farm, and move in there."

"Live with your dad?" She would have said no before. But Bert had been a good companion in her convalescence. He still launched into jeremiads about the evils of the modern age, but usually managed to avoid getting personally insulting. One afternoon he had decried the media's promotion of Godless homosexuality one moment and proudly related the results of Carla's most recent ultrasound the next.

"He's agreed we can ditch the doilies," Winslow said. "But he'd expect us to get married first if we're going to live there."

"If we try to do anything soon, I might drop this baby right in the middle of it."

"I'd be willing to take that chance."

Mary closed the cellar door and lowered herself into a chair at the kitchen table. "Okay."

"Okay? Okay, we can get married?"

"Yeah, let's get married." She smiled and held her hand out to him.

"And move to the farm? We don't have to, you know."

"It makes more sense to live at the farm." It was also a comfort to think that Roger didn't know where it was, and that Abigail would bark if he showed up.

They were married on a Saturday morning just after the New Year. Mary wore a cream-colored maternity dress and carried a simple bouquet of flowers from the market tied with a bow. She was not yet walking well enough for a processional, so she sat in the front pew next to Annie while more people than she'd expected filled the pews behind them. Winslow stood at the front in a new suit, giving her cautious looks while she breathed in short puffs and tried to stay calm.

He edged over to her. "You okay?"

She could see Bert in her peripheral vision, peering over. She saw Winslow exchange a concerned look with Annie. She thought: *What if this is another terrible mistake?*

He kneeled down in front of her. There was a fine sheen of perspiration across his forehead. "Mary? We don't have to do this if you're not up to it."

Was the poor man really volunteering to be stood up at the altar?

"No, please, let's do it. I'll be okay." She could get through this. *Breathe,* she thought.

*

"Breathe," Winslow urged her, six weeks later.

Mary had rolled over in bed that night and felt her water break. She started demanding the epidural before they'd left the driveway. She hadn't had any serious contractions, but she was bound to any minute. They'd put her in a birthing room and shot her full of Pitocin and still hadn't given her an epidural. "Fuck breathing!" she cried. "I want the good stuff! God damn it, I've waited long enough, give it to me!"

"Mary, we've only been in here for twenty minutes."

"It's been MONTHS!" she wailed.

Dr. Gupta shared a look with Winslow and told the nurse to get the anesthesiologist.

Perhaps unsurprisingly, given her luck with pain, the epidural didn't take completely, although it was probably better than nothing. Spurred by horse hormones, her labor galloped along. Six hours later she pushed her baby out.

"He's beautiful," Winslow said, when they pronounced the infant healthy and laid him down on her chest.

Mary thought William looked like a strange little red caricature of an old man, but she didn't care; he was hers. She was enormously relieved that he didn't have a little broken baby nose or show any other signs of Roger's assault. While Winslow was off making phone calls, she looked carefully for signs of Arthur — crags, dark hair, grey eyes, incipient melancholy — but William was bald, blue-eyed, and placidly content to alternate between suckling and sleeping.

Winslow smiled as he joined her in her room. His animal instincts ought to be rebelling against this: in nature and even among some humans, males had a tendency to murder the progeny of their rivals. But Winslow looked smitten as he tenderly traced his index finger along the baby's sleeping form.

"I can't see much Arthur in him," he said. "Maybe the nose?" He looked from Mary's nose to the baby's and back again.

Mary was relieved the question was not going to sit silently between them.

"I called him too," Winslow said.

Mary looked at him, surprised.

"He got a little emotional. I guess it brings back memories of Matthew."

"Yeah. He got like that when I told him it was going to be a boy."

"You didn't tell me that."

Mary wasn't sure how he meant that; was he accusing her of keeping secrets? "I knew it was a sore subject."

His face turned red. "Look, don't protect me from sore subjects."

Did he really mean that? "He also told me Lucy wanted to see the baby."

Winslow frowned. "Couldn't we just send her a picture?"

Mary supposed she owed Lucy at least that much, but she hated to think of it falling into Sharon's hands. She could imagine her sticking pins in it and muttering incantations.

Winslow lowered his head to Mary's chest, level with the baby's, and gently fingered William's tiny hand outstretched in sleep. The baby reacted by stretching his fingers and sighing. "You really don't think Arthur will try to claim paternity?"

"I think he's just relieved to be off the hook."

Winslow caressed William's tiny fingers. "What an idiot."

After some deliberation, Mary and Winslow sent photos of William to Arthur to share with Lucy, and offered her a visit. There followed an unpleasant period of weeks during which unexpected knocks on the door made them both tense. Eventually Arthur sent his thanks and said that Lucy had decided to decline for now. He also sent an illustrated children's Bible, a copy of his family health history, an old snapshot of himself , "to satisfy any future curiosity William may have about his biological father," and a book of contemporary theology for Mary. He made no mention at all of Winslow, unless he was encompassed in the closing: "Wishing your new family all of God's blessings." Mary hoped she detected a note of finality.

Winslow asked that they plan a baptism for William, and Mary felt it would be churlish to say no, although she was not thrilled that this would take place during a regular service at St. Andrew's in front of all those people who knew exactly where this baby had come from. But when Laura and Carla said they wanted to baptize their baby, too — and the interim priest didn't faint at the idea — Mary was able to take comfort at the prospect of splitting her notoriety with a lesbian couple. Even better, this meant the whole thing was put off until July, after they had moved to the farm, when church attendance was sure to be low.

Not long after they moved to the farm, Mary received a

postal forward from her old address, sent from Walpole State Prison:

Dearest Mary,

With the help of the prison ministry here I have recently been blessed to be born again in the love of our risen Savior Jesus Christ. I understand now that I was wrong to be unfaithful to you, wrong to seek a divorce from you, and wrong to judge your own behavior. I am very sorry I hurt you. I only hope that someday you can forgive me.

It has become clear to me that if I had not been drinking and if we had not been living a life so divorced from the goodness of God, we would never have had the problems we had. I would love to talk to you about all of this after my release next month, and that is why I am writing to you. Mary, would you please grant me this chance to make amends? It would mean everything to me. It could be a new beginning for both of us. I long to share the miracle of my redemption!

In the Never-Ending Love of Jesus,

Roger Mitchell Bellamy

Horrified, Mary showed the letter to Winslow. "Is he allowed to do this?"

His face darkened as he read. "No. Don't worry, I'll take care of it."

Mary looked at the grim set of Winslow's jaw and felt a qualm. "Legally, you mean."

He smiled wanly. "Are you afraid I'll go beat him up?"

That was exactly what she feared… or perhaps it was exactly what she wanted.

Winslow sighed. "What's sad is that all I'd have to do is mention something to the right person and he probably would get the crap beaten out of him."

Her mouth went dry. All he would have to do is say something? "I'd be awfully tempted if it was really that easy."

She felt that old assessing eye on her again. "But then I wouldn't be any better than Roger, would I?"

"You'd have a long way to go to get as low as Roger."

"Not that far. I'd owe a favor to the worst kind of people."

She sighed. "I guess you're right." Even in her hatred she understood that revenge would damage him more than it would help her. She read the letter again, marveling at Roger's oily mastery of religious schmaltz. Where on earth had he learned this stuff? Was there a book of ready-to-use Born Again letters in the prison library? "Anyway, if he's such a good Christian now, how come he doesn't mention his debts?"

"Good point," Winslow said. The bank had agreed to remove her from the foreclosure, but Mary had finally settled on a payment plan for the credit card debts so that she could slowly rebuild her credit. Perhaps she would sue Roger for every penny if he ever had enough to make it worthwhile.

There, a more practical reason not to beat him up.

She knew she might need that credit if she ever went looking for a job again, but for now, she was a housewife and enjoying it. She'd taken over most of the cooking, though not the bread-baking. She and Bert had planted an acre to try out the cut-flower market, although the baby and her back kept her from doing much of the manual labor and they seldom managed to sell even a quarter of their stock. Winslow said it looked real nice and was greatly preferable to a pair of llamas.

CHAPTER FORTY-ONE

WHEN MARY FINALLY met Laura that summer she thought she was a lot like her brother — tall, beautiful, stoic, and kind. Carla, on the other hand, was small and dark and full of nervous energy, like a little bird with a racing metabolism, constantly replenishing herself and everyone around her with ideas instead of birdseed. She had been reading everything ever written about raising healthy, happy, well-adjusted, intelligent and brave little girls, and she eagerly dispensed to Mary and Winslow any such advice that might also apply to William. Breastfeeding loomed large in her views and she had a disconcerting habit of popping out an engorged breast to feed Sophie without regard to Bert or Winslow's sensibilities.

"Carla, honey," Laura said once, after the men had beaten another hasty retreat, "Must you? Mary goes in the other room."

"I see no reason to hide a beautiful, natural womanly function like breastfeeding a child," Carla said, so promptly that Mary suspected she'd been eagerly awaiting an opportunity to raise their consciousness.

"This isn't California. Even if you just tried to cover it up a little —"

"They'd get used to it if they tried. Why do we live in a world where a natural act like breastfeeding is seen as immodest? Why should a nursing woman have to get up and go hide somewhere, like it's a shameful act? Women have catered to men's misogynistic anxieties for far too long."

Laura rolled her eyes at Mary, but sat down next to Carla to play with Sophie's tiny feet, which were flexing and pointing contentedly while she suckled. Mary kept her mouth shut. Carla's righteous fervor somehow felt a lot like Bert's.

The interim priest was a cheerful young woman not long out of seminary. She seemed delighted to have two infants to baptize and unfazed by the unconventional family dynamics, but she did look perplexed during Carla's long explanation that she believed in a higher power, a goddess/god, and respected many of the principals of Judeo-Christianity, but felt she must forcefully reject the Christian claim for exclusivity, as well as its long history of patriarchal oppression. After a short silence, the priest suggested, "Let's walk through the order for baptism, shall we?" and led them into the sanctuary to rehearse.

Mary gazed at the figure of Jesus on the cross and wondered whether he could possibly have foreseen that his life and death would someday be reduced to these stiff recitals. No doubt many stood here sincerely seeking eternity for their children, but so many others, like her, were merely participating in an arcane tribal social ritual. Roger, she suspected, had embraced Jesus like some sort of lucky Get-Out-of-Jail card. She held William, who was asleep, and Winslow held the prayer book as the priest talked them through the ceremony. What did all this stuff really mean to Winslow, anyway? Did he really believe that a few words and a little sanctified water could work soul-magic? Or did Christianity appeal to him as a moral code, an overarching version of the laws he enforced everyday in his job?

When Carla stopped the priest to ask how strongly she felt about keeping in that dated reference to Satan, Mary traded William for the prayer book and read ahead. The language seemed familiar, but new, too. When she read, "Will you persevere in resisting evil, and, whenever you fall into sin, repent and return to the Lord?" she couldn't help thinking of Arthur, who had presumably repented and returned to the Lord numerous times. Could a person wear existential grooves in his soul, with the same sins washed out by the same repentance over and over, forming moral gullies or valleys or even great gaping maws?

Mary felt nostalgic for all those years in which her own sense of personal guilt consisted primarily of day-to-day omissions: failing to feed starving third-world children, failing to inquire after a friend's concerns, forgetting a nephew's birthday, never getting around to a thank you note. Despite them, she'd felt relatively confident that she was a generally good person.

These days she was aware of having racked up an impressive array of faults, failures, stupidities — sins. Yet she couldn't fully regret any of them. There was the adultery, of course — stupid and wrong, but it had given her William. There was fornication with Winslow, which she did not for even a moment repent. She had not honored her mother as she ought, but then her mother was no saint either. Mary knew she was a pathetic excuse for an aunt, but it wasn't her fault all her nieces and nephews lived in Arizona. She was less than perfect as a wife or mother or daughter-in-law, but she felt she was doing her best. She still hated Roger, but surely any omnipotent being could understand that. Even so, she accepted that Roger was not the only culprit in their relationship: with the clarity of hindsight she detected avarice in her decision to wed him and a kind of willful stupidity in staying with him when it wasn't respect for the commitment that kept her there so much as a stubborn refusal to act even when reality was slapping her in the face.

It struck Mary that her greatest sin in life was exactly that passivity — that refusal to engage — which was not unlike what she was doing now. Her out-of-body experience had suggested to her that she possessed a soul, and she had even grown to believe that Jesus was at least a prophet worthy of respect. Yet she still held back from these rites. Meanwhile Winslow, an intelligent and capable adult, embraced them. Even Carla, with all her politically correct adjustments, was more engaged than Mary was.

"Are you okay with this?" Winslow whispered, as the priest moved on.

She nodded. Of course she was okay with it. She wasn't really doing it.

During the baptism the next morning Mary let the words wash over her while she coped with the logistics of fancy dress and fussy child. William cried and Sophie didn't, which Mary could tell was highly gratifying to Carla. Winslow and Bert and Laura looked happy and their guests looked happy and most of the small July congregation looked pleased, too. She really ought to be grateful these people were smiling and wishing her the peace of the Lord instead of throwing stones or forcing her to wear a scarlet *A* on her nursing blouse. They could have boycotted the proceedings, as Winslow's brother had. Stephen had told Winslow that although he might manage to gloss over the sinful origins of Mary's child, there was simply no way to protect his children from the morally confusing sight of a baby with two mothers.

Her own family had not made the trip, though not because of any moral objections Mary knew of. Patty had planned to come, even bought tickets, but her youngest had just broken his collar bone. Her mother had murmured about making it, then demurred because her new husband wasn't up to it and she couldn't leave him alone — he would never remember to take his blood pressure medication.

It was hot and muggy that Sunday afternoon. Laura and Carla went up to pack for their trip home and fell asleep with Sophie between them on the old sagging bed in the guest room. Bert had turned on the TV in the family room and was snoring his way through a Red Sox game. Mary was so reluctant to move that she suckled William right there with Bert, confident that he was asleep and Carla would not come down and make a crusade out of it. After a while, Winslow brought her a glass of lemonade and sat next to her, watching the game, but looking restless.

He hadn't driven off exploring in a long time, had he? She felt a pang — he must sometimes regret getting tied down so quickly and thoroughly.

"Bored?" she asked softly.

"Hot."

"It is hot."

"I want to show you that swimming hole."

"Now?" William had just fallen asleep, and she was in no mood to move either.

She caught his slight sag at her response. "How about when he wakes up?" she asked. She wanted to reverse that sag, but she was also thinking: diapers, water, sunscreen, hat, mosquito repellent, towels, oh my God what if he drowns?

"Give me that baby," Bert growled from where he was still stretched out on the sofa.

Winslow smiled and lifted William off Mary and deposited him on Bert's chest. The baby stretched his fingers and slumbered on.

"I thought you were asleep," Mary said. Had he seen her feeding William?

Bert yawned. "I believe I may have missed an inning or two. Go on now."

"I'll get my suit," she said to Winslow. Would she even fit into it anymore?

"Never mind that," Winslow said. "Let's go while the going is good."

They snuck out of the house, leaving Abigail even though she whined pitiably. Mary felt shy as they walked down the tractor run to the river. She was still plump from pregnancy and stiff from her injuries. She would probably never feel the same easy confidence in her body that she had the summer before, when they'd canoodled on that rock in the river. Somehow it seemed a lot easier to ignore all this at night in their bedroom than out between fields of corn in broad daylight.

"He's fine," Winslow said, when she stopped. She sighed and followed him along the river bank. Every sound, from the cicadas humming to the wind rustling in the corn to the water babbling in the river, seemed to contain muffled infant cries.

"Are you okay?" he asked.

"I'm fine."

He walked on. After a moment, he stopped and turned around. "You know, you don't have to do something just because I ask you."

"What do you mean?"

"Like this. Like the baptism. Like the wedding. Sometimes I feel like everything you do is because you think you owe me."

"I do owe you."

His face reddened. "I didn't marry you so you would owe me. We're even, okay? You need to start doing things because you want to do them."

Winslow didn't understand. Given her own druthers, she might sit on the sofa for the rest of her life. "But I enjoy being with you."

He frowned and set off again. He stopped at a bend in the river where a rough circle of boulders had bottled it up, creating a green pool half overhung by a gnarled old willow. It was beautiful. And they wouldn't be here if it were solely up to her. "You know, sometimes I just need a little push. Besides, I trust you."

He kicked off his shoes and then, to her surprise, took off his shorts and shirt and underwear, too, and laid them on a rock. He stood there in the dappled sunlight under the willow, a beautiful naked man with just the beginnings of a little paunch at his belly. Mary looked around nervously to see if anyone could see them, but it was all Jennings land on this bank and a low bluff hid River Road on the other, and in any case the willow hung down like a curtain. "You need to trust yourself, too," he said, and jumped into the water with a mighty splash. He came up and blinked water out of his eyes. His wet hair lay uncharacteristically dark on his head. "Having said that, don't jump unless you can get past that boulder there."

"I never jump." Mary removed her shoes and looked around nervously.

He shrugged and went under again. When he came up she was still standing there.

"I never skinny-dip either."

"So keep your clothes on." He was treading water.

She sighed. It was hot. She was sticky with sweat. Winslow regarded her soberly for a few moments and dipped back under the water.

Oh, hell. With another quick look around, she stripped out of her clothing and carefully picked her way over the rocks into the water. She lowered herself in. It was cold at first, but soon felt delicious.

He grinned when he saw she was all the way in. "You see? Isn't this a blessing?"

She smiled back at him and took a deep breath and slid

underwater. It was an otherworldly green down there. The light from the sky filtered down through the water like a benediction, and she let herself relax, let her arms and legs float where they would. She felt graceful and free, safely cupped in the palm of heaven. And for the first time she could remember, she thought: *Yes — I am blessed.*

NEW FROM SANDRA HUTCHISON
IN 2014:

THE RIBS AND THIGH BONES OF DESIRE

It's 1977 in a small college town in Massachusetts. Molly is a sixteen-year-old girl who thinks French kissing is gross, and her mother's notorious, sexually-themed art makes her want to curl up in embarrassment. Her summer job will be housekeeping for the newly-widowed college professor across the street. David is a 32-year-old physics professor who somehow survived the plane crash that killed his family. He's quietly plotting his own demise. Both Molly and David are about to grow up the hard way, and they're going to require each other's help to do it. And both will begin to wonder: Is there ever a time when what everyone thinks is wrong might actually be right?

Be the first to hear about Sandra Hutchison's new releases by joining her book updates email list at www. sheerhubris.com

ACKNOWLEDGMENTS

This work wouldn't exist without the support and encouragement of so many people over such a long span of time that I am probably going to forget to mention some by name, so I apologize for that in advance.

This book's greatest debt is to Lucia Nevai, friend and neighbor and far more accomplished author of fiction than I will ever be. She has generously offered excellent editorial advice, writing tips, moral support, shared laughs, and gentle nudges to take this whole enterprise more seriously.

My parents Jackie and Alexander, AKA Hutch, are nothing like Mary's parents, and have always been my biggest fans. They have also nudged me over the years, of course, but who ever listens to her parents? My brothers and sisters-in-law have also been supportive, as have stepdaughter Lourdes and her husband Edward.

Other writing friends along the way have offered practical help and support, perhaps especially my online (and eventually real-life) writing buddies Lynne Clark, Jamie Roberts, Rachel Vagts, Marie Duggan, and Ann Norman. More support came from the talented and indefatigable Jenny Milchman, along with Jessica Lipnack,

Karina Berg Johansson, and other Stump Sprouts friends, as well as friend, neighbor, and poker mystery writer Rudy Stegemoeller. My writing group listened to a great deal of this and offered many helpful insights — a big thank you especially to Nandini Sheshadri, as well as to Winifred Elze, Valerie Nicotina, Roy Busse, and Zack Richards. Thanks also to Chris Hayes MD, who helped me correct some medical errors.

I also have been blessed by wonderful reading friends like Cris Blanchard, Bridget Ball Shaw, Jill and Ben Comings, Carol Demont, Barry Richardson, Barbara Naeger, and others I am probably forgetting to list. They as well as others who have been come to this project more recently have offered their support and often served as my super-duper, ultra-cheapo ad hoc focus group as I founded Sheer Hubris Press and set about the business of producing an ebook. (Some not already listed above include Beth Heier, Jessica Brouker, Cathy Peake, Rebecca LaDine, Vonnie Vannier, and Rebecca Chaffee.) I also thank anyone who ever encouraged my online alter ego, Alelou.

Some of the professors who made a big difference for me as a thinker and a writer — and might still get have a chance to hear that — are Rosemary Jackson, John Sitter, and (most of all) Fred Miller Robinson.

There are a lot of generous bloggers in the self-publishing world, and I'd like to thank them for sharing their knowledge and expertise and lowering the financial barriers to producing a decent product. (If you're thinking of going this route, I would point you to people like Joel Friedlander, J.A. Konrath, Jane Friedman, Mark Coker, and the folks who share advice about e-publishing on

LinkedIn.) Fellow author Jackie Weger has also been very helpful.

I also thank my former boss and long-lost friend Kate Comiskey for the poet's delight she took in announcing that she wanted to go "visit Winslow at the Mini-Mart." I don't remember what that guy looked like, but his name obviously made an impression on me.

Most of all, I thank my husband Jaime DeJesús, who has supported my writing from the very beginning, even though I know he'd prefer to wait for the movie. My son Alejandro has also put up with an awful lot, including all those blank looks when he needed me to raise my eyes from my work. I just hope he appreciates that I didn't publish this book until he was safely out of high school.

If you got this far, please consider leaving an honest review somewhere for it. You don't have to make it five stars to earn my gratitude. I would also ask you to consider donating something to your local food pantry or to Feeding America. There are lots of awful messes out there, and more of your neighbors than you realize are anxious about how to keep their families fed.

ABOUT THE AUTHOR

For the last two decades or so, Sandra Hutchison's career has shifted between teaching, writing, editing, marketing, and advertising, all of which she enjoys. She founded Sheer Hubris Press in 2013 in order to enjoy using all of these skills at the same time.

Born and raised in the Tampa Bay area, Hutchison survived a transplant to Greenfield, Massachusetts in high school and has stayed in cooler climes ever since. She is a graduate of the University of Massachusetts at Amherst and has an MA in fiction writing from the University of New Hampshire. She lives with her husband Jaime DeJesús and son Alejandro outside of Troy, New York, where she teaches writing at Hudson Valley Community College.

Hutchison's next novel will be *The Ribs and Thigh Bones of Desire*. She is also a budding playwright whose short one-act play *Nude with Bearded Irises* recently premiered in the Circle Theatre Players' second original one-act play festival in Sand Lake, New York, where it won third place in the judging.

For the author's blog and other updates, visit www.sheerhubris.com or follow Hutchison's twitter feed @sheerhubris.

You can also like her on Facebook at author.hutchison.

QUESTIONS FOR DISCUSSION

1. Mary: Love her or hate her? Some readers love this character, and others consider her pathologically self-involved or too passive or too goody-goody, or at the very least annoying. What do you think?
2. Is that a religious conversion at the end?
3. Was Arthur in even the slightest way justified in his behavior in this book? What about Sharon? Who's worse?
4. What are we to make of the nosy next-door neighbor Cici? Why is she even in this book?
5. Is Mary a character a feminist can approve of, or does she require entirely too much rescuing?
6. Does Mary really love Winslow?
7. English majors might have noticed that Arthur has the same first name as Arthur Dimmesdale of *The Scarlet Letter*, and that the dangerous (ex) husband is a Roger, like Chillingworth. There are also a couple of minor direct references in the book to that novel. In what ways could this book be taken as a response to *The Scarlet Letter*? In what ways does it depart from it?

8. One of the author's interesting surprises when she went to publish this novel was that it would be unwelcome to many readers and writers in the Christian category because it has sympathetic gay characters, not to mention adultery with a priest. Thoughts on this?

9. Bert is a favorite character of many readers. Why do you suppose that is?

10. Is a man who'd rather get married before he gets laid really clinically fascinating? Is he believable?

11. What does this book seem to want to say about the concept of human dignity?

12. The author decided to release an adult version and a PG-13 version that took out the explicit sex and crudest language. (And she can tell you that it is far, far less popular, which is why it is only available as an e-book.) What do you think of this as an idea as a marketing strategy? As a literary decision?

13. Some Amazon reviewers have bemoaned the disappearance of Bob the cat for large chunks of this book. Did this bother you? Why or why not?

Made in the USA
Charleston, SC
16 January 2014